PAUL IS A DEAD MAN

A NOVEL
BY

RYAN BRACHA

Paul Carter is a Dead Man

All Artwork by Gavin Wiggan

Also by Ryan Bracha:

Strangers Are Just Friends You Haven't Killed Yet

Tomorrow's Chip Paper

The Banjo String Snapped but the Band Played on

Bogies, and Other Equally Messed up Tales of
Love, Lust, Drugs and Grandad Porn

Ryan Bracha

Paul Carter is a Dead Man

For my long suffering but truly supportive wife,
Rebecca

Ryan Bracha

Foreword.
Life imitates art. Or something.

A lot of writers will take normal things that they see and hear, and store them. They'll steal random glimpses of your life, and plant them in a little pot somewhere in the back of their mind. I'm the same. I do it all of the time. The little pot is left to incubate this thing. Over time, it grows, and grows, and becomes something different altogether. A full novel can be created from such a simple concept. The reason I created so many characters in my first two novels was that I simply had to get the things I'd seen and heard on paper, in and around the plot that I'd got bubbling away up in my tiny mind. None of the characters were based on people I'd met, but the things that a lot of them said were quoted verbatim. Jesus whip, for example. Read my first novel, you'll get it. So that's just art imitating life in whichever form the author chooses to represent it.

Sometimes, however, life does a pitch perfect impersonation of art. I'd started this novel in early 2013, as I'd been watching social media, and how outrage can be voiced from the oddest of places, when there's an outlet. I wanted to push this idea that I had to its extreme. Of course there's no way that capital punishment is going to return to our shores. Human rights and all of that. There's no way that Facebook will be the courtroom of the future where people can be hanged for swearing. There's no way that people would even want to partake in acts like that. There's no way we would accept our doors closed off to the rest of the world. Or is there? Whilst I was writing Paul Carter is a Dead Man, I was sent a link by a friend. It was a picture by some British-is-best type of social group. On it there was the picture of a man who'd been caught urinating on Buckingham Palace or a war memorial or some such. Beneath that there was the caption 'Bring back the death penalty. If this reaches one million likes this man should be hanged' or words to that effect. I'm paraphrasing but the sentiment stands. In May 2013, Drummer Lee Rigby was sadly murdered in an awful attack by two lunatics in the name of Allah. The country went into meltdown. Facebook was awash with demands to remove our troops from other countries. To stay here and protect our great nation. To kick out anybody who believed in Islam. It felt like I was basically writing our future mere weeks before it happened.

I don't condone either of those two acts. Far from it. But nor do I go in for knee-jerk reactions. This book is about an extreme version of knee-jerk reactions. About what happens when the mob mentality takes over. And about what happens when a man decides that enough is enough. I hope you enjoy it, and if I really am writing the future as it happens, next time I'll write about a millionaire called Ryan.

-    **Ryan Bracha, December 2013**

Ryan Bracha

Paul Carter is a Dead Man

A wanted man.

My heart thumps an awful beat. It's loud as hell. My whole body seems to lurch forward with every smack against the inside of my ribs. Wave after wave, lurch after lurch. My surroundings close in on me, and they were already small to begin with. The sweating brickwork of the yard drips against my back. Soaks into my already wet clothing, the exertion from chase has me pouring sweat from every pore. All I'd need would be for the heavens to open and I'd have amassed a full house. The yelping strangled noises echo through the smoky alleyway. *The dogs.* They're getting closer too. I'm not sure I have much time left. They never fail. They *always* get you in the end. *The Network Cutting Crew.* The footsteps become louder, the squeaks of rubber against concrete from somebody's pumps. A car horn bleats out. Another squeal of brakes being applied, and hard. A small voice, cursing their mothers. Ten loud voices, intimidating the lone man standing up to them. The car drives off. They continue. I hold my hand over my mouth, and nose. Only allowing so much air in, or out. I know it's making my breathing worse, denying my body the gasps of oxygen it so desperately craves, but I need to be silent. I *have* to be. The sphincter of my throat twitches involuntarily. Desperately battling against the urge to vomit. The sick wouldn't be my worry, it would be *the least* of my worries. It's the noise I have to avoid. I know what the people will say. They'll hang me, or worse. They're at the end of the alleyway. Dogs yelp. Men jeer. I'm screwed.

"Banger!"

"What?"

"Down there, go!"

"Me?"

"Yeah you, go!"

Maybe not. It sounds like only one man. No dogs. Can I do this? What have I got to lose? They catch me and it's game over anyway. What are they going to do? Kill me twice? I'm sure if they could, they would kill me a thousand times over. One day, that's what it'll come to, but today, just the once is enough.

I carefully and quietly stand, my hands against my aching knees, hoping to God they don't crack. I scan the yard for a weapon within arm's length. Not much. The bin has a lid but it's a kind of rubber, it won't offer me much, unless my assailant is allergic to it. A heavy duty yard brush seems my only hope. Banger, of all people, is slamming gates open further up the alleyway. Bins rattle. I press my back to the wall. Still my heart pounds. Blood gushing around my body with the urgency of white water rapids. I take deep, controlled breaths. I need to compose myself. Behind me, over the wall, Banger kicks open the gate opposite mine. The clanking of the metal bin hitting the floor. Banger curses his luck. He wants to be with the rest of them. Bemoans that he'll miss out on the fun. Some people just can't get a break. His footsteps fall back into the alley, he pants heavily behind my gate, I brace myself. He is huge. I know this from his reputation, and growing celebrity. The broom might simply shatter into a million pieces. *Focus man, for God's sake.* The door explodes into splinters as if it's been hit with a jackhammer. Dried crusted paint released of its years of dedication to decorating the previously intact gate, and revelling in its new job as precipitation. The ferocity of the impact takes me aback somewhat and I'm momentarily stunned. I've only ever seen him on *The Network,* but Banger is a beast of a man. Standing at least four inches over my six feet, and twice as wide as me. He hasn't seen me. With his back to me his eyes scan the shadows of the yard.

"Pointless, jackin' pointless. Ain't no jackin' crooks here, wastin' my time. Jackin' Wilson thinks he runs the show," he's muttering to himself, but how wrong he is, all he needs to do is turn around to discover that there *are* indeed *jackin' crooks,* around here. I won't allow my lungs to steal any oxygen. I must remain silent. *Turn around, Banger.* He's wallowing in the inaction. Stupid lump. He ain't turning.

"Ain't nobody here but us chickens, Banger."

"What the ja-"

I plunge the broom handle into his beady eyeball. Once, twice. Then the other. Once, twice. Banger wails like wounded dog. Howls into the night. Blood spurts from his face like crimson ejaculate and comes over the wall. His hands claw at the pain. At the broom handle jutting from his ocular cavity. It won't be long before they realise

Ryan Bracha

something's wrong. Before a neighbour clicks to what's happening and comes to investigate. I need to get out of here. Banger's still flailing, his wounded animal howling echoes into the night, stomping around the yard. I should put him out of his misery. A light clicks on in the house next door, a woman approaches the window. She can't see me in the darkness, but she'll sure as hell see Banger in his agony. Her husband joins her at the window and the pair of them look on in horror at the still squirting face of Banger. I'm crouched in the corner. A coiled spring. I wait. Watching my would-be captor, waiting for an opportune time to pounce. He blindly steps toward the wall of the house and I spot my in. I leap forward and plant the palms of my hands against his heavy back, and with every milligram of my weight I thrust the poor beast forward. The other end of the broom in his eye hits the wall long before he would, and the wooden pole jabs further into his skull, his brain. He drops to his knees. The noise no more. He's dead. I have no time to waste, and I exit the yard through the open space that Banger had created. I can't risk turning left and heading back toward the closest end of the alleyway, that's where *they* are, so without another thought I scramble through the shadows, and away to safety.

After a while.

I've avoided capture. I think. At least this time I have. My hands are shaking like hell and I have no idea where I'm supposed to go. A million eyes are looking for me. A car screams as it passes me, honking his horn for seemingly no reason as he rockets past me. There are no other cars on the road, I'm the only one around. Maybe he wanted to make me jump. Only he knows. The city around me stinks, garbage piled high around gates, some hopeful notion that somebody will be around to collect it any time soon. Not likely. Nobody goes out so much anymore, those of us that do are either on the run, or the ones doing the chasing. *The Network* is where their lives will be played out. For some of them it's always been the case, for others of us, we remember a time when we had to physically go and knock on somebody's door to interact. It wasn't so long ago either, but so much has happened. So much has changed. I rack my brains for a place to go, I suppose there're the outer limits of the city, but that's a risk. There are less people there, but the lack of people increases vigilance from those that do reside that far out of civilisation. It would only take one to see me, recognise me, and then the whole charade will happen again. Maybe that time I won't be so lucky. I need to rest, my thighs ache from running, and my chest hurts from the effort of holding my breath. My brain is frazzled from the fact that I have just murdered a paid up member of a government authorised *Network*

Ryan Bracha

crew. Banger. He was popular. This is bad. It creeps through my fried brain again. I have just killed one of the most popular members of the most popular crew on *The Network*. They're going to torture me. My pace picks up somewhat with a renewed appreciation for exactly what I've done. But what could I do? It was me or him, and I pretty much made my decision when I ran, instead of holding my hands up and accepting my fate. Names flick through my mind like a mental Rolodex, people I could trust, people I couldn't trust in a million years. I'm dismayed to acknowledge that of the few people I know, most of them fall within the bracket of the latter. I'm so screwed.

Meanwhile.

"Hey! Pete! You seeing this?"
"What?"
"Carter got away, killed Banger!"
Pete's face appeared, incredulous, from the doorway.
"You're kidding?"
"No man, it's all over The Network. Here, listen *'Paul Carter, thirty three, has evaded capture on this occasion, and in the process he has murdered one of the best loved members of The Network Cutting Crew. He has now killed two members of the British society, and is considered highly dangerous. Should he attempt to contact you then you must send a Network communication to The*

Network Cutting Crew, or any other government authorised crew. Failure to do so will result in lawful detainment, and your punishment put out for the standard twenty four hours. The maximum punishment permitted will be death.'"

Pete shook his head, a look of concern in his eyes.

"He needs to stay away from here," he said, before returning to the kitchenette, "seriously! If he comes you have to send him away!"

Without taking his eyes from the screen Danny trusted in his fingers to find the unlit end of the cigarette in the ashtray, before fetching it back blindly to his lips to take a deep inhalation of the tobacco. A heavy thump at the door. Three of them. Bang. Bang. Bang.

Pete's face shot back through the doorway with a start. Danny knew what he was going to say before he even said it, but let him speak nonetheless.

"No," he said, a definite tone of urgency, maybe even fear of the potential.

Danny waved him away, some sort of dismissive action which he hoped would result in his flatmate not worrying. No chance though. He was the worst kind of worrier. The kind that would not shut up. A silent worrier he could live with, they had their demons to battle. A vocal worrier simply upset the moods of all around them with their incessant whining.

"Danny, seriously, tell him to f-" he stopped himself in time, he was still learning, "tell him to jack off!"

Ryan Bracha

"Mate, it's probably not even him," said Danny, rising from the chair, stubbing the cigarette out in the ashtray, and locking his computer. It wasn't unknown for others to hijack another person's *Network synopsis* and declare something entirely hurtful, or untrue, to the rest of the country. He wouldn't risk it though, even if Pete was one of the few people with which he interacted with properly.

Danny approached the door, placed his eyeball against the small distorted hole which constituted his view to the rest of the physical world. Usually it was three stairs going up to the left, three stairs going down to the right. No other doors. Today however, in his small circular eye to the world, stood Pete's worst nightmare. Carter. Even if he hadn't been melted by the distortion he was dishevelled, wet, shaking. A mess, basically. His hand reached up to the door again, and had begun to tap out the same three knocks, only interrupted by the door being removed from his arm's length.

"Paul, what are you doing here mate?" Danny hissed into the corridor, tugging at the damp shirt that his cousin wore to pull him into the relative safety of the flat. Carter said nothing. His eyes were all over the place, his brain unable to string a sentence together. His face was caked in blood, as were his clothes. For a second Danny wondered that maybe his cousin had been caught between the news of Banger's death, and arriving here, maybe attacked. Maybe left for dead. But Paul didn't seem injured, just delirious from shock, exertion, maybe exhaustion too. "Seriously, what the hell are you doing here you jackin' rucksack?

Me and mine.

My name is Paul Carter. In the old days I was employed by a multi-national corporation to train their new staff. I enjoyed the job that I did and the opportunities that it brought. I devised and implemented new methods of delivering the material, taking these methods to my colleagues in India, America, and Australia. Showing them how I intended it to be delivered. I created activities designed to engage the learner at the same time as educating them. I had the respect of my colleagues, my peers, and my employers. I was well paid for what I did, and I'd like to think that I earned every penny. I was focussed, and I was committed to my role. My divorce from my wife would perhaps hint at the possibility that I was in fact married more to my job than I was Ciara, I was rarely home, always performing some task or other in the name of my job, and if I *was* home I was thinking about work. I couldn't see that I was hurting anybody with it, I was investing in our future together, and she couldn't see that, no matter what I argued. She wanted children, I wanted to create a home environment that would be conducive to raising a child. Eventually the cracks became unplasterable.

Ryan Bracha

Became rifts. Became divorce. It was expensive but I felt a huge relief when we parted ways. I immersed myself further into the job, concentrated on my ambitions, and climbed the ladder one rung at a time, the pinnacle of which was my promotion to Director of Learning and Development in 2009. Then came the bomb.

Sometime last year.

It all started with a bang. A very loud, and destructive bang. That's not strictly true, the unrest had been bubbling beneath the surface for a while, and the bang was just the straw that broke the camel's back. Over four hundred people perished. Including the most prominent members of our monarchy. Three generations of heirs to the throne decimated in one fell swoop. Religious extremists took responsibility for it, and all hell broke loose. The government was called to task over the troops who were based overseas. Asked why, when we were under attack ourselves, were we sending our armed forces to countries who really did not want our help? The red tops called for the Prime Minister's head, told him that he'd lost touch with the common man, and the common man agreed. The common man rallied together, started a revolution. Recruited more and more members through *Facespace.* First it was hundreds, then thousands, and before long it was millions. Not just one, or two million. No, we're talking tens of millions. *Facespace* groups appeared, grew, mutated. The country became united by hate. Those that opposed it were struck down. Within weeks the privately educated, greedy members of our government were overthrown, their bodies cast out into the Thames. Our old Prime Minister was strung up from the Tower Bridge, as a warning to all who might think to oppose the new regime, which included our new Prime Minister, Robert Lodge.

Lodge called for, and imposed new rules, he called them *The Guidelines.* I still think of them as the information age's version of the *Commandments,* even now, after having them forced down my throat at every opportunity. He gave the country an ultimatum which amounted to *live by the guidelines, or get out.* Those that chose not to live by the guidelines left the country in their droves. Then the ports, air, sea and rail, were dismantled. You weren't permitted to come in, or leave, the country. He cut the country loose of the EU. Told us that if we wanted a holiday then we were to take them in New Britain. *Keep it British,* he'd said. *A fresh start,* he called it. If you lived in Britain and wanted to stay then you abandoned your religion, your country of birth, your heritage. You committed to New Britain and denounced all you knew before. The royal family was never replaced, money would be better spent on the common man and his causes. There would be no money generated from tourists flocking from all over the world to see the monarchy, simply because there would be no tourists, and so there was no need for a royal family. Robert Lodge was rarely seen in public, preferring to communicate with his people through *The Network.* He gave us weekly chances to admire him, praise him, but never question him, unless it was a pre-planned and vetted canvassing session. It amazed me how easily the people allowed themselves to be swept along in the revolution, but swept along they were, and they bought in to every little thing that Lodge put to them. Especially *The Guidelines.*

Don't kill anybody, unless you're a government authorised *Network* crew.
Don't lie, unless you're performing the role of a government authorised *Network* crew.
Don't swear, even if you're performing the role of a government authorised *Network* crew.
Don't steal anything, ever.
Violence will not be tolerated, unless you're performing the role of a government authorised *Network* crew.
Don't oppose the regime.
Commit your heart and soul to the British way.

What's a government authorised *Network* crew? The law.

A government authorised Network crew.

Lodge put a variety of contracts out to tender.
The country lived so much of its life on The
Network that it was only logical to give the
country the rights of judge, jury, and executioner,
and what better way to do that than to create
open forums? These contracts would require an
organisation to form gangs, or *crews,* of not more
than ten members, although the number of gangs
allowed to operate under any one organisation is
unlimited. These people were to track, and hunt
down those who chose to break any one of *The
Guidelines,* and upon success, they would display
their catch over their Network synopsis. The
public would have twenty four hours from the
announcement of the catch, to vote on whether
or not to punish the perpetrator of the crime.
The amount of votes required to punish them
reflected the severity of the crime. For example,
should a murderer be held for all to see, and
judge, the crew would require at least ten
thousand votes. Rape would require twenty
thousand. Child Molesters would require only
ten votes, although even if it were ten million
votes, it would be achieved and surpassed within
minutes. The lesser crimes of speeding in your
car, you would need a million votes. You see how
this works. Swearing was outlawed altogether. A
Network crew would need half a million votes to
kill you for it. *If,* that was the chosen punishment.
I told you, it's an open forum. Not only do the
public vote on whether to punish, they also

Ryan Bracha

decide the punishment. In the twenty four hour voting period they will be given the opportunity to offer ideas on how best to punish the crime. I've seen a man pumped full of poison for stealing a car, and in the same breath I could tell you also that I've seen a woman walk free even after declaring that she would kill again if released. This is the country, the society, the *lives* we've created.

Facespace and The Network.

Before the bomb, Facespace was the main networking tool with which we communicated. Nobody ever really spoke face to face anymore. Barely used the telephone. People that would pass one another in the street without so much as a blink could open up, tell each other how they were feeling, whether they liked it or not. They sought advice from people who were as good as strangers. Gave them unrestricted access into their lives. Rather than invite the family round for drinks and a bite to eat they were playing electronic games that spanned the length of the country. The corporations saw the massive opportunity to sell their wares. Everything was sponsored by something else was owned by somebody else was employed by somebody else. It was an endless chain of money making, but we embraced it, loved it. Eventually we needed it. Eyes that looked anywhere but the Facespace synopsis that they had before them were treated with suspicion. Televisions were getting bigger, more advanced. Touchscreen technology at its unrivalled peak. There was so much potential to take the technology and do something good with it, but it always came back to Facespace. Television viewing figures dwindled, nobody wanted fiction anymore. They watched the comings and goings of the next door neighbour. Alerted authorities of anything untoward. They wanted the real life dramas of the girl down the street who was battling depression, struggling to keep it together on the breadline whilst she raised her tiny daughter. They wanted the lonely virgin who was on the verge of suicide. They wanted the latest funny video of the cat that couldn't jump properly. They wanted to all rally together when one of their connections was hit with the tragic death of a blood relative. This, was what they wanted. Not regurgitated stories of drug addiction spewed from the pens of washed up screenwriters who hadn't scratched together an original storyline since the seventies. The real life drama was much more entertaining. Facespace also gave the country an opinion, a platform from which to voice it, and an audience who would listen. Groups borne out of animosity began to spring up, recruited new members to help them to spout their words of hatred. Prowled Facespace, looking for individuals to troll, the aforementioned suicidal virgin poked and prodded until the time which he no longer signed in to Facespace. People would question his whereabouts for days, tell their other

Ryan Bracha

connections that they missed his ways. The inimitable passion for martyrdom. Eventually the word would get out. He was dead. Hacked into his wrists one night after one insult too many. Been discovered five days later. Pictures of his bloated corpse surfacing across Facespace, alongside a glowing tribute to his character. The world would mourn another who had been taken too soon. Then it would move on. The government largely chose to ignore the voice of the masses in the Facespace realm. They were adamant that it was just another flash in the pan craze, that we would move on when the next latest one surfaced. But we didn't. New technology was built around our passion for it, our need for it. Our addiction. We bemoaned the government for ignoring our voice. But did nothing about it. Sat in our homes. Telling our every connection on Facespace that we had had enough. Created long winded diatribes that were just our own spin on something else that somebody else had written. Nothing new. Nothing done. Then the bomb came. The hatred grew. The government overthrown. Lodge's new regime took the technologies from Facespace, VidiYou, online gaming, gambling and shopping, forums, advertising, audio and visual communications, television as we once knew it, and then put it all under the control of a government that knows exactly where you live and what you're doing and, well, you get the picture. The Network is an all-encompassing life enhancer for everybody. We were entertained.

We were informed. We were watching. We were watched.

The Crews.

There are several government authorised Network crews plying their trade today. In the north we have *The Network Cutting Crew,* touted as the original and the best. They're as vicious as they are prolific. Their 'leader' is a man named Wilson Becker. Former rugby player, from New Zealand originally but was extremely quick to pin his flag to the British pole when *The Guidelines* came into force. It is a testament to their tenacity that within their organisation there is but one crew. Their competition for business comes most notably in the form of *Tough Justice,* whose name says it all, and the altogether more efficient *Finnegan Law Enforcement.* These three are the top rated, and highest earning of those that deal with the northern contracts, which comprise any area between Nottingham and the walls of what we used to know as Scotland. In the south, and Wales there are, amongst others, *Wrecking Ball, The Network Razors,* and *The Swift Deliverers.* And in London, by far the most lucrative contract, since there is no competition, belongs to *Devine Law Enforcement,* run by the consummate professional, Tony Devine. If you're wondering about Northern Ireland then wonder no more. Robert Lodge handed the place back to the South for the princely sum of five pounds, and no more was said about it. Whatever happened in Ireland after that remains unknown. We have no access to the internet, or worldwide information anymore, except for The Network. Lodge returned industry to the country. Created a self-sufficient society. He wanted us to live by a *Made in New Britain, for New Britain* philosophy, and we embraced it. For the most part. Pockets of resistance still exist, as you might expect. These usually pour down from the cracks in the walls of the no-man's land which used to be known as Scotland, but they are being steamrollered one at a time until there will come a point where our country follows Robert Lodge and his radical ethos without question. The regime is a mere five years old, by the time the next generation comes around he will be elevated to Godlike status.

No-Man's Land.

There lies an area of land to the north of New Britain. We used to call it Scotland. When Robert Lodge came to power, and the choices were given, of in-or-out, the population of that small, yet feisty colony kicked hard against the system. They'd been doing it for years anyway. Pushing for devolution from our own government. Wanting to make their own decisions. Be seen as an actual country rather than a small piece of a much more important empire. At that time it was seen as a petulant child, always wanting something it couldn't have. England's parliament held all of the cards, and they weren't for showing any of them, so Scotland made token, and often crude hand gestures at us to our faces, to let us know exactly what they thought of us. Robert Lodge coming to power was by no means different. Scotland watched his rise to power, and when he held a hand of solidarity their way, they laughed. They swore. They killed every person who thought it wise to try to bargain with them in the process. Scotland refused to give up its identity, and it was a logistical nightmare for Robert Lodge in his mission to unite a country and close its doors to the world, so after a largely unsuccessful attack on them he simply closed the doors on Scotland. Convicts were put to work on the wall which now separates us from them, in exchange for freedom. Thousands of men worked day and night to block off the dissenters from the rest of us, the conforming society. They did this for a fresh start, looking forward with the rest of us to a new, and exciting future. He shut off their electricity, and he left them to rot. Rumour has it that the Scottish predilection toward foul language is what lay behind the guideline which forbids swearing, and forces us to replace expletive with suitable alternatives. Nobody truly knows what's happening behind that wall, but it scares us to death. I once saw a live-feed documentary on the Visual Entertainment Network, about a young man entering No-Man's Land to see what the animals beyond the wall were capable of. It ended with a quickly typed obituary for the poor stupid soul.

Back in the present.

"Seriously, what the hell are you doing here you jackin' rucksack?"
This is my cousin Danny speaking. Another of those that opted to remain in the country, pledge our allegiance, fly the flag, all that other bullsherbet. I don't know what to tell him. He's my only hope of salvation right now. I could tell him that but he knows it. Why waste my breath? "You can't stay here," he's saying, in low hushed tones, his *flatmate* Pete is around, he must be. He'll be in the background of Danny's mind, his nasal whine, complaining about everything. One time, when we got together for an *Off The Network* party, somebody dared to bring contraband into the place. Pete almost had a heart attack. It was one cannabis joint. It ended up getting flushed down the toilet, but only after being torn into a thousand pieces. To remove any possibility that a *crew* was filtering anything that was flushed down his sherbet pipe. As if he was that important that the law might wish to view his sherbet, pick through it, determine that his diet was indeed as rubbish as the rest of us on The Network knew it to be. Danny holds my shoulders, his face pulled right in to mine. I can smell the tobacco on his breath. It smells warm, and bitter. I smoke, but I hate the smell of it on

other people's breath. It must show in my face because he's pulled away slightly.

"You killed Banger," he's saying. I *know* I killed Banger. I was there.

"It was an accident," I lie. It was self-defence. Kind of. Is that as good as an accident? I guess.

"Do you think that makes a difference? Carter, they're pushing your name all over The Network, I read that they bringing more than one crew in on it. You can't stay here."

Pete, the *flatmate,* appears, he looks spooked. I cannot trust the man. He'd give up his own mother. Now I'm wondering why I came. I look at him through the crusted blood and brains on my face. He lets out an effeminate gasp, his hand slides open palmed up to his mouth.

"Oh gosh!"

"Hi Pete," I say, "in a bit of a mess."

Understatement of the year.

Pete avoids eye contact thereafter and looks to Danny.

"What did I say?" he whines toward my cousin, his effete voice reaches tones that I didn't realise existed.

"Don't worry," I say, shaking my head in defeat, "I just thought," I stop myself, no point wasting my breath, "I'll go."

I pull my shoulders from Danny's grasp, and offer a thin smile by way of acknowledgment. I suppose I'm asking too much, for them to risk their lives. Danny loosens his grip and lets me turn to the door.

Ryan Bracha

"Paul," he says, I turn to face my cousin, "be careful."

I smile another acknowledgment, but this time I don't even try to keep the disappointment from my face. All those years back. I took him in. When his dad, my uncle, threw him out for being gay, he had nowhere to stay. I let him crash at ours. Ciara, understandably, hated it, somebody encroaching upon our space, but he was blood. I couldn't see him struggling. The door closes behind me and the muffled sound of Pete wailing behind it makes me wince. Never truly liked the guy. My heartbeat kicks up some more, I know for a fact that he'll already be issuing a statement to the Crew. My feet begin to get the message from my heart and begin to speed up. The heavy thud against each step, the velociraptor squeal of the rusted hinges on the exit door. The sound of the outside world once more.

A MODERN BRITAIN #1

IN THE SPARSE LIVING ROOM DAVID SMITH SAT IN HIS UNDERWEAR. HIS FAVOURITE GREEN AND WHITE STRIPED BOXER SHORTS, AND HIS PLAIN GREY T-SHIRT. THE FABRIC OFFICE CHAIR CREAKED BENEATH HIM AS HE SHUFFLED SLIGHTLY, ALLOWING THE BLOOD TO CIRCULATE AROUND HIS BACKSIDE. HE TOOK HIS MOVE. PLAYED THE WORD *IMAGERY* AND SCORED EIGHTY NINE POINTS. USED ALL SEVEN TILES AND LANDED ON A TRIPLE WORD. A SATISFIED SMILE ON HIS FACE. HE WOULD BE TOUGH TO BEAT NOW. A TWO GAME LEAD WAS WITHIN TOUCHING DISTANCE. UPSTAIRS, HIS WIFE GLORIA CURSED HIS NAME, AND ASSESSED THE TILES BEFORE HER, WHICH INCLUDED FIVE VOWELS. SHE HADN'T DRESSED IN OVER A WEEK. WHY SHOULD SHE? SHE HADN'T HAD CALL TO LEAVE THE HOUSE. NONE OF THEM HAD.

Ryan Bracha

IN HER BEDROOM THEIR DAUGHTER, FIFTEEN YEAR OLD JENNIFER WAS CATCHING UP ON HER VOTING BACKLOG. IN THE MINOR CRIME CATEGORY SHE CONDEMNED A MAN TO DEATH FOR STEALING BREAD, DECLARED THAT EVEN HANGING WAS TOO GOOD FOR A WOMAN WHO'D SLAPPED HER CHILD IN AN ACT OF FRUSTRATION, AND VOTED THE DEATH PENALTY ON FOUR MORE PEOPLE WHO WERE GUILTY OF SWEARING. IN THE MAJOR CRIME CATEGORY SHE INDISCRIMINATELY CLICKED HER VOTES FOR THE DEATH PENALTY ON EVERY PERSON IN THERE. USUALLY SHE WOULD TAKE THE TIME TO CONSIDER THEIR CASE, WEIGH UP WHETHER THEY DESERVED IT, THE LOOK IN THEIR EYES, WHAT HER GUT TOLD HER. SHE HAD FALLEN BEHIND THOUGH, SHE NEEDED TO CLEAR THE BACKLOG, REGARDLESS OF CIRCUMSTANCE. BY THE TIME SHE HAD DONE SHE WOULD HAVE PLAYED THE PART IN THE DEATHS OF SIXTEEN

PEOPLE. SHE DIDN'T THINK TWICE ABOUT IT.

Respite.

The train to Manchester rattles overhead. It only runs once a day, so it must be around six o'clock. I daren't switch my mobile on to find out. They'll track it, they'll track me. It's so hard though. Just me, my thoughts, and the water that drips from the rails above. This is the longest I've been without my phone being on for as long as I can remember. It's just not natural anymore. The cold of the evening is settling in, and a chill grabs at my fingers, so I sit on my hands. Hope to fool my blood into circulating around to my extremities. The archway smells rotten, the garbage piled high around me, but at least it's providing some degree of shelter, a breaker against the winter breeze. Voices in the distance. Laughter. The sound of the brave. It fades and I close my eyes, hoping that my brain can switch off just briefly enough to allow my body to succumb to sleep. My thoughts flicker around, like a moth against a light bulb, jittery, jerky. The past. The present. The future. It's all a mess. Unknown. They jump from Ciara, and regret, through Banger, the blood, so much blood, to what will happen when they finally catch up with me. Would the people offer any degree of clemency? I doubt it. They're like dogs with bones. They'll string me up. Hung, drawn, quartered. Dead. This is my final thought before I drift off, a brief respite.

A memory.

I wasn't out of work for long. After the corporation that I'd been so valuable to was dismissed from our country I took the transferrable skills I'd amassed in my old life and made myself useful to the new regime. So much to do, so many people to allocate jobs to, to train. The new industrial age of Britain offered a great many opportunities. I started out small. Took the finances that I'd saved and created a business. Approached the government, trained up pockets of people in new skills. Call centre staff re-placed into advertising. Shop staff into IT. Plasterers into marketing. Bankers, quite humourously, into coal mining. We helped in the grand scheme to mould our country's self-sufficient future. The great thing about being in the learning and development industry was that we never truly needed to *know* our material, it helped, of course it did, but it's all about *how* it is delivered. The ability to ascertain whether a learner absorbed information through *seeing,* or through *listening,* or by *doing.* Visual learners, auditory learners, and kinaesthetic learners. Whatever the material, if you figure your audience out in the first ten minutes, you cannot fail. That's what I did well. My *Network synopsis* attracted a great many admirers. I charged people to take my online seminars. To give skills to those that didn't want to leave their abode. Give them something to do, to tell their *Network* friends about. I was a star on the rise, and life was great.

Ryan Bracha

Further back.

She was crying on the floor of our house. The day that led to the split. I hadn't said anything. Sat on the arm of the leather sofa, my head down. Couldn't think of anything to say. Wasn't sure if I even wanted to say anything. It had gotten gradually worse. I spent more and more time in hotels, under the pretence that I was working away. I was, in a fashion. I wasn't going away. A lot of the time I went round the corner to a small inn, settled in the room with some peace and quiet, and pored over my work. Took my mind off of the increasingly fragile marriage. Spent my time, secretly on The Network, seeing her complaining to her connections, that she was lonely. Men would ask her if she wanted some company, if she needed a shoulder to cry on, an embrace to keep her warm. It should have burned me to the core, to see the woman who had agreed to be with me for better or worse, prowled around by opportunistic men. The worst thing is, I didn't care. I had far too much on my plate. I had wave after wave of groups of people to train up, to impart my knowledge of the mobile telephone industry upon these waves. I had the three pronged training technique which would bring all three types of learner into the fray at the same time. It would save money. Time. Effort. I had to design a presentation to show the powers that be exactly how it would save those things. The marriage had become a hindrance. A side-track. Was it my fault? Probably. Did I care? Not really.

Eventually she looked up at me, her bright red eyes. A string of snot, and tears connecting her quivering chin to the carpet. She was a mess. Which made it easier to do what I was about to do. I said I wanted a break from one another. Just a few days. A time apart to take stock. She stayed at the house. I went to my usual hotel. Four days passed. I hoped that I might miss her, but in my heart of hearts I knew that the time apart would only serve to make it easier to finally end it. Three years of marriage, three years of wasted time. Three years of regret.

The running dead.

I awake with a start. A gasp. That foul stench stings my nostrils, attacks my throat like dynamite on a coal face. The dogs. They're in the distance, but getting closer. Whooping and jeering. That familiar sound. I can't risk running. They'd surely catch me. In blind panic I pull at the wall of garbage, one fly-tipped bag at a time. The smell continues to attack my senses. Flies, woken, skitter about in the air, punching my face. Punishing me for my encroachment upon their territory. I create a hole, a burrow, and drag the bags back upon myself. Creating a vantage point of sorts. A place to keep lookout. The crew still sound distant. Footsteps approach though, gasping breaths. A crew? A silhouette appears. A

Ryan Bracha

man? The figure is struggling for breath, slowed down, head looking back over its shoulder. Gets closer. Can't see my eyes peering out from the garbage mountain. Crying. High pitched, whimpering cries, gasps. She's a woman. She pauses in front of my mountain, considers the plastic, stinking mess before her. Looks back behind her again. No choice. I pray she changes her mind. I can't afford for her to bring trouble to my door. I have more than enough for the both of us. Keep going, please. She's still crying, from the pitch I don't think to attach many years to her age. Maybe teenage, early twenties? Younger than me, in other words. Admittedly, my ears for age, are worse than my eyes. Suddenly the bags are dislodging above me, she's climbing the garbage mountain. No. She's gasping, weeping, struggling to catch her breath between the sobs. She's almost upon me. I need to think fast, if she disappears above me and continues to cry she's going to get us both caught. Think. Her foot slides into the pile, planting directly in front of my eyes. As quickly as I can I pull at her foot, she yelps as she loses her balance, toppling backwards, I need to keep her quiet. Like a fly being ripped from its perch upon a plant by a lizard's tongue she slides into my hole. My hand grabbing for her mouth. "Be quiet," I whisper urgently, the girl is spooked, of course she is. She's bucking against my grasp, trying to wriggle from my sweating hands, "I won't hurt you, just be quiet for jack's sake! You'll get us killed!" I continue, hoping that she sees no threat in my eyes through the darkness. The dogs are approaching quicker still. The yapping. A handful of voices encourage them.

"Please," I beg, my tone rises slightly, from whisper to desperate voice, "be quiet."

The girl slows in her wriggling, the breath from her nose rushes past, and tickles the hair on the back of my hand. Her eyes don't blink. She just stares at me. The only noise right now is her harsh breathing, against a tinny echo which resonates through our small front door between the bags and the world, the echo of dogs yapping in an ever decreasing distance. I loosen my grip over her mouth just slightly, a show of intent, or lack of intent I suppose, to hurt her.

"Don't make a noise, please, they're nearly here," I whisper.

I remove my hand from her face fully, drawing a finger to my lips, the universally accepted sign to be quiet. She says nothing, and I roll back onto my stomach. Watching. Hoping that the stink around us might mask the scent from the dogs. Her lungs continue to gush warm air against me, it circulates around our hole, her breath is rotten. Dogs appear, strangling themselves against the chains upon which they are hooked. Their snarling, slathering faces edge further forward, their powerful bodies pulling the men that hold them. Heavy, hard yanks, close to ripping their masters' arms from their shoulders. The jackets they're sporting, from here they look dark green, the yellow thick embroidering up the arms. They're Tough Justice. They catch us and

Ryan Bracha

this ends badly. Very badly. They've been called out in some corners for their harsh punishments. The girl beside me whimpers, just slightly, holds her breath, a hand involuntarily grabs at my sleeve. She's shaking.

Then men lead their animals into our archway. The dogs snarl, but I get the feeling that this is par for the course. They've disappeared out of sight but are still audible. A voice.

"He's smellin' somethin'! Whipper! You got the scent boy? Get 'em"

The dogs respond by way of growl. The girl beside me is silent. A bead of sweat rolls from my armpit and down the side of my chest, cooling as it rolls. The dogs sound ready to pounce. The girl grips my arm ever tighter, and we brace ourselves. This is it. They pounce, the savage roar as they clamped their teeth around something. The sounds of tearing flesh. But no cries. There's no movement around the girl and I. Something's amiss.

"Jackin' idiot!" says one of the Tough Justice crew. A hollow thud. A yelp. He's kicked one of the dogs. Another thud. The other dog's taken a kick too, "supposed to be a jackin' sniffer dog, can't sniff nothin' but skanky old meat! Come on! She'll be gettin' away!"

Strangled whimpers emit from the canines. Another yelp as the girl's would be captors lay another boot into the chest of one of them. A phone rings.

"Yeah? No. No. Stupid mutts took us to a garbage dump, attacked nothin' but garbage bags, stinks somethin' rotten too. Bring the car round, we aint makin' no headway on foot."

A squeal. Choked anguish.

"Come on, stupid mutt!"

From our vantage point the men and animals come back into view, the dogs more subdued. Dragged roughly by their charge hands. Away, away, and out of sight.

The girl and I both sigh, and heavily. Nobody says a word though. I push some of the bags from above us and rise tentatively. She stays where she is, but looks up at me. In the dark I can see she's a very pretty girl. She looks as young as she sounded. Maybe twenty one, twenty two. Her face is filthy. Unwashed.

"That was close," I say, running my fingers though my blood crusted hair, pulling my hands down my cheeks to stretch the skin away from my eyes. The girl sits though, doesn't say anything, will not take her eyes from me, "you okay?"

Finally she shifts on her backside, swings her legs over the edge of our hole, edges closer to me. Still her eyes remain on mine.

"You," she says, shuffling down the garbage mountain, "you're Paul Carter."

A confession.

I have to confess before this goes any further, before you get any sort of attachment to how I might fare in the end, before you root for the

Ryan Bracha

wrong guy. I'm not an innocent man. I'm on the run for a reason, and I don't mean because of Banger. I'm talking about before Banger. The reason he was chasing me. Him and the rest of the Cutting Crew. The reason a million eyes are on the lookout for me, to get me in the public arena. To judge me. To execute me. I assure you, I'm far from innocent. I'm not talking about small hateful campaigns against homosexuality or anything like that, I didn't hurt small animals in either of my lives. My past life or this one now, in this messed up country we live in. I visited my parents as regularly as work would allow. I'm not, nor was I ever, a nasty, spiteful person. But I'm still guilty. I don't want us to have any secrets between us. I want you to trust me, as much as your knowledge of my past will allow. As Robert Lodge might say, my confession might mean we get off to a fresh start.

I killed a man. It was cold blooded, it was calculated, and it was premeditated. He threatened my livelihood, and the life to which I'd become accustomed. His name was Jacob Glover. He cast aspersions over the legitimacy of my Network seminars. Called me a fraud. It started small, as do most things, a few snide comments here and there. At the end of every seminar, in the midst of all of the thanks and praise, he was there. Pointless. You're talking bullsherbet. Only idiots would take this sherbet seriously. I took it with a pinch of salt to start with, accepted that I couldn't win everybody over all of the time. I almost took it as a compliment that the guy was paying through the nose just to insult me, that I was obviously prominent enough to bother with. After that came the pictures. Crudely created images of me with children, in lewd situations. It obviously wasn't my body beneath the picture of my head, which was taken from my Network promotional page. They would appear on the official Whistleblower synopsis on The Network, which was a synopsis whereby people would actively post the crimes and evidence of others. It was a place that most crews, the smaller ones, would pick over, choosing criminals to track, hunt, and punish. Larger crews had their own official synopses, wouldn't need to scrape the barrel. Although the pictures were blatant fakes it sowed the seeds into the less logical brains. After the Whistleblower he started to circulate images which found themselves on LOLZ!!! which was one of the few shows on The Network TV, a place where humourous items were montaged to generic music, videos of people doing 'funny' things, items that the population had created for the purposes of comedy. He'd attached my head to a video of a dog copulating with another. He made me a laughing stock, and it affected the way that people saw my work.

So I started to plot his own downfall. Followed his movements on The Network, what time he made statements to his connections, what he said he was doing, where he lived. He was a walking disease. It wasn't just me he targeted. He seemed to want to make the lives of everybody in the country a misery. They wouldn't miss him. I started to watch his house, saw that he lived alone. Of course he did. No way would a man who was happy in a relationship would treat humanity with the contempt that Jacob Glover did. He would revel in misery. His actions, to me, didn't look like those of somebody who wanted to live very long, they looked more like the actions of somebody who wished that one of his victims would eventually snap and dispatch him to the other side. So, I guess that the person who snapped was me. I walked into his dingy flat. It was dark, damp, and as miserable as the wretch that resided there. Plates piled high in the small kitchenette. Takeaway food no doubt ordered from the Sustenance Network, left rotting on the small table with a single chair pushed in. His hallway smelled awful. The only noise in the whole place was the low hum of the refrigerator, and incessant tapping of fingers against keyboard, along the stinking hall and behind a thin door. I edged slowly along, softly dropping onto my heels as I went, pausing as he snorted out with mirth. Some tinny music emanating from his speakers. Another snort of laughter. Sound effects of slapstick bangs and bongs. I gave myself a three count, and burst through the door, belt in hand. Wrapped it around his neck, and squeezed with every ounce of energy I had in my body. He jerked. Jumped. Struggled. Died. It was all so quick. There was no euphoria. Nothing like that. I'm not even sure that my heartbeat raised much above eighty. He twitched a little bit, then slumped slowly out of his chair and onto the floor. Then a gasp emanated from the tinny speakers. I'd been watched. His stupid personal channel. I'd committed murder live to the country.

A MODERN BRITAIN #2

JOE DAVIES WOKE UP AT NINE IN THE MORNING, AS USUAL. AT NINE THIRTY HE TOOK A PHOTOGRAPH OF HIS BREAKFAST MUFFINS AND ADDED IT TO HIS DAYLINE ON THE NETWORK, BY ELEVEN O'CLOCK HE HAD REACHED LEVEL FORTY ON FRUITY BASHER, SURPASSING HIS PREVIOUS PERSONAL BEST SCORE, AND THOSE OF AT LEAST NINETEEN OF HIS CONNECTIONS. HE CELEBRATED BY POSTING A SCREEN GRAB OF THE OCCASION TO HIS DAYLINE, WITH A BOASTFUL COMMENT. AS IT WAS SATURDAY HE LOGGED ONTO THE SUSTENANCE NETWORK AND ORDERED THE WEEK'S GROCERY SHOPPING, WHICH ARRIVED BY MID-AFTERNOON. IT CONSISTED OF EIGHTEEN IDENTICAL MICROWAVABLE MEALS, SIX DIFFERENT VARIETIES OF FRUIT YOGHURT, FORTY EIGHT CANS OF NON-ALCOHOLIC LAGER, AND TWO HUNDRED CIGARETTES. HE ASSESSED

Paul Carter is a Dead Man

THE FORM OF THE ELECTRONIC FOOTBALL PLAYERS FOR THE PREVIOUS MONTH AND BET UPON THREE OF THEM, FIVE POUNDS PER PLAYER. IF HE WON HE WOULD PULL IN OVER TWO HUNDRED POUNDS OF PROFIT.

BEFORE THE FIRST MATCH WAS DUE TO KICK OFF HE BROWSED THE CRIME NETWORK. THE VOTING ON A CRIMINAL THAT HE'D BEEN KEEPING AN EYE ON WAS DUE TO END WITHIN THE NEXT TEN MINUTES. THE PERPETRATOR HAD BEATEN HIS WIFE, AND CAPTURED BY WRECKING BALL. JOE HAD VOTED FOR DEATH, AND HAD SUGGESTED THAT HE BE DECAPITATED. SEVERAL THOUSAND PEOPLE HAD AGREED THAT THIS WAS A GREAT, AND DRAMATIC ENDING TO SUCH AN AWFUL MAN'S LIFE, SO JOE WAS HOPEFUL, CONFIDENT EVEN, THAT HIS PUNISHMENT MAY BE SELECTED. IT WOULD BE A GREAT MOMENT FOR HIS ACHIEVEMENT WALL, WOULD SIT PROUDLY ALONGSIDE THE QUESTION THAT HE'D ASKED OF PRIME MINISTER LODGE DURING PRIME MINISTER'S

Ryan Bracha

QUESTIONS, WHICH HAD RECEIVED A
RESPONSE. HE'D NEVER MET ANYBODY
ELSE WHO'D HAD A QUESTION
ANSWERED. THE CRIME TIME CLOCK
DIPPED BELOW FIVE MINUTES. HE
ALERTED ALL OF HIS CONNECTIONS,
TELLING THEM OF HIS TREPIDATION.
SEVERAL JOINED HIM ON THE CRIME
NETWORK, AND TOGETHER THEY
COUNTED DOWN THE CLOCK. TEN, NINE,
EIGHT, SEVEN, SIX, FIVE, FOUR, THREE,
TWO, ONE. THE SENTENCE. DEATH. THE
PUNISHMENT, SUGGESTED BY JOE
DAVIES OF MILTON KEYNES.
DECAPITATION.
WITH A NON-ALCOHOLIC BEER IN ONE
HAND, AND A CIGARETTE IN THE OTHER
JOE LEAPT FROM HIS SEAT. PUNCHED
THE AIR IN DELIGHT. AS THE MACHETE
DROPPED DOWN AND THROUGH THE
CRIMINAL'S NECK JOE TOOK A SCREEN
GRAB, AND PLACED IT UPON HIS
DAYLINE AS THE SECOND PROUDEST
MOMENT OF HIS LIFE.

I had my reasons.

"You're Paul Carter," she's said, for the third time. Her face closer up to mine, scrutinising it, a look of delight in her eyes, "I've never met a murderer before. You saved my life. Thanks."
She seems genuinely excited about this fact, and I'm unsure as to how I'm supposed to respond to it. I opt for silence.
"You killed Banger too, mental, proper mental!"
"It was self-defence."
"Stabbed his eyes out? Self-defence?"
I turn and start to walk away, I'm not getting into it.
"It was him or me," I say, "you're safe now, go your own way."
She follows me, skirting around me to get in front, walking backwards.
"What about Jacob Glover? I watched you kill him on the Repeat Network, strangled him dead, self-defence?"
I stop. She stops. I sigh. Pinch the bridge of my nose. Look at her.
"I had my reasons."
I continue walking and she sidles alongside me, the Tough Justice crew is now long gone, but we're still in danger, doubly so as a pair, but it seems like she's going nowhere so I turn it back on her.
"What about you? What's your story?"
She hums, like she's rewinding her life. Choosing a suitable place to start.
"Why don't you start with your name eh?"

Ryan Bracha

"Katie."

"Hi, Katie."

"Hi."

"Why was Tough Justice after you?"

"I was-"

A carhorn bellows from a few blocks away, so we swiftly duck into an alley, clamber over more garbage. It's a dead end, but it's shelter from prying eyes. Safety. I hope. I grab a few bags, pile them on top of the existing wall of trash. Try to raise its shelter level by a few precious feet. Once I'm suitably comfortable with it I settle, trying to make a seat, of sorts, from the trash. Katie seats herself beside me, not too close as to be invasive of space, but close.

"So?"

"So what?"

"Your story, why were they chasing you?"

"I posted a picture on The Network," she laughs, incredulously.

"Of what?"

"Robert Lodge," she says, mischief in her eyes, and laughs, "with poo on his chest."

Great. The murderer and the childish political rebel. What a pair.

I look at her, and shake my head. Close my eyes. Resting awkwardly against the cold wall of the alleyway. Music echoes out from somewhere above us. It's a song from my old life. I used to enjoy music once. When the artists had something worthwhile to say, now it's all the same, New Britain is great, what a great thing it is to be British, who needs different? That kind of thing. That's what Lodge has created. A uniform, bland, steadily declining society of robots. I followed the crowd, made my money, did what I was told, but really had no real thoughts of my own. I've been without The Network for less than twenty four hours and already my brain is threatening mutiny. Katie shuffles closer to me, and drops her head onto my shoulder. She's a curious girl. She sighs.

"So what's the plan?" she asks. The plan, I guess, is to survive. Work one minute to the next. I have no idea how I suddenly became the plan man for a girl I've just met.

"Sleep," I say.

"Cool."

She goes quiet again, but is still shuffling a little. Her head leaves my shoulder. I open my eyes. She's sitting, cross legged, looking at me.

"What?"

"Why did you do it?"

"Forget it, please."

"Did you enjoy it?"

"Not really."

"Are you gonna kill me? Are you a psycho?" Her eyes go all wide at this one.

"No to both," I say, "will you let me sleep?"

She tuts. Sighs. Shakes her head in disappointment.

"You're very boring for a murderer."

Ryan Bracha

Where's Paul Carter?

"What did he say?"
"Nothing. I didn't give him a chance."
"You didn't think to stall him? Keep him here till
we arrived?"
"No, I just panicked, the Network statement just
said to contact you if he tried to get in touch,
so we did."
Wilson Becker stared into his eyes, sizing him up,
stepped closer into his personal space. Pete was
in the chair, one of his eyes rapidly swelling,
growing purple, two of The Network Cutting
Crew hovered over him. The one that had
attacked him, Grady, eyed him menacingly.
"You know the punishment is death for
witholding information?" Wilson asked, the
question entirely rhetorical. Of course Danny
knew, "if I think for a second that you're
witholding information, I can put you up for
judgment. Do you want that?"
Danny stood firm. Said nothing.
"Grady," said Wilson, his underling approached
at his shoulder.
"Boss?"
"You think this jacker is witholding
information?"
Wilson stepped away, let the volatile Grady take
his place in Danny's personal space. His head
moved, snake-like, around before Danny's face.
Attempting to look even more menacing than he
already did. Scrutinised Carter's cousin.
"I think he is boss."

Danny shook his head.

"We're not-"

"Don't jackin' speak till you're spoken to maggot!" roared Grady into his grimacing face, before returning his attention to Wilson Becker, "Now I'm sure of it, infact I wouldn't be surprised if the creep hadn't sent Carter on his way with a little sustenance."

"You know we can check your Sustenance Network history? We have the authority to do that. If it doesn't match up against your Personal History we can hold you up for judgment," said Wilson.

"Feel free," Danny said.

"Please, we don't know anything, we tried to help," Pete whimpered from the sofa, hushed by the Crew member standing over him. Wilson changed tack.

"You're Carter's cousin aren't you?" he said, referring to Danny, who nodded.

"Yes, but-"

"As Carter's cousin I think you might want to help him out. I think you cleaned him and fed him and I think you let him get a good distance away before you decided to call it in. That's what I think."

Meet Katie.

We're on the move again. Just walking, no direction. The murderer and the political rebel. Me and my new, and probably only, friend. She's

Katie, she's nineteen, and she's always willing to stick two fingers up at the government. Her story is that her parents forced her to remain in the country when the regime changed. She was too young to be permitted a choice. They were staunch nationalists. Loved New Britain and what she stood for. She said that, they referred to the country as *she.* They gave everything to Robert Lodge and his guidelines. The house was painted with the Union Flag. Flags hung from every window in the house. They bought into the dream with everything they had. Then one day her mother and father were driving home from a rare trip out of the house, not a care in the world. A man stepped out in front of the car, and was killed instantly. He'd posted on to his Network dayline that he'd lost the will to live. His wife had taken their children abroad before the regime change, left him alone, and desperate. He'd committed suicide, but Katie's parents were held responsible. It wasn't their fault, but since it was they that killed him, they were accountable. Finnegan's Law Enforcement caught up with them within an hour, and twenty four later they were placed before a wall, and James Finnegan drove a car straight into them. The country's idea of ironic punishment, I suppose. Her mother died instantly. Her father went shortly after. They'd given all that they had to New Britain, and New Britain took their lives. I can see why she's bitter.

"You know there's more like me?" she says, looking up at me. Her green eyes glassy and blinking in the scant light of the city, her story's obviously brought things back that she'd rather had stayed in but once she started it just didn't stop.

"More what?"

"People who hate what the country's become, who never had a chance to leave."

"I can imagine."

"Can I trust you Paul Carter? Even though you're a murderer?"

"Stop saying that."

"But you are. Don't worry, I think it's cool. Can I trust you?"

"I saved your life didn't I?"

"Answer the question Paul Carter," she says. Stops in her tracks. Pulls her hands up into the sleeves of her hooded top. Wipes her glistening cheek. Smudges the dirt across her face. Folds her arms. I stop too, turn to face her.

"Yes, you can trust me."

She starts walking again, only with more purpose.

"Okay, good, because I know somewhere safe we can go, come on."

Somewhere safe we can go.

"Are you joking?" I ask, incredulously.

"If I were joking it'd be funny, believe me," she says, with a small giggle.

What we're looking at is a derelict police station. A modern, newly built before the regime change,

Ryan Bracha

but left unused after Lodge deconstructed law enforcement as we once knew it. It stands alone amidst overgrown grass, weeds, and bushes, an empty carpark. It looms large over us, dominating the immediate skyline. The building in total darkness. Any windows within rock-throwing distance have been smashed. I suppose there's a certain irony in where she's brought me. Where else better for criminals to seek solace than a disued police station?

"Come on," she says, sneaking off through the shadows, toward the building, I follow at pace. The area around us is silent, but for intermittent scuffs of my feet dragging along the floor, "pick your feet up Paul Carter," she whispers. I do.

The door to the station is not so much a door anymore. It's simply the metal frame of a door, with both huge panels of glass smashed away. In the darkness I can see a huge piece of graffiti across the face of the station. *Keep Britian Brittish.* My guess is that it was daubed by somebody who, up until a few years ago, held an overseas passport, and jumped at the chance to adopt our fair nation as their homeland. I wouldn't wish to guess the nationality. Katie spots me looking at it.

"I did that," she says proudly.

"You spelled it wrong," I retort, and she laughs.

"Soz Mr Brains," she says, her words dipped generously in sarcasm, "I *know* it's spelled wrong you wally, it's spelled wrong on *purpose.*"

"I don't get it."

"You don't need to, come on."

She ducks beneath the bar that runs across the glassless door, and into the building, a rapidly diminishing echo of her feet against the crunch of broken glass emanates from the hole of the door. Now that's she's told me I don't need to get it, I really do *need* to get it. I hate not understanding things. I hate not being *the best* at things. If I struggle to understand something, then I will work, and work, and work, to ensure that by the time I am done I am the world's foremost authority on the subject.

"Wait," I say, following her into the building. Up ahead the crunch stops, and a narrow powerful torch beam swings back from the dark toward me.

"What?"

I catch up to her, the torchlight so powerful and narrow it seems more like a bright white laser beam drawing me toward it through the black.

"Why did you spell it wrong on purpose?"

Katie sighs dramatically, her rotten breath picks at my nostrils we're standing that close. The torch beam swings up to beneath her chin, in that *spooky* way that people do when they have a torch in the dark. All she needs now is to say *whoooooo!* and you'd get the picture.

"You know how we're all British but some people aren't really?"

She means the foreigners that opted to stay. I know already why she did the graffiti.

"Yeah."

Ryan Bracha

"You know how even though we're all British some people can't even speak English?"

"Yeah."

"You know how *actual* British people are scared of the *pretend* British people?"

I know how her way of making statements through questioning isn't even nearly endearing.

"Yeah."

"Well, that's the plan, write a badly spelled, obviously pretend British statement, and you scare a lot of people away. This is where I go to hang out away from the country. I don't want every man and his wife coming to hang out with me."

"What about me?"

Katie considers the question briefly, then swings the torch back to the corridor, and starts to walk. "You said I could trust you Paul Carter. Come on."

Actual British and Pretend British.

On paper, Robert Lodge's ideas of a unified Britain were great. His illegal immigrant amnesty brought millions from the woodwork of society. People from the darkest corners of the globe appeared, hands in the air. To be fair to him he was true to his word. These wretches had previously lived in squalor, thirty people deep in a derelict squat, hiding from the law, from the potential to be cast out of our country, back to whatever they were running from. Robert Lodge offered them a chance to live as normal a life as they could ever hope to dream for, in exchange for unrequited loyalty to New Britain, and they grabbed that chance with both dirty hands. People who once belonged to places like Afghanistan, Somalia, Nigeria, and North Korea, ran amok. Communities arose in the areas that had been left deserted by former occupants who had given the country up to live their lives abroad. Although we were all *British,* there remained territorial hazards. Those of us that ventured out of a day, would continue to be fearful of stepping into an area now occupied by the Somalians, or Koreans. Pidgin English threats echo through the air. Strong regional accents, such as those around Liverpool and Newcastle, are on their ways to becoming twisted out of all recognition, absorbed and melted into a pot of African or Asian. Sometimes both. Although violence, killing, swearing, stealing, and anti-British action are outlawed we still find ways of hurting one another. Our distorted sense of right and wrong mean that we can do anything that was not outlawed by The Guidelines, no matter how wrong they once were. Bullying, bigamy, adultery, spitting, racism, sexism, homophobia, even slavery, are permitted under The Guidelines. The messed up part of it all is that reaction to any of the above can result in death. Each *Pretend Briton* could flaunt the loopholes, provoke response from rivals, and then stand entirely in the right whilst their rival

Ryan Bracha

is sentenced to death. The country, as much as we pretended otherwise, is more divided than ever.

Shelter, shade, and Shane.

"Who's this guy?"
This is the kid speaking. He's agitated and up on his feet. Fists clenched. He's as filthy as Katie, but it might be the light. His greying, tattered outfit stinks of homelessness. Standing about a foot smaller than me he seems ready to pounce. Then his features soften as recognition sinks into his brain, slowly but surely, like feet into quicksand.
"You're Paul Carter," he says finally, Katie's dancing around excitely.
"I know, right?" she sings. Almost skips toward the kid, tugging on his torn plain sleeve, "he saved my life! Paul Carter saved my jackin' life!"
"What's it like to kill people?" asks the kid, stepping toward me, wide-eyed and excited. Not this again. I sigh.
"I already asked him, he won't say," Katie interjects, for which I'm thankful, then she turns to me, "this is Shane."
Shane moves toward me, hand outstretched for me to take, which I do. His grip is really quite strong for such a small kid. He shakes my arm vigorously.
"Good to meet you, you're a legend."
Legend seems pretty strong. I'm barely even notorious.

"Thanks. I think."

"Do you know what you've done?"

"I'm pretty sure I do."

"Have you seen The Network?"

"No."

"You should, you killed Banger, you're all they're talking about."

This is bad. I don't want to be *all they're talking about*. I just wanted to silence the man who poured dirt over my name. I really don't know what I expected would happen. Something clicks.

"Wait. You have Network access?"

"Yeah, course."

Shane digs a palmtop computer from his deep scruffy pocket, and clicks it on. The pale white glow illuminates his face, which really is as dirty as I first thought. How he came to own a palmtop I don't ask. His fingers do their stuff, and he spins the screen toward me. The statements all melt into one.

PaulCartermustdiePaulCarteristhemostwantedmaninthecountryPaulCartershouldpayforwhathe'sdonePaulCarterisadeadman.

Then a jolt like a bullet in the chest.

Paul Carter's cousin up for judgment for harbouring a wanted man. Two hundred thousand votes required.

Danny.

A MODERN BRITAIN #3

FRANCIS SKELTON WAS SEATED IN JUDGMENT ROOM THREE OF THE DEVINE LAW ENFORCEMENT BUILDING. HIS RIGHT LEG BOUNCING RAPIDLY. HIS FISTS CLENCHED TIGHT AROUND ONE ANOTHER. HIS HEAD FACED TOWARD HIS LAP. TO HIS RIGHT WAS A FIFTY INCH LED SCREEN. UPON THE SCREEN WERE CHARTS AND NUMBERS. INFORMATION ABOUT HIS CASE. THE CRIME. THE QUANTITY OF VOTES REQUIRED TO PUNISH HIM, THE QUANTITY OF VOTES ALREADY AMASSED IN THE TWENTY THREE SLEEPLESS HOURS SINCE HIS JUDGMENT WAS PUT TO THE PEOPLE. AN INSET MONITOR SHOWING THE IMAGE OF HIMSELF. A SCROLLING YELLOW BAR OFFERING TO-THE-MINUTE UPDATES. THE NUMBER OF CURRENT VIEWERS. THE AMOUNT OF HITS THAT HIS JUDGMENT HAD AMASSED. THERE WAS AN INSTANTLY REFRESHING OPINION BOX, A

Paul Carter is a Dead Man

LIVE FEED TO JUST EXACTLY HOW HATED HE'D BECOME. THE INCREASINGLY VIOLENT THREATS UPON HIS LIFE. OCCASIONAL VIDEOS, TALKING HEADS FROM SUPPORTERS OF THE LAW. HIS CRIME WAS SPEEDING. HE'D DONE FIFTY SIX KILOMETRES PER HOUR IN A FORTY ZONE. THE REQUIRED VOTES WERE ONE MILLION. THE CURRENT VOTING TALLY WAS AT NINE HUNDRED AND SOMETHING THOUSAND. HE'D STOPPED WATCHING. TO HIS LEFT STOOD THE ARMED GUARD. ENTIRELY SUPERFLUOUS, GIVEN THAT FRANCIS WAS CHAINED TO THE CHAIR. DIRECTLY IN FRONT OF HIM WAS THE CAMERA. THE WORLD'S WINDOW TO HIM. THE BLINKING LITTLE EYEBALL THAT HAD UNADULTERATED ACCESS TO HIS ANGUISH. SUCKING UP HIS LIKENESS THROUGH FIBRE OPTIC CABLES. SCATTERED ACROSS THE AIR VIA WIRELESS CONNECTION. THE MILLIONS OF TINY PIECES OF FRANCIS SKELTON TRANSMITTED THROUGH THE SCREENS OF THE POPULATION THAT HAD CHOSEN TO JUDGE HIM. PEOPLE

Ryan Bracha

WITH AN INTEREST IN HIS FATE. HE'D
SPENT THE FIRST FEW HOURS ANGRILY
DEMANDING THAT THEY LET HIM BE,
THAT ALL HE HAD DONE WAS GO A
LITTLE BIT FAST IN HIS CAR. HE'D BEEN
IN A RUSH TO SEE HIS DAUGHTER AT
THE HOSPITAL, SHE'D JUST GIVEN BIRTH
TO HIS GRANDCHILD, NAMED FRANCIS IN
HIS HONOUR. THEN CAME THE PANIC,
THE TEARS, THE BEGGING. THE
BARGAINING, FOR WHAT IT WAS WORTH.
NOTHING. THEN AS EXHAUSTION SET IN,
AND THE RESIGNATION, HE'D GONE
QUIET, SETTLED IN HIS THOUGHTS.
MUTTERED USELESS PRAYERS.
APOLOGISED QUIETLY TO HIS DAUGHTER
FOR NOT BEING THERE. THIRTY MINUTES
TO GO. THE GUARD INFORMED HIM THAT
THEY ONLY NEEDED FIFTY TWO
THOUSAND VOTES, AND THAT THERE
WAS A LAST MINUTE VOTING FRENZY.
THE GUARD LAUGHED WHEN HE SAID IT.
TEN MINUTES TO GO. ANOTHER
REMINDER. THREE THOUSAND VOTES
REQUIRED. FOUR MINUTES. NINE

Paul Carter is a Dead Man

HUNDRED VOTES REQUIRED. TWO MINUTES. TWO HUNDRED VOTES. AS THE CLOCK TICKED DOWN, SO DID THE AMOUNT OF VOTES REQUIRED TO PUNISH HIM. TWENTY SECONDS. EIGHTY VOTES. TEN SECONDS. FIFTEEN VOTES. FIVE. EIGHT VOTES. TWO. FOUR VOTES. THEN. NOTHING. THE CLOCK HAD REACHED TWENTY FOUR HOURS. NO FANFARE. THE GUARD SIGHED HEAVILY. CALLED HIM A LUCKY BANDSTAND. BEGRUDGINGLY FLICKED THE KEY AROUND IN THE LOCK. RELEASED ONE HAND. THEN THE OTHER. FRANCIS SKELTON WAS RELEASED FROM DEVINE LAW ENFORCEMENT SHORTLY AFTER. TOOK A DEEP BREATH OF THE ACRID GARBAGE RIDDEN AIR OF LONDON. IT HAD NEVER SMELLED SO GOOD. HE PULLED OUT HIS TELEPHONE FROM THE BAG THAT HE'D HAD RETURNED, DIALLED THE NUMBER FOR HIS DAUGHTER, AND AS SHE WAILED OUT AN EXCITABLE GREETING INTO HIS EAR FRANCIS SKELTON DROPPED TO HIS KNEES AND WEPT.

Ryan Bracha

They've got Danny.

So they've got Danny, and he's up for judgment. Part of me wants him to rot for his blatant disregard for my wellbeing. Aside from a token *be careful.* The other part is grating at me, he's *family.* For what family means anymore. "What's the plan Paul Carter?" asks Katie, her eyes blinking from beneath her dirty forehead, they're bigger than I first thought. She's looking up at me. Cute. Filthy, but cute. *Focus.*
"I don't know," I say, and I don't. I really don't. Although he informed on me, it was I that showed up at his place. Gave him no choice. He wasn't to know that they'd do what they have done. I can't stop staring at his judgment.

Daniel Carter is hereby accused of both harbouring and assisting known murderer and fugitive Paul Carter, who has not only killed an innocent member of our British society in cold blood, but has also ended the life of popular government authorised Network bounty hunter, Barry 'Banger' Armstrong without remorse. This is notice that The Network Cutting Crew intend to offer Daniel Carter the standard twenty four hours to be judged by the British public for his crime. The maximum punishment permissable will be death, and the method of punishment shall be selected by a random drawing of those submitted by the British public. The required amount of Network votes is two hundred thousand.

Paul Carter is a Dead Man

I can't help but feel my first pang of guilt in a while. All Danny did was open his door. Pete sent me on my way before I even knew it. Pete. Something doesn't sit right here. I immediately close down the judgment, and scroll up to search. My brows furrowed, I sigh through my nose. "What's up?" asks Katie, but I don't look up to her. Don't say anything. Something's not right at all. One after the other I tap in the letters. It brings up over a hundred Peter Fergusons. I shorten it to Pete but that only serves to add more names to the results list. No use. Katie's appeared over my shoulder, and Shane over hers.

"Who's Pete Ferguson?" asks Katie, her hand drops onto my shoulder, squeezes it for some reason.

"He's Danny's flatmate, he was there when I showed up, I'm just checking something."

"If he's up for judgment too?"

"Yeah," I nod.

"Why don't you just check the Crime Network for his name?" Shane suggests, "You know? Instead of the whole Network?"

"Good lad," I say, and instantly I'm in the Crime Network. There's a Paul Ferguson up for judgment for smoking cannabis in his own home. A Pete Franklin for murder. Critically though, there are no Pete Fergusons. *Why would they only judge Danny?* I know exactly why but I can't admit it.

"You know what I think?" says Katie.

"You'll tell me anyway, won't you?"

Ryan Bracha

"Already you know me too well Paul Carter," she smiles, "I think that 'cause you nailed Banger, I think it's personal. I reckon they're using Danny to get to you. You've annoyed some powerful people Paul Carter."

I feel a cool fleck or two of spittle as she enunciates the *P* from her alliterative statement. It makes me slightly uncomfortable, but I limit my reaction to a shuffle in my seat and as subtle a wipe of my cheek as I can muster.

"It seems so," I agree.

"So what do we do?" Shane's voice comes from over Katie's shoulder.

I'm not sure whether I should be grateful that these kids have taken it upon themselves to start a band of sidekicks. I'm only going to bring trouble. But then what else do they have? The way the country's going we'll all be dead before long, either through our own wrongdoings or by having our lives strangled by this regime. I can't lie. I was a part of it. I took my pound of flesh, but the longer I've been away from The Network, the more I see what we don't have. We have garbage piled up high. Maniacal law enforcement. Minimal actual physical interaction. It's going to get worse too. This could all end in tears, but the same as Katie and Shane, what else do I have? If we're going down we might as well go down fighting.

"You up for a fight?" I ask the pair, and already Katie is nodding eagerly, Shane is slightly more tentative.

"I'm not very hard, they'll kill me," he says, but I shake my head.

"You don't need to be, they've got strength in numbers, if we're gonna do it we're gonna have to play dirty. You know how to play dirty?"

He's nodding sagely now, and already I can see his thought process clunking into life.

"Yeah," he says.

"Good, because I've got an idea."

Danny's plight.

He almost wished that he *had* harboured Paul. Taken him in and helped him. Fed him. Instead of turning his back on him. Casting him out. At least he'd have been here for a reason then. *Stupid Pete,* he considered. Hands chained to the chair. The clock read only forty minutes in. The screen beside him filled with the image of himself, flicking to a series of summary tables and charts. The judgment counter showed at eight thousand votes. A slow start, which was a positive thing. The one called Grady was seated in the corner, facing him. Sneering threateningly at him every time he felt inclined to look the guy's way. He seemed like a genuinely angry guy. His shorn head glowing red with apparent fury. He encapsulated all that was wrong about law enforcement. People who seemingly took employment in this sector to hurt people. At least the police in the old regime tried to help, instead of going out of their ways to hurt. Or kill.

Ryan Bracha

This new law enforcement was actually *disappointed* if they were denied to opportunity to punish. Robert Lodge didn't see this side of things. He sat in his ivory tower, reaping the financial benefits of the advertising revenue from the Crime Network. Danny had *always* known this, but chose largely to ignore it. The Crime Network was always so much fun on the other side of The Network. He was finding out one agonising second at a time just how *little* fun it was in the firing line. Especially when he was innocent. He refused to bow to the pressure though. They could go to Hell if they thought he was going to crack. He cleared his throat, attracting a smidgen of attention from Grady. "I'm sorry," he said to the camera. Grady twitched slightly, but still didn't move. People spoke to the camera all the time on the Crime Network. Some would say prayers, others would take the time to curse the names of everybody and their mother. Those whose judgment vote requirements had been met and surpassed would often spew expletives into the airwaves before being dragged kicking and screaming from the judgment rooms. Danny had no intention of being that man.

"I'm sorry for everything," he continued, "Paul, if you're watching this, I'm sorry I turned you away."

The name grabbed the attention of the guardsman, who turned further still to watch the performance.

"You took me in, and I'm sorry I turned my back on you. I wish I really had taken you in and helped you. It would at least be justification for these-"

He stopped himself short, he had no intention of giving them further ammunition.

"-people, to be holding me like this. Don't worry too much about me though," he laughed, "I'll live."

A video response.

"You ready?" I ask of Shane, who's holding the palmtop computer in my direction. Both hands to hold it as steadily as he can. A blinking red light beside the small retina of the camera. Behind him stands Katie, a wry smile on her face, one of her hands holds Shane's shoulder. It would seem this is what she's dreamed of since the regime dragged her parents under. Sticking it to the man, doing it properly, and doing it by fighting dirty. I still don't have an idea as to the plan, or how it might go, but what have we got to lose? Shane holds up a thumb to give me the go ahead.

"My name is Paul Carter. It would seem that I've gained a degree of notoriety for my actions. I have my reasons for why I did what I did, believe me. I don't want your mercy. I deserve to be judged. Banger, may he rest in peace, was a matter of self-defence. It was him or me. Again, I did it, I hold my hands up, I haven't recorded this

Ryan Bracha

message to plead my case. I know that right now, if the NCC catch me it's game over. You'll fall over yourselves to be that final vote that tightens the noose around my neck. Or drops the blade down upon it. That's what you do. It's not your fault. You're so easily conditioned."

This last sentence sticks in my throat. I know what I need to do.

"But that's by the by. I only wanted to try to help you to understand. You'll hear from me again. If anybody wants to join me in making a stand, I'll find you. If anybody wants to stand against me. I'll fight you. Mr Wilson Becker, this is for you. If you, or any of your crew cross me," I pause for dramatic effect, then say "or my new friends, you'll go the same way as Banger. Goodbye."

Shane clicks off the camera.

"Awesome. Properly awesome."

Katie approaches and throws her arms around my neck. Pulls me closer to her height. Whispers in my ear.

"You're gonna be a hero, Paul Carter."

I don't want to be a hero. I want to. I don't know. What I *do* know, is that I have the shell of a plan forming inside my skull. *You're so easily conditioned.* Katie kisses my cheek, and drops back to her feet. Shane shakes his head with a smile. *You're so easily conditioned.* He approaches, and turns the computer to us to watch my performance. I'm remarkably impressed by my performance, if I do say so myself. It comes from hours, days even, of speaking to myself in the mirror. Perfecting my public speaking skills. When I would have conversations with people, and there was a reflective surface in sight, I would perform to myself. Barely even aware that a conversation was happening. Practising standing before tens, hundreds of people, and being the centre of attention. If I were being honest with myself I'd say that when Katie told me I was going to be a hero. Well. I got that tingle. *You're gonna be a hero. Focus!*

"You look cool Paul Carter, like a proper cold blooded killer should," says Katie. I've stopped asking her to stop saying it, it only spurs her on. "Yeah, man. You do," Shane concurs, "so what now?"

So what now.

We've left the abandoned police station for the time being. Getting as far away from it as possible. Tramping along a barely used and partially overgrown dual carriageway, finding our way to somewhere half decent in order to upload the video. This is the hard part. We can be tracked within minutes once a video is uploaded. Once I even turn on my mobile. Location software has grown with our useless society. I don't want to upload the video using Shane's Network synopsis. The fewer people implicated with me the better. Of course they'll question my intentionally mysterious *or my new friends* comment, but unless we're caught how will they

Ryan Bracha

ever know who these new friends are? We need as many tricks up our sleeves as possible. We have no weapons. No army. Just myself and two kids. Hardly Robin Hood. Not yet anyway. As we walk I'm hearing Shane's story.

Shane's story.

Shane is sixteen, and has been living on the streets for three years. The majority of the current regime's period of power. His family wanted to move to Ireland when given the choice. Shane was an ordinary thirteen year old kid who'd developed an attachment to his friends. Enjoyed bouts of online team-gaming, hung around in Facespace forums chatting to kindred spirits, went to the local fast food restaurant to look at girls. On the eve of their impending journey to a new homeland Shane opted to run away. Left a letter, asking his parents to go without him, he liked being British too much. He had somewhere to go. Friends who would take him in.
The thing was, a thirteen year old friend's promise is nothing if it relies too heavily on the permission of unknowing parents. He was turned away from door after door after door. By the time the penny had dropped that he was homeless his parents were presumably long gone. He moved from squat to squat. Sofa to sofa. Worked menial tasks in exchange for food, money, electric to charge his computer. Learned

to embrace life on the streets. It was different to how it used to be. The streets were overrun with vagrants before the government was overthrown. When the exodus began the homeless would take residence in houses, flats, mansions. Anywhere that had previously been owned and loved by families who would now be living in political exile in France, Belgium and Germany. The tables turned. Shane preferred to stay on the move. When work wasn't forthcoming he would help himself to the things left behind by those that emigrated, like clothes, electrical products, tinned long-life food, sometimes money. A free spirit. That's what he calls himself. He'll do anything as long as it's something new. Something that keeps life interesting. He has no ulterior motives. No vendetta against governments, cyber bullies or anything like that. He just wants a story to tell when he's old. I have to admit that I sort of admire the ethos. It's not for me, nor is it likely to ever be, but for one so young, he's got a decent approach to life in this nightmare of a country. I asked him why he wanted to get involved in this fight, his response *why not?*

How he and Katie came into each other's centres of gravity is that she'd gotten talking to him on Network. Played word and puzzle games against each other on The Network until the early hours. Grown closer. Met in real life. Shane took her away from this society that's growing ever more dependent upon The Network, showed her the outside world. They'd explored derelict estates,

Ryan Bracha

grown ever more wily. He'd supported her as best he could throughout the whole thing about her parents. They'd tried to be intimate once. Didn't work out. They were best suited as friends. A pair of rebels. Now they are here, following their new hero. A murderer.

A gauntlet thrown down.

"Boss?" The voice of Oxley crept into his ears from behind the door, followed by a tentative tap of a single knuckle tickling the wood, "boss?" "Come in," said Wilson Becker, seated behind the heavyweight desk, fingers pressed firmly together before his nose. He watched the flesh turn white as he pressed firmer, then released the pressure and watched the colour flood back into them. Oxley crept into the room, mobile phone in hand, outstretched toward Becker. "Boss, you need to see this," he said, passing the device over. On the screen was a paused image of Carter. Face dirty. Eyes tired. Unshaven. The guy was a mess. He wasn't the crisp, smart character that the circulating images would suggest anymore, but it was definitely Carter, the way he carried himself, that confidence. It was infuriating. Becker watched the whole performance. Silently seethed at the arrogance of the man. Felt a pang of sadness upon mention of Banger. The way his name had been used in a threat. Becker felt his throat constrict. His nostrils twitched involuntarily in fury. His breathing grew heavy. Firm.

"When did this go out?"

"A few minutes ago. He logged on to The Network five minutes ago, Ned started tracking the location straight away. Then this video got uploaded onto the Crime Network and he logged out. The thing is, it's gone jackin' viral boss."

Wilson Becker rose from his seat, struggling to compose himself. He wanted to crush the smug skull of Paul Carter, no judgments, no twenty four hours, no nothing. The fact that it had already circulated The Network in the few minutes since it had been up spelled bad news. They needed to put a stop to this sooner rather than later.

"You got a tracker on it still?"

"Yeah, we got it triangulated to a meadow just outside the city, Teddy's gone to get the van. Joe's gettin' the dogs."

"Good man. Let's catch this murderin' bandstand, and quick."

Mr Robert Lodge discovers the situation.

"Sir, it seems that there's, ehm, a *situation*, in the North."

"Situation? What kind of situation?"

"A fellow by the name of Paul Carter is causing a fair bit of trouble for one of the authorised crews. It would appear that he eluded them on a routine hunt, and in the process has murdered one of their men."

"Oh dear."

"Indeed."

"What do they intend to do?"

"I'm not sure, as of yet, sir. We are yet to contact them. The situation has only come to light since the fellow in question has uploaded a threatening video to The Network. In this video he has also called anybody who opposes the regime to arms."

"Oh dear."

"Indeed."

"This isn't ideal at all is it?"

"No sir."

"What would you propose Garner?"

"My thoughts might be to first issue a statement regarding Paul Carter. We would look to cauterise this particular wound as quickly as possible."

"Hmmm."

"Indeed."

"And what of the crew? Which crew is it?"

"The Network Cutting Crew, sir."

"Really?"

"Mmmm."

"How unusual. They're usually so efficient."

"Yes sir, and the nature of the man's video response leads me to believe we're not dealing with your everyday garden criminal, sir. Perhaps quite the opposite."

"Tell me Garner, do you wish to marry the man?"

"Sir? No, of course not."

"Then stop talking about him as if he is anything other than a violent murderer. No more, no less. He is scum, and will be dealt with as such."

"Sorry, sir. Of course."

"We'll say no more about it. Okay Garner, go ahead, speak with Wilson Becker about working with some of the other crews to bring this man to justice as quickly as possible. Issue the statement across The Network. You put this rucksack under no illusions that we will not have him caught, and judged to the full extent of the law. Paul Carter is a dead man, Garner."

"Sir."

Wilson Becker to Paul Carter.

We've set the wheels in motion. Planted the seed. If I was big news before, you can guarantee that I'm monumental news now. Nobody's ever done this before. Stood up for themselves. Not since Lodge came into power. For the last few years all we've done is accept that what he says is the final word, lived our lives. Thankful that we didn't have to worry about immigration issues. Jobs going abroad. Industry going down the pan. We thought that what our lives had become was the best thing for us. We didn't have to worry about the next man. We knew exactly what the next man was doing because he laid his soul bare on his Network dayline. What Katie, Shane and I have done is put a cat amongst the pigeons. Upset the applecart. Choose your analogy.

Ryan Bracha

We're back at the police station, having
delivered the video in as remote an area as
possible. Now we're waiting. Shane has
refreshed the Network dayline every few
minutes. Checked the Crime Network. Opened up
a new window showing solely Networking
Cutting Crew feeds. Looking for anything to tie
us in. There are hundreds of people, all placing
the video of me on their dayline. Thousands
even. But they aren't supporting the cause. Far
from it. They're insulting me. Chastising me for
my violent actions. Showing their support for
Banger. Threatening to kill me themselves if I
ever show my face. Then it happens. A new
message. It's on the NCC feed. It's titled *Wilson
Becker to Paul Carter.*
"He looks mad," says Katie with a chuckle, at the
freeze frame of Becker's big face, close up. I
would hazard a guess that he's just this minute
arrived to find me not there. At the field.
"Start it up," I say to Shane, who obliges. The
buffer circle spins maybe one, two, three
revolutions, before Wilson Becker kicks into
action. He's in the outdoors. A breeze tickles the
microphone just slightly. The light casts jagged
shadows around his mangled, rugby-injured
nose. He looks annoyed.
"Paul Carter. Wilson Becker here. The man you
murdered. Banger. He was my colleague, my
friend, and my brother. He was in the wrong
place at the wrong time, and I will avenge him.
You may think that you can run forever, hiding
with, *your new friends,* but hear this. You can't. I

will personally hunt you. I will personally catch you, and when the good people of New Britain judge you, I will personally rip you limb from jackin' limb. Mark my words son. I hope that you'll enjoy watching your fool of a cousin being judged."

He turns away from the camera and looks out into the field. Roars in fury. Dogs yelp in the background, and then the video cuts out.

Immediately the Crime Network is a frenzied flickering moment of people sharing the same video that we've just seen. Each adding their own comments of support for Wilson Becker and his cause. Calling for them to kill Danny sooner than twenty four hours.

"These people are mad Paul Carter, you're awesome," says Katie, and her hand squeezes my shoulder. I look to her and she is smiling at me with a look that I could swear was pride.

"So what next?" Shane asks, placing the computer down upon the table, "I mean, the ball's in our court again now, isn't it?"

"Yes," I nod, but it occurs to me that I'm absolutely shattered. This day feels like the slowest that a day has ever gone in the history of time, "but we need to sleep."

"I'm okay, I don't need to sleep," says Shane, shaking his head, "I'd rather stay up and watch The Network go nuts in your name. You're welcome to my bed though. Or you can share with Katie?"

His eyebrows raise and Katie appears to have taken a turn toward bashful.

Ryan Bracha

"Shut up, you rucksack!" she whines, punching his arms, before looking to me, "but really, you can if you want? I've never done it with a murderer."

"No, thank you, I just need sleep."

I couldn't possibly say it but even if I were up to that kind of thing tonight, I couldn't do it with her, she's too young for me for a start. Her breath also smells.

"Suit yourself," she shrugs, "I'm tired too though. Shane, you good to keep guard?"

Shane nods and we disappear to our respective corners. I find the piles of materials that make up Shane's bed, and drop down fully clothed. I'm asleep before I'm even halfway horizontal.

Introducing Johnny Stiff.

"So I'm told we've all got to be a little bit more scared tonight, in case Paul Carter comes and kills us while we sleep," the bespectacled twenty something deadpanned against the familiar backdrop of his mother's living room. The edge of his straight cut dusty brown, immaculately combed fringe sliced directly across the middle of his forehead, giving it a more than a passing resemblance to a two-tone coffee bean. His fingers pulled awkwardly at the edge of the spectacles as he forced the things into a more comfortable position on his face, "don't get me wrong, I'm scared, of course I am, but I mean, come on, with my immune system, I think I ought to be a little more fearful of airborne germs than that guy!"

Johnny Stiff, born Jonathan Smith, was one of a multitude of bedroom comedians who had found the soapbox nature of The Network more than accommodating for their tastes. The classical comedians of days gone by had lost out. Made way to a new breed who could ply their trades with the ability to block out potential hecklers by simply removing their subscription rights. It gave them the chance to preach only to the converted, of which Shane was one. He loved his self-deprecating humour. The way he played his disabilities for laughs. He wasn't afraid to poke fun at those who were in a better place that he was. The way his own broadcasts played out was that he would open with a few topical jokes that in some way brought his disability into the mix, and then would open up a forum where his fans might ask him stupid questions and he would change his set based on the questions. A cross between improvisation and just the guy twisting the question to accommodate an existing joke.

"Let's think about this," he said, "Paul Carter shows up at my house, he's got a belt in his hands, gonna strangle me like he did old Jacob Glover. I'm a funny guy though, so I throw him a joke and suddenly we're friends. Like we've known each other all our lives, like he's my brother for jack's sake!"

Shane watched the typed responses from the viewers so far. A variety of LOL, which was *laughing out loud*, or TIJFS, *this is jackin funny*

Ryan Bracha

sherbet, amongst others. Johnny Stiff had a lot of fans.

"So now I've made him a cup of tea and I'm thinking, *for a cold blooded murderer Paul you're a good guy,* maybe we even have a game of Fruity Basher and he lets me win because hey, even though he kills people for fun he has to, I'm the guy in the wheelchair!"

More LOLs and TIJFS. Smiley emoticon faces. Shane laughed quietly through his nose, holding in his mirth, aware that the others were in dire need of some quality sleep. He wished he could tell the people that Paul Carter *was* a good guy, whatever his motives, Shane felt that he would have been justified in his actions. That was the feeling he got, and he liked to think he was a pretty good judge of character.

"So me and Paul Carter are now best friends yeah? I know, the cripple and the killer, we're this year's mismatched crime fighting duo," he continued, snorting laughter, building up his audience to the inevitable and predicted punchline, but it wasn't what he said that was funny, it was the way he delivered it. That snorting amusement at his own jokes, "and he's just about to leave for home, maybe he's got a pie in the oven that he needs to get back for, and suddenly you see that look in his eyes. The finger goes up like he wants me to wait a minute. The lip goes and I can see it happening. Time slows down and I'm trying to wheel away in time but it's no use, he sneezes, right in my face. Kills me dead. His new best friend."

Paul Carter is a Dead Man

Johnny Stiff paused. Sniggered pig-like. Eyes flickering left to right.

"I'd forgive him though. As I floated ever so slowly up to Heaven on my Stanner stairlift." Shane hooted a loud laugh before clamping a self-conscious hand over his mouth, but snorting quiet laughter through his nose. A flurry of typed responses followed from the audience, to which he added his own. It was a classic. He scrolled through the other responses, mostly typed variations to let their good host that they were laughing behind their Network synopses. Standard procedure. Something stood out though. A simple sentence that, on the face of it, was a mere message of support for the housebound comedian. Shortly after that it became a political rally.

London Calling.

Wilson Becker quietly seethed. Watched the dishevelled edge of the city tenements roll by behind his own reflection in the passenger side window. Oxley was driving. Teddy sat in silence at the back. Even the dogs knew not to cause a fuss right now. Carter had so far made a fool of him in a big way. He'd had help, he *had* to have had help, and they were playing him for an idiot. Becker considered the situation. Paul Carter was clever. He had ghosted in and out of their vision with ease. Tackled and killed Banger. Found and brainwashed some civilians into joining him in

Ryan Bracha

whatever it was that he had planned. The best that they could hope for was that he'd screw up sooner rather than later, maybe get spotted in society, and they could draw a line under the whole sorry mess. Worst case would be that the people bought into his bullsherbet and they had a war on their hands. That eventuality didn't bear thinking about. The government would strip the Cutting Crew of the contract faster than a Network Prostitute of her underwear at the sight of a five hundred pound credit limit. A horrifying split second glimpse into the future later the government appeared to read his mind as the phone on the dashboard illuminated and vibrated. A London number flashing on the face of it. Oxley glanced toward his boss nervously, but knew better than to take his eyes from the road for much longer than that. Wilson Becker pushed the call accept and spoke.

"Becker."

"Mr Becker, Francis Garner here, I'm calling from the offices of Mr Robert Lodge. I wonder if we might have a word."

"Okay," Becker said, wanted to let the government man do the talking.

"Does the name Paul Carter mean anything to you?"

"You know it does."

"Indeed, and it has come to our attention that this man has become something of a thorn in your side, Mr Becker."

Wilson Becker sighed impatiently. He hated dealing with these types. Too many words to use and a silver spoon in the mouths they were speaking from.

"Nothing I can't deal with."

"Indeed, but as he may be a thorn in your side Mr Becker, Mr Lodge is concerned that your failure to *deal with it,* may result in Paul Carter becoming a thorn in *the nation's* side."

"Like I said, it's nothing I can't deal with."

"Be that as it may Mr Becker, our advice to you is to seek assistance from elsewhere, perhaps look in the direction of Tough Justice? Your own crew is sadly depleted, of course, what with the demise of poor Mr Armstrong."

"His name was Banger."

"Quite, my point is that you appear to be somewhat *out of your depth,* and extra hands on the job may ease the burd-"

Becker ended the call. He wasn't hearing this. The car remained silent as he tapped the edge of the phone against his chin. Wanted to curse. *So* wanted to curse. A real, old fashioned, outlawed swear word. Thought better of it and threw the phone against the front window with every ounce of bottled fury.

He let out an animalistic roar and slammed his hand repeatedly against the plastic dash, drawing a wince from Oxley with every smack. In the foot well his mobile buzzed into life once more, but remained ignored.

"Fungus! Fungus! Fungus! Fungus!" he yelled between each angered smack, before turning to his driver, "Paul Carter is a dead man. Paul Carter is a DEAD MAN!"

Ryan Bracha

Mr Robert Lodge makes a decision.

"Ah, Garner, any news?"

"Not as of yet, sir."

"Hmmm."

"Wilson Becker is being extremely evasive, sir. He is now refusing to enter into any communications since we, ehm, *suggested* that he seek assistance."

"Really? Even through The Network?"

"Yes, sir."

"Curious. Very unprofessional. Not like him at all."

"Indeed. I do believe that he's driven by the death of his colleague. Blinkered even. It appears he may be making this a personal vendetta."

"Hmmm. Understable, but unprofessional nevertheless. Tell me, do you have the statement prepared regarding Carter?"

"Our media people are working on it, sir. They are finalising the audio track, all imagery is edited. We shall have Paul Carter running scared, of that I have no doubt."

"Excellent, Garner. Be sure to release it as soon as it's ready."

"Of course, sir."

"Anything else?"

"Ehm, yes, sir. What of the Wilson Becker situation?"

"Oh, oh yes. Well, I should allow him to continue along whichever path he sees fit, he still has a job to do and far be it from us to remove a useful cog from the wheel. If he chooses to step outside of

The Guidelines in order to avenge his friend then we shall deal with him in due course. We've enough on our plate with *rogue elements* as it is. In the mean time you should contact James Finnegan, or Kenneth Wainwright."
"Might I suggest both, sir? Three crews would perhaps bring about a swifter conclusion?"
"Interesting."
"Indeed."
"I like it. Good idea, Garner, but keep it low key. Advise them both that discretion is of the utmost importance. We cannot afford for this situation to get any further out of hand."
"Sir."

A MODERN BRITAIN #4

HE'D SEEN HER AROUND. ROSIE
WHITTAKER. ON THE SUSTENANCE
NETWORK AT FIRST, OFFERING A RECIPE
FOR HER OWN VARIATION ON AN
ENGLISH OMELETTE, WHICH ITSELF WAS
A VARIATION ON AN OLD TIME SPANISH
OMELETTE, CLAIMED AS A BRITISH
INVENTION WHEN THE REGIME CHANGED.
IT HAD BEEN A POPULAR POSTING WITH
MANY PEOPLE, ANTHONY INCLUDED,
LAUDING HER FOR THE SLIGHT ADDITION.
HE'D SEEN HER AGAIN ON THE CRIME
NETWORK, DEFENDING THE RIGHTS OF A
WOMAN WHO HAD SLIPPED IN THE
STREET AND ACCIDENTALLY KNOCKED
A CHILD OVER, CAUSING LIGHT BRUISING.
THE PARENTS HAD KICKED UP A STINK
AND SHE WAS SUBSEQUENTLY TAKEN
IN FOR JUDGEMENT BY A SMALL TIME
CREW. ROSIE HAD DEFENDED HER
HONOUR, STOOD UP FOR WHAT SHE
BELIEVED. THAT THE COUNTRY SHOULD
NOT DESCEND INTO THAT KIND OF

VIGILANTISM. ACCIDENTS HAPPEN. THAT HER JUDGEMENT WAS A FARCE. ANTHONY HADN'T DARED TO SPEAK UP ALONGSIDE HER, HOWEVER MUCH HE AGREED WITH HER WORDS. HE SIMPLY FELL FOR HER FURTHER. NOT A DAY PASSED WHEN HE HADN'T SPENT HOURS TRAWLING THROUGH THE PARTS OF HER DAYLINE THAT SHE HADN'T HELD PRIVATE. LOOKED AT THE PICTURES OF HER WITH HER REAL LIFE FRIENDS. HOVERING HIS CUSTOMISED CURSOR OVER THE REQUEST CONNECTION COMBINATION ICON. DARED HIS FINGERS TO PRESS THE MOUSE BUTTON. NO MATTER HOW MUCH HE WANTED IT HE COULD NOT TAKE THE LEAP, LEST HE BE CALLED OUT FOR UNSOLICITED CONNECTION REQUEST. IT WASN'T ILLEGAL BUT IT WAS FROWNED UPON. PEOPLE, MORE SPECIFICALLY MEN, HAD HISTORICALLY REQUESTED THAT WOMEN WHOM THEY DID NOT KNOW COMBINE CONNECTIONS WITH THEM, UNDER THE PRETENCE THAT THEY HAD ONCE BEEN ACQUAINTANCES.

Ryan Bracha

UPON ACCEPTANCE OF THE COMBINATION CONNECTION THEY WOULD PROCEED TO HARASS THE WOMEN, ASKING TO TAKE OFF THEIR CLOTHES ON SHARED VIDEO LINKS. PLACED IMAGES OF THEIR GENITALS ON PRIVATE COMMUNICATION POSTINGS WITH REQUESTS FOR A FAVOUR RETURNED. THESE PEOPLE, MEN, WERE EVENTUALLY OUTED AS PERVERTS. NETWORK GROUPS WOULD APPEAR WHERE THEY WERE NAMED AND SHAMED, AND, AS WITH THE MAJORITY OF THESE GROUPS, THINGS EVOLVED AND ANYBODY WHO REQUESTED A COMBINATION OF CONNECTIONS FROM SOMEBODY THEY HAD NEVER INTERACTED WITH WOULD BE BOTH NAMED, AND SHAMED. SO, WITH THIS IN MIND, ANTHONY LET THE CURSOR MOVE AWAY FROM THE ICON AND SIGHED.

Like a log.

A hand shuffles against my shoulder, nudging me awake, helped by a soft voice that filters into my ears. I don't know what the voice is saying immediately, but it slowly becomes apparent that it's Katie, repeating my name. My eyes try to flicker open but the lips of the lids refuse to part company from one another.

"You awake Paul Carter?" asks Katie, sensing movement on my part. I grunt an affirmation and roll my body toward her. There are suddenly hands on my face and Katie's fingers pick at the corners of my eyes.

"What are you doing?" I ask gruffly, now scared to open them for fear of being blinded.

"Getting rid of your sleep snot, stop moaning," she says with a giggle, "there, all done."

I frown at her looking down upon me, and shake my head as I drag my bones upright and lean against the wall, my legs flat against Shane's makeshift bed.

"Thanks, I guess."

"Did you sleep okay?" she asks, passing me a dirty white cup filled with some dark steaming brown concoction which I have no intention of drinking.

"Like a log," I say, "what time is it?"

"I don't know, I can't tell the time," she says with a sad look on her face, "I can't even read."

This strikes me as strange, unbelievable even, but I feel moved to ask.

"Really?"

Ryan Bracha

Her face shifts in demeanour as she laughs out loud.

"No, of course not *really,* you wally, it's half seven," she chuckles, "you're too easy Paul Carter. Come on, Shane's got news."

Shane's mixed news.

Shane's outside. Standing in the crisp morning air and listening to the sound of dawn's silence. In one hand he's holding a cup identical to the one that Katie's forced me to bring along with me. Steaming brown muck just as full as mine. In his other hand he's holding the palmtop computer, scanning The Network as usual. He looks up at me as I step beside him, and Katie wanders around the perimeter of the station car park, kicking stones and stretching her legs. The air feels cold but the sharpness of it bites into me and serves to wake me up a little. The sleep I've had was well needed, it's given me time to recharge. To accept what it is that we're faced with. Yesterday was one full of quick decisions and working entirely on impulse. Today I feel we're going to have to plan a little better.

"What do we know Shane?" I ask, before stifling a yawn, almost tempted to drink whatever it is that I've got. His look is one of slight trepidation. "Mixed news Bossman," he says, I don't know where *Bossman* came from, but I say nothing, "the government have got involved, and they don't like you."

He smirks at this, like it's all a big joke.

"What do you mean?"

"Watch." He holds the computer screen my way and what I'm watching is an offical government statement about me. It seems it's mostly a warning to the public about my danger levels, and it then elaborates as to the real danger, which is anybody who feels like they want to join my *crusade against Britishness* will be held as accountable as I will be. That we will all be made examples of. Typical posturing and empty threats made as if they are the ones who hold all the cards. It irks me somewhat but I continue to watch. It shows images of me from my old life. Pictures of Ciara. Of our wedding day. My family. Danny. It's basically a propaganda film which is intended to leave me under no illusions. That they don't know everything about my life. About my history. My skills. I get a very strong feeling that it's more for my benefit than anything else. Before long I've seen enough and I pass the computer back to Shane with a shake of my head.

"Rubbish," I remark, "it's all bullsherbet."

"What's bullsherbet Paul Carter?" Katie's voice appears shortly before she does from behind us.

"The government video," I respond, "they're clutching at straws, it's good."

"How comes?" she asks.

"They're panicking. If you're up against a clever opponent the worst thing you can do is panic. It's a sign of weakness, a clever opponent will sense that and work that to his own end."

Ryan Bracha

Shane nods wistfully, taking my words and making them mean something to his own mind. He's an *auditory* kind of kid. Katie twists the end of her hair and processes the words in her own way. The jury's still out on her.

"So what now?" she says after a short moment of quiet contemplation.

"That I don't know, it looks like we're in the same position as last night. The ball's in our court."

Shane shuffles his feet at this point and looks up to me, then Katie, and then back up to me.

"Well, I said it was mixed news, I think I might have somebody who'll want to help."

As he says this the sun breaks out above the peak of the hill that rolls down toward us, piercing the darkness of dawn in the car park, shining an orange and fantastic light over the three of us. I smile for what feels like the first time in years, and pat my hand onto Shane's shoulder, and without thinking I gulp down what turns out to be very drinkable black, sugarless instant coffee.

"That's excellent news, do tell."

Shane's excellent news.

"I were watching Johnny Stiff while you two were sleeping," he's saying as we walk back into the darkness of the police station, Katie up front with the torch, Shane and I walking behind.

"He's funny Paul Carter," Katie says over her shoulder, her feet crunching against the broken glass.

"Is he?" I ask, but not really wanting to know the answer.

"Mmmhmm." She doesn't elaborate, thankfully, giving Shane his opportunity to continue.

"Yeah, and he did a joke about you, well, not *about* you, but you were in it." *Great,* I'm being used in jokes now, half of me wants to know the joke, but the overriding half wants the news, Shane carries on.

"Afterwards all the people said how funny the joke was, me included," he states, then seems to argue with himself, "it were funny, what can you do? Anyway, there's this one bloke, he's talking about how you should be put to a proper trial, not paraded like your cousin," he pauses, "sorry."

"Don't worry about it," I reassure him, which seems to work.

"Okay, so he was going on about all the crews, said they were animals. He loves his country but they make him ashamed. Then everybody told him to stop spouting his views on Johnny Stiff's channel, so he left it."

As we enter the main downstairs room, Katie snorts with a mix of derision and affection for Shane, and says pretty much what I'm thinking.

"So what? You found a guy who wants to put Paul Carter in front of a judge instead of on The Network? How would he help us?"

Shane sighs and shakes his head.

Ryan Bracha

"If you'd shut up and let me speak I'll tell you," he whines, his voice bordering on tears, which serves to remind me that these kids are just that. I wonder exactly how prepared we are for this fight. I shake the doubt off and place a hand on his shoulder.

"Carry on Shane."

"Well, he got me thinking, how many people think like him? I mean, there's us for a start," he points at himself and Katie, "and I started looking at his history on The Network, you know? Like, people he spoke to a lot and communities he was a part of. He's always spouting off about the crews, but stays just on the right side of being anti-British. Starts everything with *I love my country, but* and then he rants about The Crews. He *hates* Wilson Becker."

"Okay, interesting," I nod, feeling a seed of something being planted but not really feeling the excellent aspect of this news that I anticipated, Shane senses it and holds his palms up, one eyebrow raised.

"Nah, hear me out, this guy, there's a reason he's so into putting people up in front of a judge, seriously."

"Which is?" asks Katie, her backside rested on her hands against the wall, her huge eyes blinking through the dirt in expectation. Shane gives her a look that almost says *I thought you'd never ask,* or *I'm glad you asked,* then steps toward us in a gesture of tension building.

"He's been up for judgment before," he says, "seven times. Always for speeding. He drives up and down in front of the NCC building, peeping his horn, shouting at them. Gets away with it every time. It looks like he's crazy as fungus, and I think he's exactly the kind of person who'd help us."

Danny's plight continues.

"Twelve hours down, Danny," Wilson Becker growled as he paced the room behind the camera which blinked away in Danny's face, "it's not looking good. You helped Paul to escape, and for what?"

Carter's cousin said nothing as Becker forced a laugh, playing it up for the audience. The guard, Grady, sneered from his chair. Pushed his clenched fist against the arm, cracking his knuckles. Seemingly just for effect. These people were cartoonish idiots with an awful, and misplaced tendency toward the dramatic. The vote counter had been extremely slow overnight, but that was no saving grace. It was par for the course, the people had been sleeping, aside from the nocturnal trolls who voted guilty on every judgment. The country were beginning to wake up and would be spending the morning crunching on their Sustenance Network provided, and cornerstone of every Englishman's breakfast, *Yawnflakes*, one eye on their Network synopsis, checking for Communication Alerts.

Ryan Bracha

Proof of their popularity would lie in the quantity received whilst they were not logged onto The Network. Once these alerts had been gratefully received and investigated, then they would begin to use The Network for recreational purposes. Children would be playing games, be they educational or otherwise. Some people may be gambling, others talking to friends, the professionals would be working hard (or hardly working) and then the rest would be judging. The recreational activity of choice for the whole country. Judging. Spending their time condemning the actions of others whilst balancing precariously on the perches within their glass houses. It's when those people fully woke up that the judgement counter would jolt into life. Danny knew this, because he had always been one of them.

Exactly the kind of person who'd help us.

"Who are you?" says the muffled voice through the door, responding to Katie's knock. She glances my way but only briefly. I'm standing with Shane, our backs to the wall along this narrow hallway. The lights at this end are out, much the same as most blocks of flats nowadays. Not many people take the initiative to call maintenance issues in anymore. It's always somebody else's problem. Luckily for us, it would seem, because it's providing an acceptable degree of cover as Katie stands in the light of one

of the few that *are* in working order. I'm not
entirely comfortable with her doing this. I'd
much prefer that I did all of the risky work
myself but then Katie was right on a couple of
counts. For one, a notorious, and fugitive
murderer would be infinitely more threat to the
man than a nineteen year old girl. The other was
that we are now, seemingly, a team.

"Hi, my name's Katie," she says calmly and
quietly, "I'm looking for Ben, uhm, Ben Turner."

"You not know how to use The Network?" comes
the reasonable question from through the door.

"Yeah I do, but-"

"Then see him on The Network then!"

"This is-"

The door pulls open, and hard, jerking against
the chain which holds it not more than a couple
of inches ajar.

"I said see me," the voice coughs, twice, says
nothing for a short while, then "I mean *him* on
The Network, are you jackin' stupid?"

Katie laughs loudly and shakes her head.

"Nobody gets in to see the wizard! Not no one,
not no how!" she mocks in a squeaky American
accent, "I *loved* that film when I was a kid," then
the joy drops from her face and she sighs,

"seriously Ben, let me in, I'm a big fan. I've got
something I want to talk to you about, and it is
not for The Network."

She beams another smile and simply stands
there in front of the door for yet another short
period of quiet, the mysterious Ben Turner
saying nothing either. Eventually the door

Ryan Bracha

quietly closes. A series of clicks and metal sliding along metal. Unlocking. Open door.

"Thank you," smiles Katie graciously, and walks over the threshold, into the apartment. Down in our darkened corner of the stinking hallway Shane looks up to face me. This kid is in serious need of a wash.

"What now then bossman?" he asks quietly.

"Now Shane," I say as my legs bend gently to take the weight as my back slides against the greasy wall, ever lower toward the floor, until I'm seated, "we wait."

Does a bear do sherbet in the woods?

It's not much more than five minutes before Katie's head peers out from the doorway. A smile emblazoned across the front of it, with those eyes twinkling from beneath the dirt. As Shane and I approach her she disappears inside the flat, and we catch the sight of her entering a room to the right, along the hallway. The hall itself is sparse, decorated only with a poster for an old film starring Bruce Lee. Quite the rarity in this day and age. The carpet is a green and brown garish patterned mess. Worn thin along the centre, especially near the door. In the room that Katie's gone into there are two armchairs. That's really it. Nothing more. Upon the arm of one of them, the blue cracked leather one, she's perched. One shoe against the padding of the seat, the other down against the carpet. That same green and brown affair. Just as worn. I doubt it's been replaced since the nineties. Maybe earlier. In the other chair, which is a pale brown fabric number, square in shape, and lower down to the floor than the leather one, there's Ben Turner. Ben Turner is rather unremarkable, truth be told. He's seated deep into his chair, his hands rested against the edges of the arms. Almost gripped tight against them, as if he's being pushed back by an unspeakable force, and they're the only things keeping him upright. His head is pressed against his shoulder as he looks up to me, his head shorn of any hair, a crooked smile upon his crooked face.

"You're Paul Carter?" This is the first time I've heard this sentence directed as a question rather than a statement of fact in the last twenty four hours. It's somewhat refreshing.

"Yes," I say, one hand held toward the seated rebel, intended as a polite greeting.

"*The* Paul Carter?"

"I guess so."

"Hmm," he says, taking my hand, not as it was intended but using it as leverage to drag himself from the chair and stand toe to toe with me, he's still smiling, "I thought you'd be taller."

"Sorry," I say. Ben shrugs and smirks.

"Don't be, can't help how you grow," he says, a swift flicker of his eyes to Katie, like the small joke was for her benefit. He's showing off, "besides, you don't have to be tall to be a murderer."

I frown, and shake my head.

"Please, don't-"

"I already told him you won't talk about it," Katie interjects, "he said he was gonna ask you anyway. I told him he was wasting his time. He said he's got plenty of time, that it doesn't matter if he wastes some."

Ben looks at her, and then back to me, and a laugh breaks through.

"That's a pretty accurate description of what was said. Well done." He rubs the shaven stubble that tops his head, with that beaming smile continuing. I don't feel any threat from the guy at all. He seems affable enough.

"I imagine Katie's told you what we need?"

"You imagine quite correctly my good man," he nods, his demeanour taking a slight twist toward the serious, "quite a risky manoeuvre if you don't mind my saying? You know what'll happen if it goes wrong?"

"Yes. I get caught. We all get caught."

"Now that little part is where you're just slightly wrong Mr Carter," he says, his eyebrows raised, "because if it *does* go wrong, me and you have never met, understand? If it goes wrong, I'm just another crazy person who wants to make trouble for some overzealous bandstands who think they're the law."

I get what he's saying, I feel almost stupid for letting him think it. I *hate* feeling stupid.

"Of course," I say, "I'm sorry that you thought that. My error."

He waves away the apology with a dismissive hand.

"Don't worry about it."

"So you'll help?" Shane says, hope in his voice.

"Hey kid, you're talking about messing with Wilson Becker's ideal little world, so allow me to answer your question with a question," says Ben Turner, "does a bear do sherbet in the woods?"

A MODERN BRITAIN #5

MAX HAD ALWAYS LOVED MUSIC. THE WAY IT MADE HIM FEEL. THE WAY IT COULD CHANGE AND SHIFT HIS MOOD WITHOUT EVEN TRYING. THE MEMORIES IT STIRRED. THE WAY A SONG COULD BE A MARKER OF LIFE. THE FIRST RINGTONE HE'D EVER DOWNLOADED, WHICH HE'D LOUDLY PLAYED ON PUBLIC TRANSPORT FOR HIS FRIENDS TO APPRECIATE. THE TOGETHERNESS THAT HAD WASHED OVER THEM AT THE BACK OF THE BUS. THEY WERE A JOYOUS, AND UNTOUCHABLE UNIT. THE FIRST ALBUM HE'D EVER ILLEGALLY ACQUIRED ON A PEER TO PEER WEBSITE, AND SUBSEQUENTLY PLAYED FROM HIS SMART TELEPHONE ON THE RECREATIONAL GROUND BEHIND HIS HOUSE AS THEY'D SHARED A THREE LITRE BOTTLE OF WHITE CIDER AND CANNABIS JOINT. THE GIRLS DANCING IN THE LIGHT OF THE STREET AT THE

OTHER SIDE OF THE FIELD. THE BOYS
CHATTING ABOUT FOOTBALL. THE FIRST
MUSIC VIDEO HE'D DEDICATED TO HIS
FIRST GIRLFRIEND ON FACESPACE VIA
VIDIYOU. ALL OF THE COMMENTS AND
THUMBS UP AT THE SENTIMENT FROM
THEIR ASSOCIATED FRIENDS. THE LAST
MUSIC VIDEO HE'D DEDICATED TO HER
MISERY AFTER SHE'D ENDED IT. THESE
WERE HOW HE REMEMBERED HIS LIFE
BEFORE THE REGIME CHANGE, BEFORE
THE INCEPTION OF THE NETWORK, WHEN
HIS WHOLE LIFE COULD BE MARKED BY
THE VARIOUS ACTIONS HE'D DONE ON
HIS DAYLINE. HIS WEEKLINE. HIS
MONTHLINE. AND SO ON. HIS LOVE OF
MUSIC NEVER WANED, AND WITH THE
TECHNOLOGY AVAILABLE TO HIM HE
ENDEAVOURED TO CREATE HIS OWN. TO
TRY TO BRING INTO OTHER PEOPLE'S
LIVES THE JOY THAT HAD BEEN
BROUGHT INTO HIS FOR ALL OF HIS
EXISTENCE. HE HAD PURCHASED A
PERCUSSION SOFTWARE APPLICATION
USING HIS WEEK'S RECREATION CREDITS.
WORKED ON A WHISPERING SNARE

Ryan Bracha

EFFECT. A 4/4 AT A HUNDRED AND THIRTY BEATS PER MINUTE. A LOOPING BASS. ADDED SOME REVERB ON THE SNARE. WIPED IT CLEAN. STARTED AGAIN. PERFECTED THE BEAT, THE FOUNDATIONS OF HIS MASTERPIECE, UNTIL HE COULD AFFORD A SYNTH SOFTWARE APPLICATION A WEEK LATER AND BEGIN THE MELODY. STARTED TO ADD LAYERS. SAMPLES HE'D RIPPED FROM THE MUSIC NETWORK. FREE EFFECTS THAT OTHERS HAD LEFT TO BE USED. HIS FAVOURITE WAS A ROBOTIC CHANT WHICH REPEATED THE WORDS 'KEEP BRITAIN BRITISH'. HE HAD SPENT SO LONG TRYING THE SAMPLE OUT OVER THE VARIOUS MASTER TRACKS THAT HE'D CREATED, EACH ONE GAVE HIM GOOSE BUMPS. A CHILL THAT STROKED THE BACK OF HIS NECK. GAVE HIM AN ENORMOUS SENSE OF WORTH. OF PRIDE IN HIS COUNTRY. THE NEXT WEEK HE PURCHASED A MICROPHONE WITH YET MORE OF HIS RECREATION CREDITS AND BEGAN TO LAY DOWN THE VOCALS. HE

Paul Carter is a Dead Man

HARMONISED WITH HIMSELF OVER THE ROBOTIC CHANT. HIS CAREFULLY CONSTRUCTED LYRICS WHICH GLORIFIED HIS COUNTRY OF BIRTH. HIS RASPING AND VIOLENT THROATY HIP HOP VOCALS DECLARING NEW BRITAIN THE BEST PLACE ON EARTH. DECLARING ROBERT LODGE THE SAVIOUR OF ALL THINGS BRITISH. DECLARING ALL WHO OPPOSE HIM AS THE DEVIL. FINALLY, WEEKS LATER, HE HAD FINISHED. HIS THREE MINUTES AND TWENTY FOUR SECONDS OF UNADULTERATED PATRIOTISM. UNASHAMEDLY INSPIRED BY ALL OF THE MUSIC THAT HE'D LOVED THROUGHOUT THE YEARS. THEY WOULD GO CRAZY FOR THIS. THEY HAD TO. ALL OF THE EFFORT, ALL OF THE SLEEPLESS NIGHTS PERFECTING THE LEVELS. REDUCING THE BASS OVER PARTS WHERE TREBLE WOULD REALLY STAND OUT. ALL OF THE RECREATION CREDITS HE'D INVESTED INTO HIS WORK. IT WAS THE SOUND OF HIS YOUTH, OF HIS FIRST KISS, OF LOVE, OF PAIN, OF JOY. IT ENCAPSULATED EVERYTHING

Ryan Bracha

THAT WAS HIM. HE NAMED IT *BE BRITISH (NOT BRIT-ISH)*. HE EAGERLY FILLED IN THE TALENT NETWORK APPLICATION. THE FIRST STEP ALONG THE POSSIBLE PATH TO STARDOM. IF THE CELEBRITY TALENT SPOTTERS, SPEARHEADED BY THE INIMITABLE BAZ LE SHAZ, LIKED WHAT THEY SAW THEN HE'D BE INVITED TO PERFORM LIVE ON THE ASPIRATIONAL NETWORK BROADCAST *TALENT TONIGHT*. MILLIONS WOULD SUBMIT THEIR WORK TO TALENT TONIGHT. A HANDFUL WOULD FIND SUCCESS, WOULD BE GIVEN THEIR OWN SPONSORED NETWORK BROADCAST CHANNEL, A GUARANTEED AUDIENCE, GUARANTEED NETWORK RADIO PLAY, THEY WOULD NEVER HAVE TO WORK FOR A LIVING EVER AGAIN. THE REST WOULD FALL BY THE WAYSIDE AND WATCH THE RISING STARS OF PEOPLE FAR LESS TALENTED THAN THEY THOUGHT THAT THEY THEMSELVES WERE. BY THREE DAYS LATER IT BECAME APPARENT THAT MAX WAS DESTINED TO BECOME ONE

OF THE LATTER. BY THE END OF THE WEEK HE WAS HANGED AFTER BEING FOUND GUILTY OF A FOUL MOUTHED RANT NETWORK BROADCASTED AGAINST BAZ LE SHAZ AND HIS INABILITY TO SPOT ACTUAL TALENT WHEN HE SAW IT. IRONICALLY, IN THE NOTORIETY THAT HIS DEATH BROUGHT HIM, HIS SONG BE BRITISH (NOT BRIT-ISH), WAS THE MOST POPULAR SONG ON NETWORK RADIO FOR EIGHTY THREE DAYS STRAIGHT. IT WASN'T COMMON KNOWLEDGE, BUT THE ROYALTIES WERE FUNNELLED DIRECTLY INTO THE BRITISH JUSTICE REPARATION FUND, AND PAID THE WAGES OF ONE HUNDRED AND TWENTY GOVERNMENT AUTHORISED NETWORK CREW MEMBERS.

Ryan Bracha

A big fish in a small pond.

The car rumbles along the barren dual carriageway. The burned out and rusted skeletons of other vehicles are sporadically scattered along the side of the road. Stolen, borrowed or inherited by whoever and abandoned when their use has expired. Ben is driving us to our *centre of operations,* as Shane prefers to call it. He may be a self-vaunted free spirit, but in my old life the kid would have excelled in business. He's got a very driven, very focussed head on his young shoulders. A credit to the *operation* I may have once declared him in a post training evaluation. He sits in the back alongside Katie, whose fingers tap a mildly irritating beat against the beaten faux leather of my seat, by my shoulder. I already know her well enough to know that this means something's on her mind. She's almost *too* quiet. Mulling something over. She'll be chewing her lip and staring off with a confused look on her face. Trying to figure out how she wants to broach the subject.

"Paul Carter, can I ask you a question?"

Bingo.

"You can, whether I answer it or not is another thing."

Shane snorts a quick laugh before Katie thumps him hard against the thigh. He groans, but remains quiet thereafter. I feel my seat drag back a touch as she pulls herself upright, and to my ear. I can feel her warm breath against the side of my neck and ear, which I further present to her in order to protect my tender nostrils from her rotten mouth.

"Why did you stay here? Y'know? In Britain? When you had the chance to go, why did you not? I would have if I had the chance."

I say nothing for a while and consider my answer. Another learning from my old life. Don't speak too quickly, you'll give yourself away. You might say something that you can't take back. Something that could be held against you. Consider how it might be taken before you give it. *I've been on far too many HR courses.*

"Greed," I say, "plain and simple."

"Really? You stayed just for money?"

"No, not just for money. For influence too. Reputation. Power. Name your vice."

"I don't get it."

Of course you don't.

"Before it all happened I was successful. I worked hard and I made all the money I could want. I didn't make friends that I didn't think could take me anywhere. Figuratively speaking. I cast aside people that I had no use for. I even let my marriage go to sherbet for my career. So when the doors got closed I saw opportunity. I wanted to be a big fish in a small pond, like, the star of the show," I explain, "and if I'd left the country I would have had to start again. I put far too much of myself into this country, into building up a reputation to allow it to all fall apart-"

Ryan Bracha

Suddenly I'm aware that I'm in danger of opening up more than I want to, and I shut up to watch the derelict cars pass us by. There's a thud as Katie slumps back into her seat, then the whoosh of her exhaling in quiet frustration, and then we simply roll along the carriageway in silence for a mile or two, and I get a time to reflect.

People I had no use for.

In the grand scheme of things I was a real cold hearted bandstand in my old life. I still am. I struggle to relate to people. To empathise with them. But I could sure as hell do a good *impression* of somebody who gave a jack about your wellbeing. I would put on a happy go lucky, approachable front to the people I worked with and the people I worked for. Always happy to help. Anything to aid the cause. That was me. Paul Carter, go-to guy for all things in the name of progress. But only when the right eyes were looking. I believe the phrase is *Fight whilst the general is watching.* But behind the warm hearted, chirpy exterior I was ruthless. I happily took the credit for other people's successes. Offered smoking shelter promises of using any influence that I had to push the careers of others, but with no intention of ever doing so. If my department came under any kind of fire owing to my own shortfalls it was always *somebody else's fault.* Be it a temp, or an employee several steps down the food chain from me, or my direct assistant. Whoever I blamed would take the full force of disciplinary proceedings. I'd instruct an underling to replace them with another bright young thing and the whole process would repeat. They were willing and disposable robots to use to my advantage and then cast aside without any sniff of unrest from the powers that be. I was saving them money in the long term. Leading people on with promises of development and nurturing, only to bleed them dry. Those former employees and useless professional friends would fall by the wayside, broken and jaded, much like the cars we pass on our way to the abandoned police station that we now call home. I would continue on my upward trajectory, and to the untrained eye my sherbet almost definitely did *not* stink. Do I hate myself for the actions of my previous life? No, not yet, but I have a feeling that it's in the post.

My daydream disappears back from the fore of my mind as Katie leans in again behind me.

"You killed somebody Paul Carter," she says, not a hint of malice in her voice.

"Two people," Ben corrects without taking his eyes from the road.

"You killed two people Paul Carter," Katie repeats, "if you didn't want to mess with your reputation you shouldn't have done that."

"I'd rather not get into it, not yet, please."

Katie is about to say something else when Shane brings about a gratefully received interruption.

Ryan Bracha

"Turn off at the next junction Ben, you see that big tall building there?"

"Yeah."

"Aim for that."

We'll be seeing you.

"Mr Wilson Becker, it's me again," I say to the camera. Shane's holding it in my direction, behind him Katie stands smiling, and behind her Ben is sitting on one of the makeshift beds, watching my performance, "I'm sure you're aware that your holding my cousin has done little to affect the situation. If it helps the country to make any kind of decision, you should know that Danny turned me away. I went to him for help, my own cousin, I asked him for help and he turned me away. His fear of recrimination overruled his family obligations. His fear of what *you* would do to him. He is innocent, in as far as you could call a man who would turn his back on family innocent. Yes, he is a man who defines the word coward, but he is a coward on *your* side. You choose whether he decides to die for helping me, if that's what you believe he did, and you choose whether he deserves to die for turning his back on me. He is in a *lose lose* situation."

I feel a pang of guilt for Danny. Regret. He will feel the knife twisting in his back when he sees this, but it's for the greater good. I have to remember that.

"Wilson Becker will carry on in his relentless pursuit of me. The man who killed his dear friend Banger. Wilson Becker will forget quite easily that he framed an innocent man in order to catch a guilty one. Will you, the people of New Britain allow that? Of course you will."

I pause, for effect, take a breath and look away from the camera. A pensive gaze to the left. A smile at nobody. Then I turn back to the blinking camera.

"You ought to know that my circle of friends has grown. Multiplied. Massively. I am fast becoming the least of your worries. I am a small part of a large problem. We are growing tired of the way our country is run. Mr Becker, you are only the start. Once we have finished with you then Mr Robert Lodge is our next issue. We will not stop. Nor will we be stopped. Not yet anyway. We have so much more to do before we call it a day."

I clear my throat. Close my eyes. Drop my head just slightly. Then with my face toward the floor I raise my eyes toward the camera and smile malevolently.

"We'll be seeing you."

As Shane cuts off the camera and exhales sharply Ben Turner claps a slow applause from his place on the bed. Katie squeals some sort of appreciative noise, and she charges toward me, throwing her arms around my torso.

"Paul Carter, that was *awesome!*"

I say nothing, but allow my hands to drop onto her shoulders, then slide down her back, my

Ryan Bracha

fingers gripping into her slender body, as I look at the boys.

"Do we need to do that again?" I ask of Shane, "Did it look okay?"

"It was brilliant, bossman," he says with a shake of the head, *"We'll be seeing you,"* he mimics my signing off statement, and laughs, "really, I framed it perfectly, it's fine, you're a pro."

Katie finally releases her grasp of me and steps away, looking up at me with a smile.

"I would *so* like to do things to you right now Paul Carter, that was hot."

A prickle of embarrassment picks at my skin, and I can feel my face heat up. I can no longer hold eye contact with her and flick my vision to Ben, which creases Katie up, she really does know how to push my buttons, I've never known anything like it.

"What did you think, Ben?"

He gives a slow, and confident thumbs-up, as he nods.

"I liked it, let's hope it does the job Mr Psycho."

The plan, if that's what you could call it.

"I want to do it, Paul Carter."

This is obviously Katie speaking, as we sit around the table discussing our next plan of action, she really feels this need to prove herself to be an integral part of the operation. No matter what I say to her to reassure that she already is, she wants to take that one next step too far, be the star of the show. She's definitely tenacious, I'll give her that.

"But you'll be alone," I start, "it's dangerous out there."

She snorts a laugh, and shakes her head.

"Please, I was looking after myself long before you came along killer, I can do it, just give me a chance," she says, and then looks to the other two, "besides, would you rather I came with you? What options have you got?"

At this juncture I have to concede that she has a point. Ben will be already otherwise engaged with his part of proceedings, and I think I'd trust Shane more at my side than Katie, but then there's this small itch at the back of my mind. I need to protect her. I saved her once, I would hate myself if I let her come to any harm now. I look her in the eyes, and as I scrabble around my brain for a way of saying this she seems to be figuring it out. Maybe it's the way I looked at her, but she responds with her eyes, and smiles. It's not a smile I've seen from her before, but she gets it. For whatever reason she places her hand on mine.

"I'll be fine Paul Carter, I promise."

I look at her sadly, before remembering myself and I clear my throat.

"Okay, so I guess Katie is our only option- OW!" She's nipped the skin on the top of my hand and is grinning mischievously.

"Katie is our *preferred* option," she cackles, and I pull my hand away, rubbing the upset nerves.

Ryan Bracha

"Okay, so she's our preferred option," I say as she nods sagely in acknowledgment, "for taking the video."

"Same place as before?" asks Shane. I shake my head, no.

"No, we need Katie to be able to get out of there, or at least somewhere to avoid the dogs."

"What about she just comes with me?" asks Ben, his body slouched back deep into the chair he's in, his finger picking at something on the old desk. Everybody looks my way.

"Go on."

"Well, I'm driving, why don't we just head out somewhere, play the video, and then get back to doing what we're doing? She's got back up then."

What I don't say is that I'm not sure we can trust him yet. He's not proved anything to us, that we've just taken him on his word. I settle on something else.

"But you want to distance yourself from this, you're the *crazy person,* remember? You take her and you're in it as much as we are."

Ben mulls this over, his teeth chewing at his bottom lip as he stares off into the corner of the room, then he shrugs.

"Fair point, but I heard your speech, you might be on to something here. I don't think you're on your own with the way the country is run. I think there's millions who want to play out, and I think you're the man to give them that power. And you know what? I want in on the ground floor."

I sigh. This was never intended to be a revolution, but people seem to want it. I just wanted to get rid of a creep who sullied my good name, and now I'm the leader of a small team of rebels who want that revolution, and it doesn't seem to be showing any sign of abating.

"It does sound better than anything else Paul Carter, then at least you know I'm safe," Katie says, that look in her eye again. She thinks she's on to me. Like she's broken beneath my exterior. Like there's an attraction between us. Like fungus.

"Okay. So Ben, you take Katie far enough away to give us an advantage, air the video, and wait. Get back and do your thing, and then Shane and I, well, we do our thing."

I look around the three of them, and am treated to a trio of conspiratorial faces. They're in.

Everybody feels responsible.

"Boss," said Oxley, his chubby sweating jowls appearing beside Becker behind the two way mirror as he stood watching the beaten figured of Danny in the chair of the judgement room.

"What?"

"Mr Garner from Robert Lodge's office has been calling reception."

"So?"

"They seem pretty eager to talk with you, boss."

"I don't care."

"They asked you to call them as soon-"

"I said I don't care Oxley! Are you deaf?! If they call again, tell them to go and fungus themselves, okay?"

Oxley flinched beneath the fury of his superior, the cold flecks of spittle dotting across his cheeks and spectacles as Becker roared into his face.

"I said, okay?" Becker repeated himself, which he hated.

"Okay, sir," said Oxley, pitching a rapid retreat from the room, closing the door as quietly as he could as he left. Joe looked up from the video monitor to view Becker, then turned to refocus upon the screen.

"We all miss Banger boss," he said, without looking back up. Becker twitched in irritation, but said nothing. Joe continued, "with respect, we *all* feel responsible, it ain't just you."

"You all feel responsible?" said Becker, finally looking down to his seated employee.

"Sure we do."

"You *feel* responsible?" he repeated. Joe shifted uncomfortably in his seat, wishing silently that he'd kept his thoughts to himself.

"Yeah, I mean, ehm, we all-"

"Yeah, you *feel* responsible, you said that already *Joseph,* but are you *actually* responsible for his death? Are you the one who's got to sit down in front of his wife and tell her that you sent her husband to his death? Are you *all* going to have to explain to his mother and father that you ordered him to go and search for a murderer *alone?"*

"Well, no, but-"

"But nothing Joe, you might all *feel* responsible, but." Becker stopped and turned away. His cheek twitching. His head struggling to switch his heart off. This was a situation that threatened to spill out of control. Becker had *never* been a man out of control. On the rugby pitch he was a born captain, he demanded the respect of everybody he came into contact with. Referees, opponents, and colleagues alike. This was the worst position he had ever been in. Emotion felt like it was in charge of the show. Not Wilson Becker.

"I'm just saying, boss. We're with you on this. That's all I'm saying," said Joe. His fingers scrolling the mouse to zoom in slightly on Danny. The criminal just watched his lap, no real visible evidence that his current plight was affecting him too much. It seemed like plain resignation scrawled across his face. Becker continued with his back to Joe, sighed heavily, and regained what little composure he had left.

"How long we got left?" he asked, feeling it right to change the subject.

"Seven hours fifty three," Joe replied. The judgement counter was continuing to climb. They were three quarters of the way there. It was slower than usual. He'd clearly got a silent population behind him who were refusing to click that *guilty* button. All that was available to them was hope. Hope that Carter would hand himself in, to save the innocent Danny.

Bing.

A communication alert appeared on the screen beside The Network Cutting Crew's dayline. A

Ryan Bracha

public communication. These were a common occurrence for them. They'd be open pieces of information regarding a criminal at large, or more often than not a simple message of support. Joe flicked the cursor over it absent-mindedly and pressed to see the alert, to remove it from sight and clean up the Network synopsis more than anything. A black box appeared on the dayline, belatedly joined by a triangle, and then a title for the video.

"Boss," said Joe, sitting upright in his chair, his arm reaching out to grab at the material of Wilson Becker's suit, as he clicked upon the link to play the video, "boss, I think he's back."

"Mr Wilson Becker, it's me again," said the speakers of the room as the video lurched into life, throwing Becker into action. He pulled Joe from his seat and replaced him there, intently watching the video, his fists clenching ever more rapidly, *"I'm sure you're aware that your holding my cousin has done little to affect the situation. If it helps the country to make any kind of decision, you should know that Danny turned me away. I went to him for help, my own cousin, I asked him for help and he turned me away-"*

The screen went black, owing mostly to the massive fist that Wilson Becker had slammed through it, before he stood, and exited through the door that he almost ripped from its hinges. In the judgement room Danny's head rose to watch the video, before dropping again, through the shame that his cousin had reminded him that he was feeling. Joe, for all of the responsibility that he was feeling for Banger's death, simply sat down, and attempted to fix the broken monitor. There was no way that he was hanging around a Wilson Becker in the state of mind that he was currently in. The door was ripped open once again, this time by Grady. His bald jittery skull swaying from right to left, looking for Becker. "Where'd he go?" he asked of Joe.

"I dunno, he just left," he responded with a shrug. Grady eyed him suspiciously, but accepted the response, and nodded toward the captive in the other room.

"Keep yer eye on that bandstand, I'm gonna go find the boss, we'll get the murdering rucksack this time," he laughed maliciously, "I can't wait!" Grady disappeared, leaving Joe to the broken monitor, and the broken man in the judgement room.

Ben and Katie make their move.

"Go go go Ben Turner!" Katie squealed as she clambered into the passenger seat of the car, a gleeful look across her face, sliding the palmtop computer into the pocket of her hooded top. The complicit driver pressed his feet onto the clutch then accelerator and spun the car out of the car park of the abandoned shopping centre. Meadowhall. Another remnant of times when Britain was a vibrant and social country. When people wanted to go out and see the products first hand, rather than in the form of thumbnail

Ryan Bracha

images. When food courts were full to the brim with shoppers eager to ease their sore feet after a heavy few hours of retail therapy. Now it was a broken shell of a building. One that housed a variety of vagrants from time to time, the wares that remained from when international brands ran the place now long gone. Stolen by whoever. Clothes that once cost a week's wage ripped from the shelves for free, to provide an extra layer of warmth in the winter months. Jewellery now rendered worthless. Things like gold and silver used to be regarded as luxury, people once queued for hundreds of meters to get their hands on charm bracelets as gifts. No more. It was now as valuable as tin. Technology was the new gold. And technology was only attainable via The Network.

The car raced along the Tinsley viaduct and past the old steelworks. Another reminder of times before times before times. An occasional car passed them in the opposite direction. Sneering faces trying to capture their license plate numbers in order to pass the information on to whichever Network Crew felt like picking up the issue. No use, of course, the car that carried two of Paul Carter's most valued team members was moving with far too much speed to be picked up.

Wilson Becker's on the move.

The vans thundered on at way over the legal speed limit. Sirens blazing. Lights flashing. Dogs yelping in the cage at the back of the first one. Grady driving, Wilson Becker beside him, in his usual spot.

"This is it boss, this is when we get him," Grady spat, dropping his foot deeper onto the accelerator as if to drive the point home, "he thinks he's gonna hide in Meadowhall he's dead wrong."

Wilson Becker refused to be drawn in to a committal, they'd let the rucksack go once before. Twice before. He wouldn't believe that they'd got Paul Carter until the jacking bandstand was on his knees, crying before Becker for mercy. Mercy would never come.

"I'm gonna slap him up, and then I'm gonna-"

"Give it a jackin' rest Grady, just jackin' drive yeah?!"

The pair in the back said nothing. Watched their boss and his second in command bickering between themselves.

"Just sayin' boss," said a suddenly more subdued Grady. Becker slammed his hand onto the dash.

"Well don't *just say,* I'm sicka you gherkins *just sayin',*unless you got somethin' interesting or useful to *just say,* then jackin' keep it to yourselves! You hear me?!"

Grady nodded nervously, his eyes flickering just slightly off the road and toward his boss.

"Yeah, sorry boss, I didn't think, sorry boss."

"Just drive, Grady."

The van fell into silence as it sped toward Tinsley viaduct and the abandoned shopping centre, the red lights of a car up ahead braking grew slowly

Ryan Bracha

closer. What grew closer still, and far more quickly was the vision of an oncoming car, seemingly going even faster than the law enforcement vehicle, but in the opposite direction. Grady squinted to focus on it, his face leaning closer in to the windscreen.

"Boss, this bandstand's going awful quick like," he said, not taking his eyes from the oncoming car or the road. Becker shook his head.

"Forget it, he's the least of our worries, just drive," he said, "we ain't giving up Paul Carter for a jackin' speed freak."

Grady sat back in his seat just slightly and watched the faces of the people in the car on the other side of the road. A guy and a girl. The guy in the driver seat looked familiar though, as he peered up to Grady as they passed one another. The inane grin on his face as their eyes met. It wasn't just the guy though. The *car.* Grady knew him from somewhere, but said nothing. The girl was faced forward, fake innocence all over her like a cloak, looking everywhere but the two NCC vans. Something didn't sit right but there was nothing else to do. It was a case of Wilson Becker said jump and the rest said *how high?*

Cool as fudge.

Shane and I watch the building. Nothing happening just now. We saw the video go live on the NCC dayline. Watched the response. Still the majority are calling after my blood, but there are small, and ever so slightly subtle pockets of people. People who won't fully commit to the cause. People who remember themselves when they feel like acting *anti-British.* But they're there. The mob mentality. They think I have a rapidly growing gang and they want in. It doesn't matter that there are only four of us. If I tell them that I have a massively increased following they're scared to miss out when the revolution comes. *Just in case.*

We watched Becker leave in one van with three others about ten minutes ago, then another four in the second. We're waiting for Ben and Katie to arrive. If there are eight in the two vans then that leaves one inside the building, *I like those numbers.*

"Do you think it'll work?" asks Shane as we stand behind a whole stinking pile of NCC garbage, out of sight of the cameras. I shrug.

"They've gone to chase me, it seems to be so far," I say, but I've been asking myself the same question for a while. We're here, ready to attack a Government Authorised Network Crew headquarters. If it doesn't work we won't have far to travel to be judged. In the back of my mind I already fancy that Ben has sold us out, grabbed a hold of Katie and is heading back with Wilson Becker. Maybe he was even waiting there, in the upstairs car park of Meadowhall, ready for our future captors, so that they could come back and shake us down. *Katie,* I hope she's okay. Nothing about that sentiment is sexual, or based on love, in any way. As much as she irritates me I feel this

Ryan Bracha

overriding sense of duty. I need to protect her from harm. This country has let her down. I can't do the same.

"If it, you know, goes wrong, I've right enjoyed this. Just so you know," he says, genuine sincerity in his voice, "I think you're cool as fudge, and Katie thinks you're fit. You know? Just so you know."

I nod with a tight smile.

"Thanks for the sentiment, I appreciate it, but tell me that when we're on our deathbeds yeah?" I say as I pat his back, I've really grown to like the kid over the last day. I feel inclined to say something else about the Katie remark when there's a sudden roar of an engine being pushed to its limit which comes echoing down the thin road to which the NCC headquarters opens onto. Joined by the engine roar are a laughing shout, and a whoop. Shane and I crane our necks over the wall of garbage to see the brown car of Ben Turner rocket past us, the self-proclaimed crazy person leaning out of the driver's side and honking the horn. Beside him is the laughing form of Katie, looking like she's enjoying herself.

Joe Fatso.

It was no use. The monitor was fudged. Becker had officially killed it, so Joe lugged the thing out of the room and swapped it with one from an unused viewing chamber. They had all been unused over the last day, all of their efforts focussed upon the current situation, so he could afford to just swap it rather than drag it all the way down to the stores, for the time being at least. Wilson Becker *hated* jobs half done, Joe would see to it that he finished the task when the others returned, hopefully, with the thorn in all of their sides that was Paul Carter.

Carrying the replacement monitor he made a laboured effort to open the door with his elbow, keeping the thing ajar with his foot, and sliding into the room. A cursory check of the prisoner showed him to be in exactly the same place as when Joe had left him. He was going nowhere. He hooked the computer up to the monitor, and switched it on, before allowing himself the luxury of taking a seat, and pulling a non-alcoholic beer to his lips. On the screen he saw that the response to Paul Carter's most recent video was massive. A variety of tirades launched about who did Paul Carter think he was? That he wasn't their voice, he was just a mad man, a murderer, and he had no right to think that he could speak for New Britain. Some more ambivalent messages were coming through too. People who sat suspiciously on the fence. Never pulling up the courage to say what they were thinking. They made Joe sick.

As he poured the last dregs of his beer down his neck he choked violently as the CCTV from the front of the building showed *him* to be back. Ben Turner, a glutton for punishment. Always with his moronic gestures and actions. Screaming profanities toward the NCC

Ryan Bracha

headquarters, and slamming his hand down hard on the horn and he raced back and forth up the road. Joe was torn. He'd got Danny to keep an eye on, but he was going nowhere, he'd thought as much himself only seconds earlier. Surely he could afford to go and tell Ben Turner where to get off, to not give the guy the satisfaction of being judged, and just tell him he was wasting his time. But Joe was only one man. What if Turner became violent? Joe felt his hands shaking as they gripped the arms of the chair he was in. He didn't know what the heck to do. He reached for his phone and dialled Becker, but hung up before the connection started. Becker was in a foul mood, Joe would feel the brunt of it if he bothered the boss when he was feeling like that. He stood, tentatively stepping toward the door, refusing to take his eyes from the prisoner, as if blinking might give the guy the powers of escapism. Joe gulped, then sighed, and exited the room leaving the clueless Danny to his own fears. With each heavy footstep he convinced himself that he was doing the right thing, tackling a criminal, that's what he was paid for, surely? He grabbed a baton from the wall at the top of the stairs and grew more confident with every step that he descended. He would be lauded as a hero. Taking the initiative to deal with Ben Turner, shackle the guy in the next room to Paul Carter's cousin, and see how Becker liked that. There might even be a promotion in it for him, watch the stupid look on Grady's face when Joe got to be the one who told *him* what to do rather than the other way around.

He approached the front door, and witnessed the familiar brown car was Ben *jackin'* Turner speed past, from right to left. Slammed the door open and flicked the telescopic baton to unleash it. Ready for action. Another base profanity echoed into the air as Turner spun the car around and began his way back past the building. Joe frowned slightly as the realisation hit him that Turner wasn't alone. He had a girl with him. A smiling, laughing, *complicit* girl with him. She leant out of the car and squealed with delight, and the car edged ever closer to the now worried figure of Joe. He hadn't anticipated this. The girl fixed her eyes on him as they sped toward him, a gleeful sparkle in her eyes. Her faced blackened from days, months, years of dirt. *A street girl.* What would Ben Turner be doing associating with a street girl? He was a mischievous political rebel, nothing more, but he was clean. The car raced past him and the girl blew a kiss, and then pointed at something. Smiled at something. Then leant back into the car, which screeched to a halt, a good thirty or forty metres up the road. Joe's feet felt glued to the spot. He couldn't move, but he was suddenly inclined to look at what the girl pointed at, or more specifically *who* she was pointing at. A boy, a street boy. He was smiling at the shaking crew member. Stepping once, twice, toward him.

"Don't move," Joe whimpered, holding up the baton toward the street kid, "seriously, don't move or you'll be dealt with."

The kid laughed. Looked over his shoulder at the car. Ben Turner had climbed out, as had the girl. Neither of them moved. Just leant easily against the car. Watched them. The kid took another step.

"I said don't jackin' move, alright?" he wailed, swinging the baton wildly, as if it were some kind of threat. Still the kid said nothing. Took another step. Joe had had enough and began lurching toward the kid, flailing the baton, until his world went dark and his knees buckled. Somebody had hit him from behind. He screeched desperately, crying for somebody to help him, until a heavy blow threw stars into his darkness.

"Be quiet," a calm voice spoke, older than that of the street kid, "we aren't here to hurt you, but if you don't zip it we will have no choice, okay?"

Joe bit his lip. Fought the urge to speak out. To cry. He felt the material over his head go tight, and heard the tearing of tape before it was wrapped around his neck to keep the hood in place. Two pairs of hands helped him to his feet, before one of them disappeared.

"Okay, so here's what we want to know," the older man's voice said, "how many are up there?"

Joe said nothing, shook his head in a final weak effort at defiance. A thump hit him in the eye.

"Answer him fatso!" said a girl's voice. *The* girl's voice. A man muttered beside her and she giggled, "Joe Fatso, how many people are up there?"

"Who are you?" he asked, "what do you want?"

"You're not in a position to ask questions, Joseph," said the unmistakeable voice of Ben Turner, "I don't think there's anybody else up there, I say we just go straight in. Before the rest come back."

A MODERN BRITAIN #6

THE THIRTY FIVE YEAR OLD MAN
FINGERED THE COLOUR CODED
SELECTION OF USB STICKS. DOZENS OF
GREEN ONES LEFT UNTOUCHED. THEY
WERE FILLED WITH MUSIC THAT HE NO
LONGER LISTENED TO. HE REFLECTED
THAT HE REALLY OUGHT TO GET
ROUND TO THROWING THEM OUT, OR
WIPING THE DATA, BUT HE WAS A
HOARDER. THE MINUTE HE THREW THEM
AWAY THEN IT WOULD BE TYPICAL
THAT HE WOULD IMMEDIATELY BE IN
THE MOOD FOR LISTENING TO ROBBIE
WILLIAMS, OR WILL YOUNG. IT WAS
ALWAYS THE WAY. YOU ALWAYS
WANT WHAT YOU CAN'T HAVE. THE
YELLOW DEVICES WERE HIS FAVOURITE
TV SHOWS. OLD AMERICAN ONES, ONES
THAT WERE NOW CONSIDERED WORKS
OF THE DEVIL. ONES LIKE FRIENDS, AND
THE SOPRANOS. THESE WERE HIS AND
HIS ALONE TO ENJOY AWAY FROM THE
PRYING EYES OF THOSE PEOPLE WHO

Paul Carter is a Dead Man

REJECTED ALL THINGS FOREIGN. HE
WOULD WATCH THEM WITH HIS
NETWORK BROADCAST CHANNEL
SWITCHED FIRMLY OFF, LEST HE BE
CAUGHT ADORING ANYTHING NOT
BRITISH. FOR THE PURPOSES OF HIS
PUBLIC PERSONA, HE HAD HUNDREDS OF
OLD EPISODES OF CORONATION STREET,
INCLUDING THE VERY LAST EPISODE
BEFORE THEY SHUT THE DIGITAL SIGNAL
DOWN FOR GOOD IN 2012. IT WAS ONLY
TWO YEARS AGO BUT ALREADY IT FELT
LIKE AN AGE. HE LOVED HIS COUNTRY,
AND MOST OF THE THINGS ABOUT IT,
BUT SOME PART OF HIM LONGED TO BE
ABLE TO APPRECIATE THE CULTURES
OF OTHER COUNTRIES. TO BE ABLE TO
JUMP ONTO A PLANE AND WITNESS THE
BUSTLING THRONGS OF MOROCCAN
MARKETS, OR BE ABLE TO SIT AT A
STREET SIDE CAFÉ IN PARIS AND
WATCH THE WORLD PASS BY WITH AN
ESPRESSO IN ONE HAND, *LE MONDE* IN
THE OTHER. THIS WAS OUT OF THE
QUESTION NOW, AND HE LIVED WITH
WHAT HIS COUNTRY HAD BECOME,

Ryan Bracha

FORCED HIMSELF TO EMBRACE THE CHANGE. HE FOLLOWED THE CROWDS TO WITNESS THE MUSICAL ARTISTS OF THIS NEW DAY PLY THEIR TRADES ON THE NETWORK. ONE SUCH ARTIST, DECLAN MCGREGOR, A SINGER WHO HAILED FROM THE FORMER COLONY, AND CURRENT EMBARRASSING WASTELAND OF SCOTLAND, HAD BECOME A FIRM FAVOURITE. HIS MODERN CLASSIC SONG, *BEST LAID PLANS*, ABOUT HIS OLD HOMELAND'S ENFORCED DETACHMENT FROM THE REST OF NEW BRITAIN WAS ONE WHICH STRUCK PARTICULAR CHORDS. IT HAD A HAUNTING MELODY, AND FEATURED A SAMPLE OF BAGPIPES, THE NOW DEFUNCT INSTRUMENT FADING OUT AT THE END AS IF TO DRIVE HOME THE COUNTRY'S LACK OF TRUE IDENTITY ANYMORE, AS ANYTHING OTHER THAN THE SOCIAL TOILET OF THE GREAT NATION THAT WAS NEW BRITAIN. THERE WAS NO ENGLAND, NO SCOTLAND, AND NO WALES. ONLY NEW BRITAIN. TO THE THIRTY FIVE YEAR OLD MAN THIS WAS

THE WONDERFUL PART OF THE WHOLE SITUATION. HE SAW IT FOR WHAT IT WAS. HE SAW SOLIDARITY, AND HE SAW UNITY, AND DECLAN MCGREGOR'S SONG ENCAPSULATED IT ALL. THAT WAS WHAT HE TOLD HIS FRIENDS, AND HIS NETWORK CONNECTIONS. INSIDE, HOWEVER, HE SAW YET ANOTHER SHEEP ON THE ROAD TO MISERY, ANOTHER SYCOPHANT WHO HAD BEEN BRAINWASHED INTO CONTINUING TO LOVE THE RAPIDLY DECLINING NATION, BUT THERE WAS NO CHANCE THAT THOSE OPINIONS WOULD EVER MAKE IT TO THE LIGHT OF DAY.

SWITCHING OFF HIS NETWORK BROADCAST, CITING ILLNESS AS THE REASON FOR DOING SO, THE THIRTY FIVE YEAR OLD MAN PULLED OUT A YELLOW USB STICK, INSERTED IT INTO HIS COMPUTER, AND SELECTED A SHOW TO WATCH. HE SANK INTO THE LEATHER OF HIS ARMCHAIR, FLIPPED UP THE RECLINING MECHANISM, AND WENT TO A PLACE WHERE EVERYBODY KNOWS YOUR NAME.

Ryan Bracha

Take us to Danny.

We're all of us tramping into the NCC building with not so much an air of victory, more a curious wondering of what's the come next. Ben's pushing the poor trussed up figure of the crew member up ahead of us, a human shield, if you will. The guy's muffled vocals alternating between threats of what will happen when Wilson Becker finds out, to which Katie responds with mocking tones about him getting his dad on to us, and weak, whining bargaining about letting him go and he'll not say anything. Katie walks alongside me at one side, and Shane stalks along the wall at the other.

"Ben," I say as we top the stairs, he stops, tugging the arms of the hostage who wobbles unsteadily, his chest expanding rapidly like a wounded animal which sits, downbeat and still but for the laboured breaths it takes, close to death, "take his hood off."

Ben looks at me as if to ask if I'm sure and I offer a small nod, time to show our cards. The hostage whimpers, and cries, as Ben removes the tape from around his neck, pulling the sack from his head. The guy has his eyes closed tight, a weak effort at bringing his tied arms to protect himself amid a fear that he's about to meet his maker. I step to him urgently, and slap him hard across the face.

"Joe," I say firmly, still he's not playing the game. I slap him again, "Joe, open your eyes."

He does, and they dart from each of us to the next. Katie. Shane. Ben. Me. Katie. Shane. Katie. Me. Me. Me. His face creases in confusion.

"You're," he says, his hands are tied together but still they attempt to point at me, "you're."

"Yes, I am," I confirm.

"Oh God, oh god, oh god," he repeats his mantra as his feet attempt to pull him away from me and into the corridor. Ben Turner tugs him firmly back before me.

"Joe, I need you to listen to me, okay?"

"Oh God, oh God, oh God," he chants, his chubby face twists, as if not looking at me will make me disappear, like a child playing peek a boo.

"Joe!" I raise my voice just slightly and handle his cheeks, squeezing them together and pulling his face directly into the line of mine, he physically flinches under my touch.

"Please don't kill me, I have kids," he says to a hysterical response from Katie.

"So do half the people you put up for judgment just for swearing you stupid bandstand!" she laughs, about to go in for a second shot but I place my hand on her shoulder and shake my head, not the time. I look back to the hostage.

"Joe, if you behave yourself you'll be perfectly safe, but I need you to listen to me, okay?"

He nods, his eyes daren't leave mine now.

"Is there anybody else in this building, apart from Danny?"

He shakes his head.

"Are you telling me the truth, Joe?"

He nods.

Ryan Bracha

"You're aware of what could happen if it turns out you're lying?"

He nods.

"Okay. Good. Now take us to Danny. My friend Ben here is a bit of a loose cannon, and if he thinks you're going to try anything stupid then he has my permission to do as he pleases to you, do you understand?"

He nods a third time, this time with a cautious look at Ben's grinning face.

"Good, now take us to Danny."

Not what it used to be.

He deserved it. He was well aware, and accepting of that fact. There was no way that Paul would give himself up for him. He'd been asking himself if *he* would risk anything for his cousin had the roles been reversed, he'd raised various situations, and conditions, and he was ashamed to admit that no, he wouldn't. Family wasn't what it used to be. Back in the old days it stood for at least *something.* Not anymore. When they were kids and they all gathered at their grandmother's every Sunday. The four uncles – Danny's dad Keith, and his brothers Mark, Gavin and Carl – would descend upon Nana Joan's house with the wives and kids in tow for a family dinner, and a few hours of socialising. Danny could sit and play silly games with his youngest cousins Patrick and Cara for ages, under the watchful eye of his Uncle Mark. Making stupid faces to see them crack up with laughter, little Cara clapping her hands and blowing spit bubbles of delight, whilst her older brother Patrick, although he'd called Danny a dork for being so stupid, secretly loved it. They'd been shipped to Paris with Uncle Mark and Auntie Natalie a few years ago, Paddy would be about ten, Cara seven. Danny shook his head in regret. He'd not thought about them at all recently and wondered what they looked like now. What they'd be doing. *How* they'd be doing. He wondered if they'd thought about him at all. If they'd missed him. Probably not, family was definitely not what it used to be.

A briefly considered realisation shook him from his reminiscence. There hadn't been a guard here in ages. Obviously there'd be one behind the two way mirror, but nobody had been in to intimidate him in a while. Had they finally managed to catch Paul? He wasn't sure how far they'd have to travel to track him down, and they'd undoubtedly let the world know if and when they did that. But then what about his *friends,* whoever they might be? Danny shook his cousin from his mind and refocused on the timer, nine hours something. The digital countdown flicked slowly but surely toward his judgment. He'd not even considered that there might not be enough votes to punish him. He'd voted enough to know that not many people ever really got away. The public *always* had their way, and the nature of the reasons for holding him in the first place ensured a high enough profile for the numbers to count against him. These were going to be Danny's last nine hours, give or take, on Earth, and he was almost certainly to spend them watching the minutes drip away. He closed his eyes and dropped his head. Watched one of his thumbs rub over the texture of the nail on the other one. He was tired. Danny let out a short chuckle through his nose, how much of an annoyance might it be for the public should he choose to spend his final hours asleep? Take away their satisfaction of judging a man begging for forgiveness. For a chance at redemption. His eyes blinked heavy as he allowed the idea to evolve into an option, his breathing grew heavier through his nose, and his mind drifted. Back to Nana Joan's. To a time when people, although some would force their opinions to a wider world, would leave others be, would focus on what was happening in their own lives and leave everybody else to it. A tapping foot jolted Danny from his reverie. How long he'd been asleep he couldn't say, if indeed he'd even been asleep at all. Danny dragged his head upright, to see a girl before him, standing beneath the blinking form of the camera. She was a petite thing, the hood of her jacket raised over her head, leaving what looked like a very pretty face in shadow. A partially covered, but no less iconic cartoonish circular egg-and-sperm logo of Queens of the Stone Age, an American band from the old days emblazoned across the front of her T-shirt. The kind of thing which could have her struck down for anti-British behaviour in the wrong parts of town. Danny didn't know what to say. What the heck what she doing here? In the NCC headquarters? Her tapping foot continued to hammer out a subtle beat as she brought one of her folded arms upright in front of her face and held a single finger over her lips. The universally recognised symbol for be quiet. Danny did as he was bidden and watched as the girl took down the hood from her head, revealing a tight pony tail of greasy dark brown hair. Her huge green eyes blinked beneath the smeared black forehead. Still she watched Danny. Her face betrayed nothing, as she watched him neutrally, one finger across her lips. The foot still tapping. Satisfied that Danny understood to be quiet she slowly turned her head toward the two-way mirror and gave a broad, dirty toothed, beaming smile, followed by a wink. Danny didn't understand, was this a dream? How had this girl even managed to get into the building, let alone into a supposedly secure judgment room with him? It *had* to be a dream. Danny shook his head violently, squeezed his eyes shut tight, held them closed for what could have been minutes. Opened them again. She was still there, shifting her attention from the mirror, and him, still her finger pressed hard over her lips as she offered Danny a mischievous wink. Her shoulders began to twitch. Just slightly at first, then heavier as she struggled to keep her mirth to herself. Danny frowned. This wasn't a funny situation, far from it, and it was growing less and less funny by the second. Danny turned to watch himself watching

Ryan Bracha

himself on the Network screen. The messages of condemnation. The judgment counter. Three quarters of the way there. Turned back to the girl. Holding in her laughter. He continued to remain silent even as she slowly she pulled her finger away from her mouth, and with her eyebrows beckoned him to look at the screen again.

"What the-" he said, unable to stick to the quiet instruction. The Network screen was black. Empty. Dead. The girl finally burst out in laughter. A dirty, mischievous, and sleazy laugh.

"Who are you?" Danny asked, but the girl continued to laugh, ignoring his question, turning to leave the room, "wait! What's happening?"

The girl was gone, taking her laughter out into the corridor and out of earshot.

"Wait!" Danny called, struggling against the bindings that held him firm to the chair. Pulled his feet against the leather strapping that held his feet in placed. Tried in vain to push himself up away from the seat, "wait!"

It was no use. He was stuck, and she was gone. Whoever she was. Maybe some make-a-wish kid who wanted to come and see the real life workings of a Network crew headquarters before she finally croaked it. Unlikely. Maybe the daughter of one of the crewmembers who'd come with dad to watch the criminal get judged. Again, unlikely, but there was no logical reason for a random street kid to be standing there laughing. And the screen dying. What did it all mean?

A set of footsteps clacked toward the door. A figure waited on the other side. Taller than the girl. A cleared throat. The handle twisting. The door opening. A man. A man he didn't recognise, closely cropped hair and leather jacket, with a smile on his face.

"What's going on?" Danny spoke, this time with a more assured tone. Something wasn't right here and Danny wanted to know what, and why.

"Busting you out old chap," said the guy, crouching to Danny's feet to unlock the strapping.

"But who are you?" he asked, no feeling of relief at the revelation, only confusion.

"All in good time Daniel, yeah?"

"What's happening?"

"You've asked that already, and I already told you the answer, so can we keep it to a minimum yeah?"

The guy stood up to unlock the arms, one and then the other. Danny had no idea of what to do next. For all he knew the second he attempted to get out of here then there'd be some cruel joke of a gunman standing ready to dispatch him to the other side nine hours sooner than anticipated. The guy took a step back and looked down at him with a smile.

"Welcome to your first day of freedom Danny boy!" he said, arms aloft by his side. Danny didn't move, and the smile dropped from his rescuer's

Ryan Bracha

face, "seriously, get up, we've got sherbet to do and not much time to do it in."

"But who are you?" Danny asked.

"Who I am isn't important," he replied, turning as if ready to leave the room. Danny rubbed at his wrists, noting for the first time how tight the NCC bandstand had strapped them down, "now, who my *friend* is, that's probably a more important piece of information."

The guy opened the door, and made to move. Danny was growing impatient of the guy's reticence to give a straight answer. He sighed, and rose unsteadily from the chair, following the guy out of the room.

"Okay, who's your friend?" he asked, matching him step for step until they approached the room next door. The viewing room. The room on the other side of the two way mirror. His rescuer stopped by the door and turned to smile once again.

"I'll let him introduce himself eh?" he said as he opened the door to reveal various things that challenged his belief. One was the shackled form of the crew member he knew as Joe, blood seeping from a cut above his eye. The other was his cousin, Paul Carter.

"Hi Danny," he said, pulling one hand from the pocket of his coat to wave at him slightly, "surprise!"

They have a ride.

Nothing, again, save a handful of vagrants that Grady had to be warned from assaulting. Paul Carter continued to treat the entire crew with a contempt best saved for foreigners and paedophiles, and Becker was reaching breaking point. They had scoured every last broken inch of the abandoned Meadowhall shopping centre, the dogs let loose to track Carter and any evidence of the friends he'd been claiming to have acquired. Nothing.

Wilson Becker stood at the epicentre of where a circular food court had once been. Smashed tables and chairs scattered around him. A carpet of broken glass from the smashed windows of the former restaurants coated the floor, which Grady crunched through to reach his employer.

"No dice, Boss," he said, shaking his head through disappointment, "we've looked everywhere, he's gone."

Wilson Becker contemplated Grady's words. Kicked a chair through frustration, but instantly regretting the action as a delayed pain shot through the length of his leg. Spoke through gritted teeth.

"I don't think he was ever here."

Grady tilted his head, eyebrows furrowed.

"Boss?"

"He said as much himself, he has *friends* to help him," he said, "what if the bandstand was never here? What if he's got stupid cronies doing the work for him while he lives it up somewhere

Ryan Bracha

else? Maybe the jacker ain't even in Sheffield anymore."

"I don't know, boss, it's an interesting theory," Grady said. A crunch of glass attracted his interest. A vagrant attempting and failing to pass them by without being noticed. Grady started toward the guy, already pulling his NCC identification card from his pocket.

"You! Here, now! Network Cutting Crew, I need to ask you some questions."

The vagrant paused. Contemplated making a dash. Thought the better of it. Turned to await the approaching Grady. Wilson Becker stood and watched the scene.

"You seen anybody here that shouldn't be?" asked Grady of the bum, a slender and dirty white man, hands tensing in fingerless gloves to keep warm as he hopped from one foot to the other. The vagrant blinked once or twice and shook his head.

"I no see nobody," he said with broken English, more than a hint of Eastern Europe to his accent, he was a *pretend British* man, "stay shelter for warm. No see anything."

Grady sneered at the man, and turned to Becker, looking for permission to strike him. Becker shook his head.

"You no see nobody eh?" he mocked, "stay shelter?"

The man nodded, and looked to Becker for help.

"So you ain't seen anybody who shouldn't be here? What about your friends? They see anybody?"

The man shook his head, no.

"I keep to self, no friend, only me. Stay-"

"Yeah yeah, stay shelter, I got it," Grady interrupted, before turning to his boss.

"He ain't no use to us Boss, stupid *pretender*."

"Watch your mouth Grady, he's as much right to stay in this country as you or I," said Becker, the former New Zealander bristling at his employee's attitude to those not born in the country. Grady moved to speak but thought better of it, and pushed the vagrant away.

"Go on, get outta here!"

The man shuffled off muttering broken English thanks and disappeared out of sight, Grady returned to Becker, who was still mulling over his original theory. The pair began a stroll back to the rest of the crew and the vans.

"If he has friends helping him how are they doing it? We have his profile tracked. How are they getting him here and then disappearing?"

"Probably got a car, boss," Grady said, before pausing for thought, "Oh, wait. No, no, he can't be," he continued, a hand rubbing against his shorn skull, playing out a possibility in his mind, finally placing a two alongside another to create the four he was looking for.

"You wanna tell me what you're going on about?"

"Ben Turner, jackin' *Ben Turner!*" Grady said, almost whispered, inwardly cursing for not making any kind of link sooner. Becker shook his head.

"No, not his style, he's a crazy idiot, but I don't think he's *that* crazy."

Ryan Bracha

"No, hear me out boss, on the drive here, I tried to tell you about the guy speeding, remember?" Becker nodded, bidding Grady to continue.

"Well, as he passed us I *knew* I recognised his face, and his *car.* It was Ben jackin' Turner, and he had some girl with him. They were coming *away* from Meadowhall, they didn't look like they wanted to see us at all, something didn't sit right, he's involved, boss, I know he is."

Becker continued to doubt it, Turner was a fruit loop who got off on winding him up, that was all. He wasn't in the market for violence and murder. It wasn't his thing. His thing was swearing and speeding and getting himself arrested on purpose because he was an attention seeking rucksack. Grady sensed it, but continued regardless.

"Think about it, Paul Carter's been directing everything at you boss. Every time he sends out one of these videos it's for *your* benefit, Ben Turner does what he does to get on your nerves, he said as much himself. I think Carter tracked him down and I think he's a part of it. It's just too damned convenient for him to be in the area. It makes too much sense, *that's* how they're getting in and out. They have a ride, and I think Ben Turner's the bandstand doing the driving."

Becker rubbed his fingers against the short beard of growth he'd begun to cultivate since this whole Paul Carter debacle started two days ago. Wilson Becker was not a man who liked the unkempt look. He was always so well groomed. It reflected badly on his business. How could he be expected to be taken seriously if he couldn't keep his facial hair in check? He made a conscious decision to shave as soon as they returned to the office. He mulled over Grady's theory some more as they passed broken shells of old retail outlets. Hangers disrobed and scattered around the mouths of the old stored, faeces dumped in corners by those who were too lazy to take it somewhere more private. Becker curled his nose up in disgust.

"This is revolting Grady, how can these people live like this? Where's their self-respect?" he said, the question entirely rhetorical, "okay, so say you're right, say that lunatic has joined forces with Carter, and there was a girl with him, right?"

Grady nodded to the affirmative.

"So that's three people. That's *not* an army, it's hardly even a gang. We don't know the girl, but assuming you're right, all we need to do is track Ben Turner and if we find him, we find Carter."

"Assuming I'm right, boss," Grady said, squeezing in a kind of disclaimer, he didn't want to be the man who took the hunt off-piste in error, "like I say, it's just a feeling I got."

"But it's all we got Grady, we need to sort this out, and we need to sort it soon. Lodge is riding my back to bring in Finnegan or Tough Justice. We've put too much in, and lost too much to let one of those rucksacks take the credit. This is ours."

"Boss."

"Call Joe, get a tracker on Turner."

Ryan Bracha

"Boss."

More refined than that.

"What's happening Paul?" Danny's asking as
we're helping ourselves to whatever's available
in the NCC stores. This is the fifth time he's asked
the question but, to be honest, I still don't really
know myself. The plan was to get him out, which
we have. I truly didn't think it would be this easy.
For the fifth time, I ignore the question, and pull
from the shelves whatever I think is of use. All of
the weapons are non-lethal. Tasers and batons.
Some guns, but the beanbag, rubber bullet
variety. This is another result of the Robert
Lodge effect. If crews were to take responsibility
for law enforcement, then he didn't want unruly
crewmembers taking it upon themselves to go
out killing criminals indiscriminately. This was
New Britain, he'd said, not some god-awful
country like America. We were more refined
than that. Justice was for the people, the crews
were simply facilitating that process. If a
criminal got out of hand then an electrical charge
into the back would be the way to bring about
that facilitation. Not bullets. Shane is in the
corner poring over the electronic technology.
"Bossman, look at this!" he's saying excitedly,
holding up a tablet computer before sliding it
into his backpack, "top of the range, this is
awesome!"

I smile but return to my own foraging. I have a Taser in each pocket. Three more in my own bag. Danny stands by the door, nervously leaning out every now and then, keeping an unofficial lookout since he's still not really processed what's happening. Ben and Katie are upstairs looking after our hostage. Danny's refused to leave my side since his release.

"I'm sorry Paul," he's saying now, having shifted his thoughts from what's *happening* to what's *happened,* "it was Pete, you know how he gets."

I mumble an acknowledgment but the truth of it is that I've already forgotten about it. Too much has happened since yesterday for me to dwell too much.

"Yeah, and he lets you get busted and goes on with his life like nothing's happened, good friend eh?" This is Shane talking, not turning to Danny to say it. From the corner of my eye I see Danny's head drop. He sighs.

"Thanks for reminding me," he mutters.

"My pleasure," chuckles Shane, shaking his head, already he's side-tracked. He holds up another piece of kit, "check this out Bossman, a tracker. Can't believe how much stuff they have here. It's *awesome.*"

Danny's head disappears out of the door as the sound of approaching footsteps draws his attention.

"It's Katie," he says, as she skips into the room.

"Paul Carter," she says, calmly, "we need to get going soon, they've been ringing every phone in the place. They're gonna be onto us soon if they aren't already."

"Okay, I think we've got enough now," I say to her, before turning my focus to Shane, "alright?" Shane nods and zips up his bag before throwing it over his shoulder. I look to Danny, my young cousin looking ever more youthful with his little-boy-lost features and blinking sad eyes. Instinctively my hand pulls up to the side of his head, my thumb rubbing against his hair.

"I'll tell you everything as soon as we're out of here and safe, yeah?"

He nods with mournful complicity and follows us as we pass him in the doorway and head back upstairs to Ben and the hostage.

He ain't there.

"He ain't answering boss," Grady said with a wince. His forehead, covered with just slightly too much skin, wrinkled into deep ridges as he spoke, awaiting an outburst, "maybe he's in the toilet?"

Becker shook his head. Climbed into the car. Into the driver's seat.

"Keep trying," he said as his employees clambered aboard. Shifting the clutch and spinning the van out of the car park. The second van shunted into life and began a rapid chase. The worst of possibilities were racing through Becker's mind as quickly as the van rocketed through the outskirts of Sheffield. The worst case scenario was that they were going to return to an empty building, save for the splayed open corpse of Joe. A warning served. A second NCC member dead at the hands of Paul Carter. Wilson shuddered at the thought. Best case was that Joe really had been on the toilet and would answer shortly that everything was fine, and then find himself on the receiving end of an almighty dressing down. Grady huffed in frustration and shoved the call button once again, pulling the device to his ear. His eyes flickered as he listened to the ring tone before once again pressing the thing to disconnect.

"Boss?" said a voice from the back, Oxley, it was weak, almost frightened.

"Mmm?"

"Something's wrong-"

Slam! Becker's hand rammed down onto the horn, interrupting the meek man in the back seat.

"I know something's wrong you jackin' idiot!" he roared, his eyes burning into the sweating jowly face of Oxley through the rear-view mirror, "you want to tell me something I don't know?!"

Oxley shook nervously, inwardly bemoaning the fact that it was he that was about to make this particular revelation.

"No, I mean. Something different."

"Spit it out then you fat, stupid bandstand!"

"It's, ehm, I mean-"

"He said spit it out you rucksack!" Grady had joined in, thankful of a reprieve from being the one in the spotlight.

Ryan Bracha

"It's… Look," he said, passing the palmtop computer to Grady, as if it were a bomb with mere seconds left on the clock. Grady pulled the thing closer and allowed the image to seep into his logic filter. The judgement window for Danny. Or, more specifically, where the judgment window, and *Danny* should have been.

"No way," he said.

"You wanna let me in on the secret boys? Huh?!" Wilson Becker shouted at nobody in particular.

"Boss, he's right, something's wrong. He ain't there."

"Who, *ain't there?*"

"Danny. Carter's cousin. He ain't jackin' there!" Becker let the words to work their magic. *He ain't there.* Joe had not gone to the toilet. Joe was dead. He had to be. Paul Carter was an animal. He wouldn't allow the poor soul to live. Everybody knew what he was capable of. The situation was out of control. Wilson Becker sighed. He wanted to get angry. He wanted to do something stupid. He wanted to drive the car straight into a wall and end this whole sorry mess once, and for all. He didn't though. He simply pushed his foot further down onto the accelerator and pulled out his phone, found the contact and pushed to dial. Grady and Oxley eyed each other nervously. The boss was on the edge of breaking here. Becker awaited a connection.

"Yeah. Wilson Becker here. Yeah. *The* Wilson Becker. I need to speak with James Finnegan. No, I can't call back. Get him for me *now!*"

How's this for a turn up?

"Okay, Joe. We're not going to let you go, because, well, just because. We'd be stupid to. But, and you'll be glad of this, you behaved yourself, so my friend Ben is going to leave you intact. How's that for a result eh?" I say to the trussed up hostage, and I have to say, this whole leader thing is starting to grow on me, like the confidence I'm feeling about our situation. The hostage nods his head but says nothing through the gag.

"Now, we're taking my cousin with us, because he doesn't belong to you, and he's done nothing wrong. You tell your boss that, and you tell him how well we treated you, okay?" He's nodding again, even more eagerly, like he senses his nightmare is about over.

"We helped ourselves to a few things, but I'm sure the insurance will cover it. Thanks for being such a good hostage Joe, it's been a pleasure." Katie chuckles throughout this, her hand over her mouth so as not to kill the magic which, it seems, would be Ben's job.

"We need to go now Paul, they'll be back any minute I reckon," he says, and he's right. We can't get *too* confident until we're out of here. I nod in his direction and look to the others.

"You're right, come on."

The hostage breathes a huge sigh of relief through his nose, he'll get home to see those darling children he was so eager to protect from being without a father. Like his children have

Ryan Bracha

more of a right than those of the people his organisation has sent to the other side, Katie had it spot on. I know we should get out of here quickly, but an idea sparks into life, and although Ben, Danny and Shane are already out of the door, I can't help but stay rooted to the floor. Katie's looking at me from the doorway, her hand reaching up to tug my finger. Just the little one, and it strikes me as tender. My hand balls into a fist out of her reach.

"Come on Paul Carter, we've got what we came for," she says, self-consciously pulling her own hand away and tucking it into the pocket of her hooded top, I don't move. Ben returns to beside her.

"What's up killer?"

"Nothing, just, I had an idea," I say, my focus entirely upon the hostage, who can sense his nightmare isn't *quite* over. Katie picks up on my vibe and is moved to ask.

"What kind of idea? Are we taking him with us?"

I shake my head slightly, but step toward the hostage. He flinches and closes his eyes but I'm not going to damage him, I'm a little hurt that he would think that, after we've quite clearly come here with no intention of doing so. We got what we wanted, but I don't think there's any harm in allowing the country front row seats to the situation.

"Come on, help me," I say, grabbing a hold of Joe's shoulders and pushing hard against them to wheel him toward the door. He's not a small man, and the flooring doesn't help matters any, but Ben's quickly alongside me and heaving to push the chair.

"What's happening Paul Carter?" asks Katie, head tilted to one side in confusion.

"Just, a little, reminder," I say, through the exertion of pushing the fat rucksack out of the room. The wheels are as good as pointless on this floor. Plus they're ruining what looks to be expensive carpet.

"Of what?"

"Of," is all I can get out before the wheels clunk heavily over the metal bar across the doorway and onto the laminate flooring of the corridor, thus ensuring a cleaner, and less painful trip to the room next door, I continue, "of the fact that we aren't going away. Becker won't just let us get away with this. He'll keep coming. Might as well strike another blow."

Ben's grinning now, and his eyes light up at the prospect. He seems like an absolute mental case, but an extremely good mental case on your side in case of an emergency.

"Shane," I call out to him as he stands beside my cousin, who continues to look like a deer caught in headlights, twitching and dancing to get out of here. Shane nods.

"Bossman?"

"Get in there and be ready for my nod, yeah? I want you to switch the NCC network synopsis back online, okay?"

"Yep."

He eagerly darts into the room, behind the two way mirror. The judgment room is a lot brighter

Ryan Bracha

than I thought it would be. Almost clinical. A hard pale blue linoleum floor with darker flecks spattered across it, almost hospital quality material. It's wipe clean. Perhaps that's the point. The guy in the chair is whimpering through fear now, much the same as a dog in a pound, awaiting extermination. It seems to be getting on Ben's nerves somewhat as he slaps the guy around the head. His inane grin continues, but with an air of disbelief as he pauses to look at me and then the tubby hostage who's shaking.

"Shut up will ya? It's pathetic, man. God."

Joe does his level best to hold in the noise, lest he be punished further. We wheel him before the camera, pushing him left to right. Trying to centralise him within the view of the lens. We then move out of shot, and I nod to the mirror. The monitors blink into life, and as they warm up the trussed up figure of Joe appears on each one of them. The image of him strapped down, defeated. A strip of pale tape across his mouth. He refuses to look into the camera. Concentrates on his lap. The timer still runs down from Danny's own plight, and the guilty verdicts continue to mount up steadily. A series of confused messages begin to filter in as the man the public anticipated is not there. I give it a few moments to let the image sink in, and then I lean in beside Joe.

"Mr Wilson Becker," I smile, "how's this for a turn up?"

Three nil.

Becker's hands gripped the wheel ever tighter as the van thundered along St Mary's Road, listening to the tinny message from Carter. "Consider this three nil to us. Danny is now free to go. He never did anything wrong, you set him up in order to provoke me. Well, guess what? You provoked me. Just, you did a very bad job of it."

Grady's nervous hand shook as he held the device. His twitching eyes darting from the screen to his employer, and on to Oxley and Teddy in the back. Each of them hanging on to the words of the fugitive as he spoke.

"Now. For you people of Britain. This is for you. Yes, I've killed two people, and yes, I had my reasons. Maybe one day I'll have an opportunity to share those with you, but right now see this," I say, a hand beckoning my audience to view Joe, the hostage, "my associates and I have had every chance to harm the poor man you see beside me. We have had him alone for some time now. Yes, he looks in some degree of discomfort, but have we hurt him? Have I, the monster that you have reviled so far killed him and feasted down on his tubby backside? Shall we ask him?"

On the screen Carter leant in to Joe, ran a hand across his sweating head, and quickly pulled the tape from across his mouth. Becker wouldn't watch. Only heard the words as the van screeched a harsh right onto Bramall Lane. His only hope was that this was live right now, and

Ryan Bracha

that Carter would keep talking, because they were mere minutes from the office. Finnegan had taken his call, and agreed to meet there within the hour to discuss the matter, but if Becker could get back to the office in time there might be no need. His teeth clenched in pure rage at the audacity of Paul Carter. On Becker's *turf,* who did he think he was? The video continued.

"Okay, so Joe, I want you to be truthful," he said, "have we hurt you?"

A moment of silence.

"Come on, don't be shy, tell the country. Have we actually hurt you, or come close to taking your children's daddy away from them? You have kids remember. Be truthful."

A small noise.

"What was that?"

"No."

"No, we haven't. If I was this cold hearted monster that you all believe me to be then would I allow you to live Joe?"

A small noise.

"Come again?"

"No."

"I see. Interesting. Very interesting. Worth thinking about, wouldn't you agree?"

No noise.

"Ah well, it was a rhetorical question anyway. So people of Britain. Whilst you munch down on your generic branded noodles for lunch. Just bear that in mind. Wilson Becker, until next time, I'll remind you again. Three nil."

Then silence, but Grady continued to watch the screen. Carter had returned the tape to Joe's face and disappeared. Wilson Becker twitched in his direction.

"Well?"

"Well nothing, boss. He's gone. Joe's sitting there looking like he's about to start bawling."

On the screen Grady witnessed a variety of ambiguous messages come through. People who, although they hadn't come outright and said it, had started to doubt not only the credibility of Becker and his organisation, but the guilt of Carter. It wasn't what they typed. It was the tone in which they typed it. All the while Joe refused to look up to face what he knew would be the sickened eyes of his boss.

The van screeched through the car park of the old football ground and hammered through an old fence that ran behind the NCC building. Wilson Becker didn't say anything but he hoped among hopes that they had arrived in time. That Carter was still inside. And his *friends.*

Mr Robert Lodge doesn't like the sound of this one bit.

"Sir, there has been a development of the most sinister of natures."

"Go on."

"Paul Carter-"

"Again? Again with this Paul *blasted* Carter?"

"I'm afraid so, sir."

Ryan Bracha

"But I thought that the other crews have been involved?"

"As of yet, no sir, but please, I need to tell you."

"Very well. Go on."

"Paul Carter seems to have gained quite a crew of his own, they have stormed the headquarters of The Networking Cutting Crew, and somehow managed to free a young man who was open for judgment."

"Really?"

"Yes sir."

"I don't like the sound of this one bit, Garner."

"Indeed. The young man in question was Carter's cousin."

"Hmm."

"Yes, and they thought it necessary to goad Wilson Becker live, using his own NCC network synopsis to do so."

"Oh dear."

"Indeed."

"Any news of Becker?"

"Not really sir."

"Not really?"

"James Finnegan called to notify us that Becker had finally called him to request assistance in the matter."

"Well, that's good then."

"Indeed."

"And how does he plan to assist?"

"Not sure as of yet, sir, but he has agreed to keep in constant touch regarding the situation."

"He's a good man James Finnegan. Always said that. Very good man."

"Indeed."

"So what of this Carter? Has he escaped again?"

"Well, sir. This is another development. It seems that Becker and his crew returned as they made their escape. Most of the fugitives got away, but Becker managed to capture one of them. A girl."

A MODERN BRITAIN #7

IN COLCHESTER, RUSSELL HUNT, A
SELF-PROFESSED LOVER OF THE ARTS,
SHARED A RECENT DISCOVERY WITH HIS
FRIEND, CHARLES BENSON. RUSSELL
LOVED TO SCOUR THE NETWORK,
LOOKING FOR THE UP AND COMING
INDEPENDENT ARTISTS OF THE
COUNTRY. THOSE THAT WOULD USE
THE NETWORK IN ORDER TO
DEMONSTRATE THE QUITE
CONSIDERABLE SKILLS THEY HELD IN
PLEASING THE NAKED EYE. USUALLY, HE
WOULD DISPLAY, AND SHARE THE
PIECES THAT HE'D DISCOVERED ON HIS
WEEKLY NETWORK BROADCAST, THE
IMAGINATIVELY TITLED *HUNT'S HUNT
FOR ART.* HE'D AMASSED A
REASONABLE FOLLOWING FOR HIS
BROADCAST, AND WOULD REGULARLY
ATTRACT FIGURES OF TWO OR THREE
HUNDRED PEOPLE VIEWING IT. THESE
KINDS OF NUMBERS COULD OFFER THE
ARTISTS THAT HE'D DISCOVERED A

Paul Carter is a Dead Man

WHOLE NEW AUDIENCE FOR THEIR
WORKS. ONE MAN, A COLLAGE ARTIST
NAMED GARETH HALLIDAY, HAD
RECENTLY GONE ON TO HAVE HIS WORK
DISPLAYED ON THE GOVERNMENT'S ART
CHANNEL, AND WAS NOW CONSIDERED
TO BE QUITE HIGHLY THOUGHT OF
AMONGST THE ELITE. SUCCESS STORIES
LIKE THAT DID NOT COME AROUND
EVERY DAY, BUT THEY DID INCREASE
THE SUBMISSIONS OF WORKS TO
HUNT'S HUNT FOR ART QUITE
CONSIDERABLY. HE WOULD BROWSE
THE WORKS, QUIETLY ADMIRING THOSE
THAT HE FELT COULD BRING IN THE
ADVERTISING REVENUE. QUIETLY
HUFFING AT THOSE THAT WERE QUITE
CLEARLY WORKS BY AMATEURS
CHANCING THEIR ARM WITH A CRUDELY
DRAWN PICTURE OF ROBERT LODGE, OR
BLATANT RIP-OFFS OF EXISTING WORKS.
ONE PIECE, HOWEVER, CAUGHT HIS EYE
FOR AN ENTIRELY DIFFERENT REASON,
HENCE, RUSSELL HUNT KEPT THE
AUDIENCE DOWN TO THE BARE MINIMUM
OF ONE FOR THE PURPOSES OF SEEKING

Ryan Bracha

ADVICE. CHARLES BENSON. IT WAS A PIECE BY A YOUNG ARTIST BY THE NAME OF GAYLE KARABELEN, ENTITLED *OLD BRITAIN NEW BRITAIN ANY BRITAIN.* THE IMAGE UPON THE SCREEN WAS SIMPLY A MAP OF THE COUNTRY, USING SOME SORT OF DESIGN SOFTWARE. TO THE NAKED EYE THERE WAS NOTHING AT ALL DIFFERENT, OR WRONG ABOUT THE IMAGE. BUT UPON CLOSER INSPECTION, THE PLACES NAMES HAD BEEN REMOVED, AND EACH ONE HAD REPLACED WITH PROFANITY. OLD BRITAIN SWEAR WORDS. ONES WHICH WOULD MAKE THE COMMON MAN SHUDDER IN THIS DAY AND AGE. ON TOP OF THE PROFANITY, THE ARTIST HAD DECLARED SEVERAL DEFAMATORY STATEMENTS AGAINST MR ROBERT LODGE. ASIDE FROM THESE THERE WERE WORDS THAT INSINUATED THAT THE OUTCAST POPULATION OF SCOTLAND WERE THE LUCKY ONES. THAT THEIR HOME SHOULD BE SEEN AS UTOPIA FOR THE DISILLUSIONED. CHARLES BENSON DID AGREE THAT, ALTHOUGH THIS WAS

Paul Carter is a Dead Man

A DARING AND RISKY PIECE, THE YOUNG ARTIST SHOULD BE BROUGHT TO TASK OVER HER FLAGRANT DISREGARD FOR THE GUIDELINES. THEY HANDED THE ART OVER TO THE NECESSARY AUTHORITY AND THOUGHT NO MORE ABOUT IT. THE YOUNG ARTIST WAS HANGED THE NEXT DAY. HER ART SOLD FOR OVER ONE MILLION NEW BRITISH POUNDS, AND, DUE TO HIS ROLE IN THE CONTROVERSY, RUSSELL HUNT NOW BROADCASTS TO OVER SEVEN HUNDRED PEOPLE EVERY WEEK.

I got cocky.

None of us has said anything for the last five minutes of walking. Ben is up ahead, a purposeful walk which, if I didn't know any better, would hint at him trying to distance himself from the situation. From me. From a way back I can see his fists clenching and unclenching. Eventually he plants them into the pockets of his jacket. Shane struggles to keep up behind him, hands grappling with the strap of the backpack that hangs from his shoulder. Full of stolen electronic goods. I'm walking at my own pace, Danny beside me. He's been making throaty coughs, and half noises, obviously wants to say something but I don't prompt him to take it any further. I have way too much to consider. Such as how the hell we're going to fix this. I play the escape out in my head, where it went wrong. And it always, no matter how many times I replay it, it always comes back to me. I messed up.
We were there, we had our out, but I took it one step too far. I had to go and push our luck. Played with the lives of four other people to show Wilson Becker how much better than him I was. How I'd outsmarted him at every turn. Then I came unstuck. I got cocky. The five of us were fast, as soon as I'd finished the video we got out of there, but as we left the building one of the NCC vans came screeching round the corner. We ran. Couldn't get back to Ben's car in time. I followed Danny followed Shane followed Ben,

and Katie followed me. She wasn't fast enough. They got her. And it was my fault. It was my stupid fault. I let her get caught. All the big song and dance about wanting to keep her safe and I let her get caught. We're back at square one, except we traded Katie for Danny. This isn't fair. Ben blames Danny, Shane blames Danny. I blame me. The reason any of us are anywhere right now, is me.

"I'm sorry, Paul," my cousin finally pipes up. I shake my head. I don't want to hear it, "for everything. Not just for Katie. For turning you away."

"Don't," I say, focusing on the two up ahead. I'm not good at this kind of thing, but he goes on.

"I want to help you, with everything. You risked everything to get me out, I want to repay you for that. I want to be a part of your gang."

My gang?

"Yes, we risked everything, and we lost. We lost Katie."

"But we can get her back, like you did with me, we can get her back."

"I don't think Becker's going to fall for the same trick twice. Besides, I'm not sure that they still have faith in the cause. Not after I messed it up." I nod toward Shane and Ben.

"They don't blame you, they blame me. You lost her breaking me out."

I try to respond but the words don't come out. It doesn't matter what anybody says, this was *my* fault, and there's not much I can do to change that. The only silver lining right now, is that

Ryan Bracha

although we're back to square one. We'll have another twenty four hours to come up with something. Assuming, that is, that there's no mutiny on the horizon. Danny takes the hint that I really don't want to talk about it, and shuts up, thankfully. We walk in silence for the rest of the journey.

Smarter than you.

"Katie Fleming is hereby accused of assisting known murderer and fugitive Paul Carter. She has continually aided Carter in his recent attack on both The Network Cutting Crew and New Britain. She has also aided him in the violent and successful attempt to release Daniel Carter from The Network Cutting Crew headquarters whilst he was being held for judgment for his crimes. Add to this the fact that Katie Fleming was herself a fugitive for the treacherous crime of depicting our Prime Minister, Mr Robert Lodge, in a compromising position with a crudely created image. For this multitude of crimes Katie Fleming will be held for judgment for the standard twenty four hour period, and the required number of votes is fifty thousand."
Becker stood over her, reading from the print out in his hands, before looking down at her, eyebrows raised.
"How do you feel about that then Katie? Regular little law breaker aren't you?"

Katie threw her head back and snorted with laughter, her green eyes twinkling up at the law man.

"Paul Carter'll break me out, like he did Danny."

"You think?"

"I *know,* you saw how easy it was to get in here," she said, then tossing a nod toward the still ashamed, and red-faced figure of Joe, "you gonna leave Joe Fatso in charge again?"

"Very good," Becker smiled malevolently at the girl, "but I have no intention of getting my fingers burned again, young lady. You see, I've changed my mind about Carter. He's a smart guy."

Katie beamed a huge smile of affection for Carter toward Becker.

"Yeah he is, smarter than you."

"You might be right, but there's such a thing as *too* smart. As *too* cocky with it. He's already tripped up once, and look where that left you. He got his cousin out, but that's because he's family, what are you? Some street kid he managed to brainwash into doing his dirty work?"

"He saved my life."

"You think he'll try to do that again? He's used you for what he needs, he can find somebody else, another tramp to take your place."

Katie moved to say something, but a memory of her conversation with Carter earlier in the day flashed into her mind. *People that I had no use for.* She stumbled over her words. Emitted a series of beginnings of retorts but nothing came. *People that I had no use for.* Carter wasn't like that with *her* though surely. She'd seen the way

Ryan Bracha

he looked at her, he had a warmth behind his eyes when he looked at her. A smile. An affection. Yes, he was cold, and distant sometimes, but that was his mask. That was what he hid behind. Katie *knew* that Paul Carter would come through for her. But that niggling doubt. That sentence. *People that I had no use for.* Katie slumped back into her chair, pulling and crossing her arms tight into her body. Shutting up shop. Wilson Becker smiled, a knowing and wicked smile. "So, how about you help yourself instead of that murdering rucksack, why don't you tell us where he is?"

Yippeekayay muddy funsters.

"Look, I'm not blaming anybody, but I'd say that this was definitely all Danny's fault," says Ben, looking to my cousin, over my shoulder and behind me. Whether he's aware of the contradiction I'm not sure, but I say nothing about it. I can hear Danny's head slump toward the ground in shame for the ten millionth time. I don't think there's any way he could feel worse about proceedings.

Where we are is back at our base, Shane is at the table fiddling with the goods he stole from the NCC, blinking them into life, and then shutting them down. Checking battery levels and the like. Ben is up close to me and Danny stands away from us. Still taking it all in.

"I disagree," I shake my head, sniffing in defiance, "it was *my* fault. It *is* my fault. None of you would be doing any of this if it weren't for me."

"I'm not being funny, bossman," Shane says from the table, the glow of another tracking device illuminates his face with fluorescent green, "but you didn't force any of us to do anything. We came because we wanted to. I joined you because there was nothing better to do, I told you this. Ben, well he's just a nutcase. No offence Ben, I mean, you're an excellent nutcase," he says.

"None taken. I am indeed a high quality nutcase."

"And Katie, well, she likes you doesn't she? You saved her life. She's totally got it bad for you. She'd follow you off a cliff if you asked her to. You've seen how she looks at you. You've got to have seen how she looks at you. Unless you're blind."

"You blind, killer?" asks Ben, surely rhetorical, but his face seems to expect me to answer. I shake my head, no.

"So don't blame yourself for all of this, sure we risked a lot to save the cousin who turned you away." Danny's head drops. Again. "But none of us would've come if we didn't see something in what you're doing. Katie included. She knew the risks, and she accepted them. I know you feel bad and everything, but blaming yourself isn't really the plan we need to get her back."

I let his words sink in. Slowly they chip away at the grating feeling I have. This new under-coat of self-loathing remains, but that's my own issue to

Ryan Bracha

deal with. Shane's right. It's not helping anything. Shane should be running this thing, not me. He's so mature for his years, and his technological skills are second to none. He should be running his own business. Not running the streets with a snotty nose and a penchant for spontaneity. It's his choice though. He's probably happier for it. What does money get you? What does success get you? It gets you noticed. It gets you targeted by slimeballs for online campaigns of abuse. It gets you so mad that you kill the slimeballs and end up in a whole heap of trouble. No, he's definitely been living a better life than me. I shake the thought off and clear my throat.

"Okay. Thanks, Shane," I say, genuinely grateful for the words, but still I can't seem to reflect that in my voice, and I wonder what my problem is. He nods and mutters an acknowledgement before returning to his device.

"So, what now?"

We turn to Danny, who hasn't spoken much at all, besides continued efforts at apologies in my direction. Ben scowls and says nothing, obviously still playing the blame game. Danny senses it and his cheeks flush red, his eyes dart toward his shoes.

"Well, we need a plan. We lost Katie trying to get you out, so it's back to the drawing board. I don't think Becker will fall for it again. Shane, check the NCC synopsis, see if she's up yet."

"We got most of their weapons, killer, why don't we just bust our way in and grab her?" Ben suggests, as if this is a viable option.

"We're outnumbered, and they still have their own weapons, and dogs. Too risky."

"Yeah, but how about we sneak in and pick 'em off one by one, like in the old movies? You ever see Die Hard?"

He's referring to an old American film from years ago. Not one I was ever truly enamoured by, but I get his drift. Still, we're just ordinary people in a completely bizarre situation. We can't expect our luck to continue in an armed siege.

"Yippeekayay muddy funsters!" Ben laughs, looking to Shane, who's too young to get the reference, and the moment passes as quickly as it arose. Shane's focus is upon the palmtop, his fingers tapping away at the touch-screen, making the line apart from each other to enlarge the image. His face creases, before he fetches it up to look at me.

"She's not on there bossman," he says, "there's no word about any of it. I mean, there's still people talking about us, and you, and Danny, but Katie's not been mentioned at all."

I grab the device, and look myself, as if I have some magic power to make news of Katie just appear. It doesn't. He's right, there's increasing unrest over what we did, but Katie doesn't feature at all. My stomach turns somersaults as I flick from synopsis to synopsis. Inputting Katie's name into the search filter. Nothing, aside from her previous indiscretion regarding Robert Lodge with faeces on his chest. My heart bangs hard. She *has* to be on here somewhere. They don't usually take this long to put somebody up

Ryan Bracha

for judgment. In my mind they caught her and they've killed her. Punished her without giving the public their right to judge. But they can't do that. It's against the guidelines. Something's wrong. As I'm passing the device back to Shane a rumbling begins to echo into the room, the crunching of pebbles against the ground. Vehicles. Already Shane's sliding what he needs back into the bag, whilst I clamber up onto a cabinet in order to press my face against the blacked out window, and my eye against the tiniest of holes in the covering. From ground level I see two vans. One is NCC and the other is Finnegan. This is bad.

"What's going on?" Danny asks, we really should get that chiselled into his tombstone when dies.

"Network crews. Two of them. NCC and Finnegan. They've brought dogs. I can't see Becker."

"Huh? *Two?*" Ben asks, incredulously.

"Mmhmm, we need to get out of here, *now!*"

I climb down from the cabinet and usher Danny out of the door behind Shane and Ben. How they found us, I don't know, but I hope amongst hope amongst *hope*, that Katie didn't sell us out.

The barking of dogs.

Shane led the way, electric Taser in one hand, torch in the other, skipping over bars and broken glass, trying to keep the noise to a minimum. There were four exits to this building, and they needed to get to the back one. The one that was polar opposite to the front that the crew members would undoubtedly be entering through. If they could get there then they'd been met by a steep, but soft and grassy decline. It wasn't ideal but it's all they had. He knew the building like the back of his hand, and could negotiate it in the dark with ease. He had three novices in the art of building navigation however, so was forced to keep a torch on for them to follow. The crews would be coming down the central stairs, so he led the others around the maze of corridors which once held a series of cells, for holding olden day criminals. Back before crews took over the law. The floor was thankfully less glass covered in that area, so as long as they kept the heavy breathing and shoe squeaking to a minimum they might be okay. Easier said than done, he conceded, given the adrenalin and urgency with which they sped along the rabbit warren beneath the disused station. The echo of dogs filled the corridors. The shouting of men. The slamming of metal into metal. He didn't have to look over his shoulder to know that they were all still there. Ben with his joyous cackling at this most dramatic turns of events. Danny whimpering. Paul not saying much. Keeping to himself, as usual. Shane liked him, he really did, and Katie was smitten by the guy, but he needed to open up more. It didn't do for people to bottle up their emotions. To pretend. Shane didn't see the point in it. He shook off the notion and rounded the corner.

Ryan Bracha

They were almost there. Where *there* was, was the subterranean fire escape. It led to a steep set of steps which then led to the aforementioned grassy decline. The building was on a plateau halfway up one of Sheffield's seven hills. On the other side of the hill they would have been able to see most of the city itself, but on this side it gave way to nothing but waste ground, barely used roads, and eventually, in the distance, an old shopping centre. Crystal Peaks. It had been a centre of unlimited promise and potential back in its formative years, but one which had faded into irrelevance when Meadowhall reared its ugly head.

Shane slowed to a halt as he approached the fire exit, trying to catch his breath back. The others tumbled into him a touch as they struggled to slow their own pace down, but it was nothing to hold them up. Still the dogs yelping and men yelling rattled through the narrow corridors. They'd have found the room empty by now, and begun a scent based hunt, led by the canines. Time was not on their side.

"Okay," whispered Shane, "this door takes us out. There's a hill. We need to get down it. Okay?"

Three blackened silhouettes nodded. Each too out of breath themselves to speak.

"If we can get down there we should be able to put some daylight between us and them, ready?"

Again the silhouettes nodded and Shane's hand grappled against the metal of the door. Found the bar of the door release, and pressed down gently. Trying to keep the noise to a minimum.

The blinding light of the mid-afternoon poured into corridor, illuminating the grey interior of the building. The four of them ploughed on, each with one arm raised to shield their eyes from the sun, and using the other to heave themselves up the railing beside the steep stairs as if traversing through the custard-thick atmosphere of some distant world. Shane reached the top and turned to ensure that the rest were behind. Ben ascended with his manic grin, clearly enjoying himself, Carter followed, his face dripping with concern, something going on behind the eyes. Danny was close behind, head twisted hard to watch what was coming behind. The barking of dogs rattled from the corridor and out into the air. Shane saw it coming. Danny was so focused on what was behind him that he failed to watch his step. His legs did their best to help his ascension, but without focus they failed. His toe slipped down against the face of the top step and his balance was lost. Danny's body slid down, one hand gripped tight around the railing, but not enough to keep him upright. Behind him a snarling dog, a British Shepherd, slid out of the building and into the stairwell. The dog clamped its teeth around Danny's shoe and twisted its head, left to right, tugging at the poor guy's leg. Danny wailed in fear. His free foot kicked hard against the dog's face, succeeding in nothing but riling the beast up further.

"Shane!" A voice called. Ben. It was Ben. He stood halfway down the stairs alongside the writhing combination of the dog and Carter's cousin.

Ryan Bracha

Shane shook his head, he felt sick by Danny's agonising wails. For all of the death and violence he'd witnessed on The Network, at the hands of the crews, he'd never seen anything like this in real life and he'd frozen.

"Shane! Wake up!" Ben again. His hand holding out, asking for something. What did he want? Shane followed his line of sight down his own body. The Taser. He wanted the Taser. Shane fumbled nervously with the weapon, struggling to approach Ben. He didn't want to be the dog's next victim. Still Danny cried, Carter pulled at him. Hands under the arms. Shane edged closer to the top of the stairwell. Ben stepped up. With a look that bordered on disappointment he quickly snatched the Taser from Shane's hand jabbed the thing into the neck of the dog. Immediately the dog's jaw released Danny's foot and yelped. An anguished, ear-splitting squeal of pain. The dog turned on its heels and disappeared back inside. Confused shouts echoing. Carter dragged Danny up away from the stairwell. His cousin crying, wiping his eyes with the back of his sleeve. Shane said nothing as Ben eyed him with a look that this time not so much hinted disappointment, than it did walk up to him, pull down his trousers and continually kick him in the backside whilst declaring that he had let them down.

"I'm sorry," he muttered to Ben. The older man shook his head as if shaking away his expression and starting anew, and smiled.

"Ah, it happens to the best of us kid," he said, ruffling his hair with his free hand, as if realising exactly how young Shane was, before turning his attention to the others, "come on, we need to get out of here."

Carter nodded, and looked to Danny.

"Can you walk?" he asked. Danny shook his head. "No, I think the nasty bandstand might've broken it," he gasped through pained breaths. Ben seemed to dance with impatience.

"Well, this all went wrong quick didn't it?" he scowled at the injured man, "you know I wouldn't be surprised if you did all this on purpose just to get yourself outta the sherbet."

"What? Get myself attacked by a jackin' *dog?* To catch you?" he asked incredulously, "I wouldn't flatter yourself Turner, really. You know what? Just leave me here, they've had me once, I can handle it."

"Sounds good to me, old bean," Turner said, nodding his head, already his legs taking him toward the edge of the decline.

"No!" Carter spoke up finally, "if we go, we all go. Okay?"

Shane's head dropped, his face refusing to commit to any cause. Just wanted to hear how it might go. Until an unfamiliar voice, followed by several grunts, both human and canine, broke the tension.

"Yeah, that sounds like a good idea, why don't you *all* go, eh?"

Ryan Bracha

It's hardly a revolution.

I sit in the back of the NCC van, behind the wall of mesh caging between me and the rest of the vehicle, hands cuffed behind my back. I was walked there by James Finnegan and two of his goons, jostling and arguing over who would get to push me harder toward the van. Behind me Ben was dragged by four of them, laughing manically as his body jerked and bucked against every effort to get him there. Danny was pulled along the floor by his bad foot, his wails of pain ricocheting from every surface around us and drifting off across the valley. Shane just did as he was told, sniffing tears back and trying to use his own shoulder to wipe away the tears and snot from his face. The game's up. We were valiant in our efforts but ultimately they were for nothing. We'll be judged, and executed before every pair of laughing eyes in the country. We'll be talked about for a few days and then something else will take our places. There was a saying, back in my old life. Today's news is tomorrow's chip paper. That's the most apt phrase for our situation, and the way our country is. We're conditioned to move on. Whether it's death, or pain, or news. We let it hit us, we moan about it, and then we move on. This is never anything that's changed.

"Well this is fun," laughs Ben through trying to catch his breath as they throw him into the van beside me. I shake my head and frown, but say nothing. Beyond his laughing face I see Shane and Danny cast into the back of the Finnegan van. The bald figure of the man I know as Grady speaks excitedly into his phone. His arms gesticulate wildly. I see him punching an imaginary victim, then kicking the same nothing. He's likely speaking to Wilson Becker, either lying about what he's done to one, or all of us, or he's telling him what he's *going* to do to one, or all of us. Suddenly he stops and nods with a laugh. He approaches the van, and comes to my side. Opens the door.

"Smile for the camera, you jackin' rucksack," he says as he holds the phone toward me, "yeah, not so tough now eh?"

The door slams as he turns, laughing and pressing all manner of things on his device.

"He acts hard but he's a total pansy," says Ben, nudging me, "all the times I got caught and judged, he always looked like he wanted to, y'know?"

"What?"

"You *know,*" he emphasises the words this time with a raised eyebrow, I do know.

"Oh," I say, the man's sexuality the furthest thing from my concern just now.

"Total pansy," he repeats, his attention through his own window, watching Finnegan's van start into life, a rumbling of the engine, "how you think they found us?"

"I don't know," I say, and don't take it any further. I don't want to reveal my fears that Katie sold us out, lest I be shouted down for my lack of loyalty.

Ryan Bracha

"You won't get judged, you know that?" he says, turning to me, "I mean, they won't judge you guilty."

"How's that?" I ask, curious.

"Well, you're Paul Carter, man," he shuffles, his knees edging toward me in the back of the can, he grimaces as the cuffs bite into his wrists, "you might think that they judge everybody guilty, but they didn't with me."

"Where are you taking this?"

"Well, seven times I got judged, put up for judgment I mean, and seven times I got off scot free, and I'm just your friendly neighbourhood nutcase. You're a man who broke into a *Crew's headquarters,* and broke your cousin out. *Then,* you stand in front of a judgment camera and call out the boss of the most feared crew in the country."

"With help," I correct him.

"That doesn't matter killer, you're the face of this revolution, you're gonna have a lot more support than you think."

"It's hardly a revolution," I say.

Ben laughs hard, his head rocked back so that I can see the rotten series of teeth that hide behind the ridiculously manic grin he often wears. He shakes his head.

"Oh man, killer, you're as messed up as I am. You know all your performances for Becker, for Lodge? People buy into it. You're the voice of millions of disillusioned people right now. The sooner you get that into your stupid skull the better for everyone."

I don't respond to this. I let Ben's words seep into my brain as Grady approaches the van with three others and they climb into the seats in front of us. The two men in the seats between us and the driver turn to peer at us as if we were some sort of mythical creatures trapped in a zoo. Hardly able to believe that we're there at all.

"I got a telly on my head?" barks Ben at the smaller of the pair, his gnarled face twists as he pushes himself further toward the mesh. The man recoils in fear, but remembers himself and his company.

"Shut yer mouth Turner, you're going down this time. Ain't no acting the fool gonna get you out of it," he laughs loudly, and goes to speak again but is halted very quickly by the loud slap of phlegm which strikes the back of his throat. Ben grins and nods.

"Bullseye," he says sinisterly, before adding, "I've got hepatitis, you know that?"

The crewmember chokes and gags violently as he tries to bring up the spit from his throat, but it's no use. As he rattles the cage and screams that he'll kill us, struggling to keep from spewing outlawed, and more than likely now diseased profanity our way, Ben shrugs and looks to me with a cheeky wink.

"Share and share alike, that's what I say."

I have no idea how to respond to that. The man is truly a law unto himself.

Ryan Bracha

A MODERN BRITAIN #8

BRAD WALKED THE OUTSKIRTS OF THE
HOUSING ESTATE TENTATIVELY.
STICKING TO THE SHADOWS AND
KEEPING THE FOOTSTEPS GENTLE AND
MEASURED. HE SHOULDN'T BE HERE AT
THIS TIME. HE SHOULD BE HERE AT ANY
TIME, BUT HE HAD A JOB TO DO, AND
HE WAS DETERMINED TO DO IT RIGHT.
HE WAS A MAN ON A MISSION. HIS
ENEMY WAS A MAN FROM THE
NETWORK, WHO WOULD POINT BLANK
REFUSE TO ACKNOWLEDGE HIM AS THE
BRITISH PERSON THAT HE WAS. HE
WOULD RALLY FRIENDS UP TO HARASS
BRAD. SHOW HIM EXACTLY HOW
UNWELCOME HE WAS IN HIS OWN
COUNTRY. PALE BLUE LIGHT GLOWED IN
EACH OF THE WINDOWS OF THE
HOUSES THAT HE PASSED. THAT TELL-
TALE BLUE OF THE NETWORK. EACH
HOUSEHOLD FIXATED ON THEIR OWN
VERSION OF REAL LIFE. HE HEARD
VOICES IN THE DISTANCE. YOUNG

Paul Carter is a Dead Man

VOICES. THERE WERE MAYBE THREE OR
FOUR OF THEM. THE EMPTINESS OF THE
NIGHT ALLOWED THE VOICES TO CARRY
CLEARLY TOWARD HIM. THEY WERE
PURE BRITISH CHILDREN, SPEAKING
PERFECT BRITISH TO ONE ANOTHER.
MAYBE TWELVE OR THIRTEEN MAXIMUM.
BRAD HELD STILL. EDGED BACK
TOWARD THE GRASS BANKING,
TOWARD, AND UNDER A PUSSY WILLOW
TREE. THE BRANCHES HUNG OUT FAR
FROM THE TRUNK, LIKE THE LID OF AN
UMBRELLA, GIVING HIM A DEGREE OF
COVER FROM THE KIDS. THEY
CONTINUED IN THEIR APPROACH, ONE OF
THEM REACHING UP TO SNAP THE END
FROM ONE OF THE BRANCHES. HE
CHASED HIS FRIENDS WITH THE
IMPROVISED WHIP, LAUGHING, AND
JOKING. SCARING THEM AWAY. BRAD
HOPED THEY WOULD GO SOON, BUT
THEY DIDN'T. ENCOURAGED BY HIS
FRIEND'S BEHAVIOUR, ANOTHER OF THEM
SNAPPED A BRANCH AWAY, AND A
FULL BLOWN WILLOW BRANCH FIGHT
ENSUED. WHEN THEY EDGED BENEATH

Ryan Bracha

THE BRANCHES HE MOVED AROUND THE TRUNK OF THE TREE. HE SHOULDN'T BE SEEN. HE DIDN'T WANT TO INVOLVE THE CHILDREN. HIS FIGHT WAS WITH SOMEBODY WHO SHOULD HAVE BEEN ALTOGETHER MORE MATURE, BUT HE WASN'T.

EVENTUALLY THE CHILDREN MOVED ON AND BRAD WAS ALLOWED TO BREATHE ONCE MORE. HE TIPTOED ONWARD, UNTIL HE FOUND THE HOUSE OF HIS ENEMY, THE BLUE GLOW EMANATED FROM THE LIVING ROOM, AND FROM THE UPSTAIRS WINDOWS. THERE WAS MORE THAN ONE IN THE HOUSE. HIS HEART BEAT RACED AS HE KNOCKED ON THE DOOR. HIS EYES CONSTANTLY SCANNED FOR PEOPLE WHILST HE AWAITED A RESPONSE TO HIS KNOCKS. NOBODY CAME. HE KNOCKED AGAIN.

"WHAT THE FLUFF ARE YOU DOING HERE?" SAID A VOICE FROM ABOVE. HIS ENEMY.

"I COME FIGHT," HE SAID, HIS BREATH FOGGING UP BEFORE HIM IN THE COLD WINTER NIGHT, "I COME KILL."

Paul Carter is a Dead Man

"LISTEN, VLADIMIR," SAID HIS ENEMY.

"I BRAD," HE RESPONDED ANGRILY, NOBODY EVER CALLED HIM BY HIS OLD NAME EXCEPT HIS ENEMY.

"LOOK, VLADIMIR, THERE ARE A FEW MATES OF MINE ON THEIR WAY. THEY DON'T LIKE *PRETEND BRITISH* ROUND OUR END, AND AIN'T NOBODY GONNA BE TELLING A CREW ON US WHEN YOUR BODY SHOWS UP, SO YOU WANNA JUST DO YOURSELF A FAVOUR?"

"I SAY I BRAD!" HE ROARED AS HIS ANGER GOT THE BETTER OF HIM, AND HE KICKED THE DOOR FROM ITS HINGES. THE WOOD SPLINTERED HARSHLY AROUND HIM AS HE STALKED UP THE STAIRS. HIS ENEMY APPROACHED HIM, FISTS CLENCHED BUT BRAD WAS TOO QUICK. HE HELD THE MAN'S THROAT, AND ONCE, TWICE, PUNCHED HIM IN THE NOSE. THE MAN LAUGHED.

"WHY YOU LAUGH? NO FUNNY!"

STILL HE LAUGHED AS HIS BROKEN NOSE WEPT BLOOD AND SNOT. BRAD PUNCHED HIM AGAIN. ONCE, TWICE. DROPPED THE MAN WITH THE BROKEN

Ryan Bracha

FACE TO THE FLOOR. SPAT UPON HIS PRONE BODY.

"NO LAUGH, MY NAME BRAD. NOT VLADIMIR."

THE MAN CONTINUED TO LAUGH, AND LOOKED UP AT THE FURIOUS FIGURE OF BRAD. FISTS CLENCHED. CHEST INFLATING AND DEFLATING. ADRENALIN COURSING THROUGH HIS BODY. BRAD MADE TO ATTACK HIS ENEMY ONE MORE TIME BUT WAS HALTED.

"WHOA!" SAID HIS ENEMY, HANDS OUT ABOVE HIM. BRAD PAUSED. HIS ENEMY NODDED TOWARD THE COMPUTER IN THE CORNER OF THE ROOM. TOWARD THE CAMERA WHICH SAT ATOP IT. TOWARD THE SERIES OF SHOCKED FACES. TOWARD THE SERIES OF FEEDS THAT HAD JUST RECORDED HIS ATTACK. HIS ENEMY HAD DONE THIS ON PURPOSE. GOADED HIM. TO TRAP HIM. AS BRAD STEPPED OVER HIS ENEMY AND RETREATED FROM THE ROOM, THE LAST THING HE HEARD BEYOND THE SCREECHING OF TIRES OUTSIDE OF THE HOUSE, WAS THE LAUGHING, MOCKING

Paul Carter is a Dead Man

VOICE OF HIS ENEMY, INFORMING HIM THAT THERE WAS INDEED NOWHERE TO HIDE.

A magician never reveals his secrets.

"We got your boyfriend Katie," Wilson Becker
announced proudly as he stomped into the room.
His gait a lot more assured than the one he was
previously wearing. Before now he was weary,
annoyed, beaten, all of those things and more.
Now he stood taller. Prouder. Katie frowned.
"Who? Banger? But he died. My poor darling
Banger is dead," she teased with mock drama.
Becker felt his eye twitched in irritation, but
would not allow the young girl to get to him at
his happiest moment.
"No, Katie, not Banger, show some jackin'
respect," he said sadly, before clearing his throat,
"no, Carter. Remember him?"
Katie regarded the man suspiciously, her head
tilted to the left, he looked right at her, a wicked
glint in his eyes. She had no reason not to believe
him.
"But how?" she couldn't stop herself from asking.
Wilson Becker waggled a finger with a
previously unseen mischief, and smiled.
"Now, a magician never reveals his secrets."
"Was it Finnegan? Did you need a bigger boy to
help you? Were you too stupid on your own?"
she asked, genuinely wanting to know the
answer but unable to keep the mockery from her
tone. Again Becker twitched in irritation.
"You've got some mouth on you, don't make me
punch it from your face," he growled.
Katie hooted with laughter, pleased that her
arrows were hitting their targets.

Paul Carter is a Dead Man

"So it was eh? Ah well, there's no shame in admitting you needed help Mr Becker, it happens to the best of us. But seriously, how'd you find him?"

"You told us where he was," Becker said mysteriously, waiting for confusion to register in Katie's face, watched her mouth attempt to form words. They wouldn't come, "not so chatty now huh?"

"But I never said anything," Katie stuttered, no longer enjoying the jolly fun that winding the law man used to be.

Wilson Becker chuckled, and crouched in to match her level. Used his considerable hand to squeeze her cheeks, pushing her mouth into a makeshift pucker, and kissing her hard on the mouth.

"No, we tracked Ben Turner's phone, but they don't need to know that do they?"

Becker stood and made to exit the room.

"Your breath jackin' stinks by the way."

Katie ignored the final comment as the door closed. Didn't even hear it. Her brain was already building up conclusions about what Paul Carter would think about her when he heard the false claims of her treachery. She would never sell him out. She'd only known him less a day but she already knew that she'd rather die than see a hair on his head harmed. Wilson Becker's words reverberated around her skull, and for the first time since her parents died Katie Fleming's head dropped and she began to cry.

Ryan Bracha

Cross promotional revenue.

He was annoyed with himself more than anything else. The street kid had pushed his buttons and he allowed her to get to him. He'd enjoy executing her when the time came. He'd choose something slow, and painful from the public's suggestions. Maybe something where he could flay her skin an inch at a time. Watch the mocking grin disappear from her stupid dirty face. Replace it with that of agonising pain. Yeah, that would be great. The thought soothed the annoyance from his mind, and he gave himself the opportunity to smile again. Besides, they knew how to find Carter by the time Finnegan showed his ugly face. Grady had it bang on the money. Ben Turner was helping the rucksack out, and they got sloppy. Carter's cousin and some other street kid were just side helpings of satisfaction. Turner was dessert. Carter was the main course. The main event. Joe, the useless lump, was being put to use away from overseeing prisoners. He was in talks with various Sustenance Network providers, discussing cross promotional revenue. They'd already managed to bag their usual electrical providers to advertise on the hour, but the real money came from the food industry. Rolling advertisements to entice those of society who enjoyed marathon Crime Network sessions. Barely able to leave their chairs as they devoured every minute of a prisoner's discomfort. They'd need feeding. Their bellies, not their hunger to see criminals put to justice. That was down to Wilson Becker. With a smile he pulled his phone out, and dialled.

"Yes, it's Wilson Becker," he said, "I need to speak to Mr Garner."

Mr Robert Lodge receives good news.

"Sir."

"Garner? You know not to interrupt me when I'm taking lunch."

"Indeed, sir. But I have some good news."

"Good enough to interrupt when I'm taking lunch?"

"I would say so, sir, yes."

"Very well. I'm waiting."

"Wilson Becker has captured Paul Carter, sir. He is being transported to the NCC headquarters as we speak."

"And what of his *friends*?"

"It's our understanding that he was, shall we say bluffing, sir. Only three others, on top of the girl."

"That's hardly an army, is it?"

"No sir."

"That's barely even a gang, Garner."

"Indeed, sir."

"Oh well, that is good news Garner, well done."

"-"

"Garner?"

"Sir."

"If you don't mind, I have a meal going cold here."

Ryan Bracha

"Well, sir. I thought it might be a good time for you to address the nation about the whole thing. There has been quite the unrest regarding the situation. The people need to know your stance on it. They need to be *reminded.*"

"What? Now?"

"Perhaps after your lunch? I've taken the liberty of arranging a session in the transmitting station."

"Have you now? Tell me Garner, have you also taken the liberty of poisoning my pudding?"

"Sir?"

"Do not let those ideas get the better of you, I'd kill you dead before you got anywhere near my desk."

"But sir, I haven't-"

"I'm only half-joking, Garner, I'll be there when I'm ready, now leave me to enjoy my food."

"Sir."

Come on, you sherbet head.

"I'll kill him, I'll jackin' kill him."

"What? And find yourself up for judgment? Grow up Teddy," Grady growled at the still whining bandstand behind him as the van slowed in front of the gate. Turner had done a number on him with the whole spitting in his mouth, but he was being a real girl about it. He hadn't shut up since it happened, and it was grating on a hundred per cent of Grady's nerves. He didn't see the bigger picture. They'd caught the most notorious criminal out there. Sure, one of the dogs took a bit of a beating, but that was what the dogs were for. Getting a bit of spit in his mouth from the eternal wind-up merchant that was Ben Turner should be the least of his worries. He should be sitting proud, they were going to be heroes by the end of the day. They'd taken Paul jackin' Carter off the streets. They were about to give the country the power they deserved.

"But I need a jackin' *doctor,* man."

"You need to grow a pair of beanbags and shut yer jackin' mouth, Teddy," Grady said, before sniggering, and adding, "mind, if you'd kept your mouth shut in the first place. Know what I'm sayin'?"

Oxley stifled a laugh beside him as Teddy silently murdered him with his stare.

"Yeah, Teddy, you know what he's sayin'?" Ben Turner piped up from the back, before Teddy turned and smashed a fist against the mesh caged.

"You pipe down, rucksack!" he snarled, his hands clenched tight around the wiring. So wishing that he could rip the mesh away and beat the skull off of Ben Turner's neck. Turner leant forward, a malevolent grin on his face.

"Psst. Teddy boy," he said, doing his level best to remain balanced with his hands shackled behind his back. Teddy never took his eyes from those of the psychotic prisoner. Never flinched as his face neared the mesh between them.

"Come on, you sherbet head, a little closer, let me poke yer jackin' eyes out," Teddy whispered.

Ryan Bracha

Grady watched in the rear view as he waited for the gates to the open. Teddy could be a real reactionary sometimes. Grady had a temper that was up there with the best of them but he was calculating. He was smart. Teddy was just an idiot. A violent, and stupid idiot.

"Oh you wanna poke my eyes out eh?" Turner said, his hushed threatening tone just willing Teddy to make a move. Grady had an idea of how the guy had made it through seven judgments without punishment. He was charming, that was for sure, but he was an absolute lunatic. New Britain loved a character. That was the crux of it.

"You girls wanna dance?" Grady called out finally from the front with a laugh. It broke the tension somewhat as Oxley exhaled with a nervous chuckle, and Teddy turned to shake his head with a smile. He was a split second from a witty retort when something registered. Pain.

Kicking and screaming toward judgment.

I can actually hear the gristle in Teddy's finger snap as Ben's teeth clamp down onto it at the knuckle. The poor crewmember squeals in agony as he tries to pull his hand away from the snarling mouth of my accomplice. The guy next to him can't do anything but look on in shocked horror as Ben's face becomes ever more covered in the blood of Teddy. The guy up front, the balding bespectacled one I know as Oxley, the colour drains from his face and he looks ready to vomit. Only Grady leaps in to any kind of action as he jumps from the driver's seat and comes round to the side of the van. He pulls open the door and half climbs into the vehicle at the same moment Ben's head yanks back, with half a finger in his mouth, and smashes Grady in the nose. The crunch of his face breaking is even more sickening than that of Teddy's finger snapping, and it's now not just Oxley struggling to hold the contents of his stomach down. Grady flies back through the air and his head bounces off the concrete on the gateway as his unconscious body lands. Teddy is crying and watching the blood pump from his now missing middle finger, his back seat friend is scrabbling round clumsily, talking about stemming the flow of the blood, but Teddy isn't listening. Oxley does nothing. Ben chuckles as he spits the chewed-off finger into the foot well, and he slides off the seat and out of the van. He looks at me. His face resembling that of an impatient cannibal. His eyes have taken on an altogether more wicked glaze, and he laughs.

"That, was jackin' excellent," he says, and crouches by Grady's body. Before he's even upright his hands are free, and he pulls me from the van. Turns me around. Unlocks my shackles. Teddy continues to wallow in his own misery. Grady continues to wallow in his pit of unconsciousness.

"What now?" I ask of Ben. This is *not* what I expected to happen. For whatever reason I feel like Danny all of a sudden. Ben is rifling through

Ryan Bracha

the pockets of our knocked-out captor, and he passes me a phone, and a Taser.

"Now, killer, you get the jack out of here, and you save yourself, okay?"

"But, what about you? And Katie? And Shane?"

"They'll live, they're stronger than you think, just go on. Get gone. I'll look after things here."

"What about-"

"Seriously killer, go. I've got a plan. Just keep your eye on the NCC feeds. You'll know what to do."

I feel I should argue more, but he pushes my chest, and that manic glint in his eye grows ever more fierce. I step back. Once, twice. Again. Then I turn and walk away. My footsteps feel heavy as I pick up pace. My mouth dry. It occurs to me that it's been ages since I've eaten, but then that thought skulks back into the corner of my mind as I hear Ben talking.

"Now what am I gonna do with you?"

I turn to see him drag the still whimpering body of Teddy from the van and lay heavy boot after heavy boot into his face and torso. Ben howls into the night and as I turn the corner I pause. He sits down beside the beaten crewmembers and he waits. Suddenly there are two or three men on top of him. They've finally emerged from the building. Before I make my exit I hear him make an expletive laden threat to the life of Wilson Becker as they drag him kicking and screaming toward judgment.

A message from your leader.

The screen flickered just slightly, and a caption informed viewers that a very important message from Robert Lodge would be imminent. Games of Fruity Basher were put on hold. Shopping orders for the week's sustenance were paused. Criminal voting counters held still. There was nowhere on The Network which wouldn't be interrupted for this. There never was. Then he appeared. His white hair appearing juxtaposed against his war-weathered face. The sign of aging against the face of a man who had killed hundreds, and was capable of killing hundreds more.

"People of New Britain. I am your Prime Minister, Mr Robert Lodge. As I'm sure those of you who follow the Crime Network with great interest will be aware, there has been a man, a very dangerous man, stalking the streets of our country. *Your* country. This man is called Paul Carter. He has murdered not only one innocent victim in cold blood, but he has also savagely murdered a well-loved Government authorised Network crewmember in his escape. He has brainwashed various people into doing his bidding. This fugitive had been making various well-aimed threats at not only myself, but at you. At *your* safety. At *your* country. At *your* freedom as citizens of this great great nation. This man has displayed an absolute lack of respect for *you.* He assumes that you wish to be freed from some imaginary despot, but people of New Britain, we are all of the same mind. When given the choice, you decided to stay and fight to make this country great again. You agreed that this way to live was the *best* way to live. This man, this Paul Carter, has been making a mockery of your beliefs. Of your decisions. Of you. But people of New Britain, do not fear. For the fugitive, Paul Carter, has now been captured, along with the disciples that he brainwashed, and will be held for all to see. To *judge.* An example will be made, you mark my words. You, the people of New Britain, hold the power in your hands to destroy this parasite on our great nation. I know, that I can rely on you to do the right thing. I know that. I know."

Robert Lodge appeared side-tracked. Paused in his speech. Either he'd seen a ghost in the distance or something was happening behind the camera. Somebody was communicating something. He coughed as the blood flushed into his face. Then it happened. It cut to black. Nothing.

I'm better than you at everything.

Back to square one. Only this time I've managed to screw up the lives of three more people. Katie. This revolution was stupid. A stupid idea. I was stupid to even buy into it, but what's the old saying? In for a penny, in for a pound. I saw what Ben did back there, I knew he was nuts, but *that,* was animalistic. He only struck me as the mischievous type. But. He acts like he's immortal.

Everything's one big joke. But. He's smart. He's got a plan. What else have we got? I need access to The Network. I don't trust that they won't track Grady's phone so I've destroyed the thing. I'm holding on to the Taser as if it was the meaning of life itself though, and I'm striding through the city purposefully to my intended destination. It's a place I can't trust, but I don't have much choice. Plus he owes me a favour, and I'm not in the mood for accepting it at a later date. I stick to back streets and fields as much as I can, the dusk chasing me, catching, and then passing me as night-time follows shortly after by the time I arrive at the door. The rusted velociraptor wail as I pull the thing open. At the bottom of the stairs I pause. Take a breath. Pull the Taser from my coat pocket and I take the steps slowly one at a time. I'm reminded of yesterday afternoon, for obvious reasons. I have to be more careful this time.

"Alright Pete?"

His bruised face freezes mid-expression and he's willing his body to make a run for it but it just won't take the hint.

"Paul?" he gasps, conscious that I have the Taser jammed into his skull. His hands hold up in a flouncing surrender, "what are you? I mean, why are- I thought they captured you?"

"They did," I respond, and I push his chest gently to edge him back inside the flat so I can close the door and give us our privacy. I'm pulling on all of my skills as the cool player in my old life. That confidence. When I was the centre of attention.

Ryan Bracha

That buzz. I felt it there when I spoke to Becker in the videos we made, and again when we had Joe trussed up. I need to stop fighting it and just accept that something big is happening, and for whatever reason I am at the centre of it. It was all I ever dreamed of in my old life, so why am I fighting it now? It's bigger than I am. That's why. I wanted more and more and more by the way of attention, and now I have everybody's attention I'm bottling it. Not anymore. Time to show what I can do. I'm better than you at everything. There's nothing you, or anybody else can do to stop me.

Pete's still spluttering. Tears welling up in his tiny marble eyes.

"Surprised to see me, eh?" I ask, but the shock's still rattling around the marrow of his bones. His shivering hands still held aloft. His eyes claw desperately at a glimpse of what I've got held to his head, and he's whimpering.

"Pete!" I say sharply, as my hand strikes his cheek, jolting him out of his jabbering state, "get a grip, man."

Pete stops whimpering, but his bottom lip quivers just slightly.

"What are you doing here?" he asks quietly.

"I needed somewhere to stay," I say, "with somebody who seems to have NCC immunity."

"But-"

"Don't bother Pete, I know what happened and why, but you owe me something, I'm calling it in."

"I owe you?" he moans. I nod.

"It's because of you that this whole mess is in the state it is."

Pete gasps.

"*You* killed a man Paul, not me," he says as he stands up straighter, obviously affronted by my accusation, but he quickly remembers our current predicament which finds us with me holding a Taser to his head, and cowers.

"You couldn't just let me go my way though, could you?" I feel tenseness in my stomach and a tingling in my neck as I hiss the question into his face. My fingers pressing tighter onto the Taser. Pete crumples to the floor as he wails pathetically into the arms he has wrapped around his head. I drag him upright and pull his arms away. Crouch down to his level, "you had to do your duty as a New British citizen and save your own skin eh? Is that how it was?"

He shakes his head, a bubble of snot expands from his nostril, and pops a wet droplet into his knee.

"So I don't have time to spell it out. You need to man up and start paying attention, because certain things are going to happen, you're going to help them to happen, and you don't have much choice in the matter. Do you understand?" Pete weeps. Nods his head sadly. I pull the Taser away from his head, and grab his chin.

"But *do* you understand Pete? What did I just say?"

Basic technique for checking the understanding of your audience. Ask them to repeat what you said, in their own terms.

Ryan Bracha

"Paul, please-"

I slap him again.

"Pete!"

And again.

"Pete. Listen to me. If this goes right, then I won't have to hurt you. For this to go right, I need to pull yourself together, okay?"

He nods.

"Okay. Stand up. Right. I need to you to turn off all of your Network video settings. Switch everything to browse, okay?"

He nods. A narrow string of spit connects his chin to the chest of his shirt.

"Anybody asks what's happening you have a headache," I instruct as his focus seems to return to the situation, his nod becomes firmer, "I just need access to your Network connection, that's all. I don't want to hurt you, Pete. You help me out now then I'll forget you sold me out, you make things difficult again, and I'll make it my life's work to destroy you. Do you understand?"

He nods again, and robotically walks into the living room. Flicks his settings to one which registers Pete online, but simply browsing the various forums and synopses of The Network, without the option to respond to anything unless he chooses to re-join The Network in an active capacity. I watch from the doorway, my Taser focused on his back, should he feel it necessary to make a thinly veiled SOS call. Once he's done he turns to me. I think the penny's dropped with him about now.

"What now?"

Shackled.

"So you lucky muddy funsters have the distinct
honour of judging one Benjamin Turner today
ladies and gentlemen," Ben laughed into the
camera, a bead of sweat navigated against the
raised ridges of the prominent vein which ran
across his forehead, his hands shackled, "accused
hereby of knocking the sherbet out of a coupla
crewmembers, helping Paul Carter push you to a
life you know you want to live."
Ben looked off-screen, gave a nod toward the
guard.
"You know I bit your pal Teddy's finger off? Is he
gonna get it reattached? I hope they could save it.
Really, it was a moment of madness, I'm not
proud of it. Could you buy his wife something as
an apology? I dunno, something lacey? Where
you can see her- HEY! HEY! WHOA!"
Ben sat upright, his hands raised as best in
surrender as they could, given the
circumstances, as the guard stood and
threatened to charge in.
"Nah, I'm only joking," he smiled, "don't get
Teddy's wife's knickers in a twist."

Paul Carter's "Army".

Katie said nothing. Did nothing. Just allowed the
situation to play out. Watched the Network
screens carefully. Watched the messages. Looked
for anything which might be from Paul Carter.

Ryan Bracha

She had every faith in him. Wilson Becker sat in the guard's chair. He'd been trying to toy with her since she'd been here. He's was just a grown up boy. She could handle this. On the screen there were three other images. Ben, Shane, and Danny. There were tags by the NCC, sneeringly dubbing them as Paul Carter's "Army", with the quotation marks. She'd seen Ben acting up. Couldn't hear anything he said, but she saw his demeanour. He was enjoying himself. Katie forced herself to believe that it meant that Paul Carter was alive and well. That there was a plan in place. Or something.

Just a thought.

"Johnny Stiff. This is a message to Johnny Stiff. You don't know me but I'm a big fan," Shane said, sincerely gazing into the lens, "Paul Carter's a good guy. You were right. I wanted to say last night but I couldn't."
He toned it to perfection.
"Baz Le Shaz. Again. I'm a big fan. I always thought you were missing a trick though. Singing judgments or something. Make celebrities out of them who get found not guilty? Something like that?"
Ben had told him how to act. In their long walk back to base after Katie had been caught. Told him how he'd managed to survive seven different judgments. He said it was because he didn't take it seriously. Took it as a twenty four

hour audition. Didn't crack under the pressure of the counter. Wasn't afraid of death. Shane resolved to follow, and replicate at least some of those traits.

"Really, you could make a *fortune* off the Crime Network. People don't get judged it's for a reason, right? It means New Britain likes them, right? Just a thought Mr Le Shaz. Just a thought."

Raspbrilliant.

His foot was agony. The dog had broken at least one bone in there. The throbbing ache pounded against the inside of his skin up the whole leg. The rucksacks that dragged him to the van by it didn't help matters. Laughing whilst he roared in anguish. Telling him to shut his stupid mouth. Danny shivered at the memory of the British Shepherd with its teeth wrapped around his limb. That snarling sickly sound. The panic. Paul pulling him against a seemingly immovable force. Ben trying to help. The Taser. All of it. Suddenly his gut rolled and hot, bitter bile poured up his throat and out of his mouth. He'd not eaten enough recently to make it a proper gusher, but there was enough to coat the front of his shirt, and leave an unmistakable bad taste in and around his mouth. The guard sneered in disgust and shook his head, before returning to his handheld device. The tell-tale sound of the strawberries and apples popping on Fruity Basher. A very British voice exclaiming that it was a *Raspbrilliant* move that he'd played. He clearly had no intention of cleaning Danny up at all. The smell of the vomit scratched at the insides of his nasal cavity. Threatened to entice a further portion from his stomach. Danny crooked his neck as far as he could to remove the bile from his chin against his shoulder, succeeding to a point, but his face felt cold with the moisture cooling in the less than comfortable temperature of the air conditioning. He made an effort to put the discomfort from his mind and returned his attention to the guard. He'd been through enough recently to have accepted his fate. If they were going to hang him then so be it.

"What level are you on?" he asked of his keeper, who frowned, said nothing, and then returned to his game, "I'm up to a hundred and nine."

"Shut yer mouth," was the impatient reply. The guy was obviously concentrating hard on that particular level. Danny chuckled, and felt the urge to upset him further.

"I bet you're on level three, you dumb rucksack. Are you struggling? Are you getting *fruity bashed* every time?"

"I said shut yer mouth gherkin, or I'll come shut it for yer."

"Banana, strawberry, apple, apple, pineapple, banana, banana," Danny laughed, "orange, banana, apple, banAAAAARGH!"

The guard was up out of his seat and had slammed his boot down onto Danny's broken foot, giving his nerves a complete meltdown. The pain seemed to fill his entire body, all flooding from the epicentre at the end of his leg. The guard returned to his seat without saying another word, leaving Danny whimpering, tears streaming down his face as his head rolled in delirium. Eventually the guard tutted as his game ended in vain, he rolled his eyes and looked up to Danny.

"For jack's sake, that's your fault, you bag of sherbet. Got to start again now."

A devilish rogue.

"People of New Britain," Ben said, clearly and loudly, "let me tell you something about Paul Carter."

His head turned one way, and then the other, as if somewhat amusingly looking out for eavesdroppers, and he was about to disclose some secret, before he dropped his tone to a hushed whisper.

"Paul Carter is going to change your country for the better. He's going to make you sit up and realise what Robert jackin' Lodge, and Wilson jackin' Becker are doing to you. What you're doing to *yourselves.* Sure, they might catch him, and you might judge him to death, but guess what? Next time, there'll be three Paul Carters to take his place. Then you'll do what? Judge and kill those. Then there'll be a hundred, then a thousand. Each and every one of you will eventually wise up to what a mess New Britain actually is. So I ask you now, why not just grow a

Ryan Bracha

pair of beanbags, and stand up against this ridiculous regime that controls your lives."

He paused. Frowned. Chewed his bottom lip.

"He doesn't control *my* life, by the way. I'm a free spirit, a handsome outlaw, a devilish rogue. I'm not even joking. I know at least a million women out there are thinking about what it'd be like to have a go on me. Well let me tell you. It'd be jackin' *awesome,* seriously, if I weren't me I would definitely go the way of the gay for me. Anyway, I've gone off a little bit there, where was I?"

Ben shook his head violently, trying to get his train of thought back onto the right tracks.

"Oh yeah, this ridiculous regime. Do you really enjoy your life right now? Is it how you thought it would be when you got the chance to stay here? I mean, yeah, it probably is if all you ever wanted was to sit at home in your undercrackers playing stupid games, and killing actual living breathing people from the comfort of your armchair, living like virtual kings with all of the attention you get for your online achievements. All the while your rubbish, and bin bags pile higher and higher on the streets outside. If *that's* what you wanted out of life, then congratulations, you're living the dream, but surely to a God I don't believe in, this isn't how every single one of you wanted to live. Maybe it is, but eventually you'll find your way into this seat. This exact same seat that I'm preaching from. It's fun while you're out there, clicking away at the guilty button, but all you need to do is slip. Just the once. Then what'll happen? You find out how it feels to be anonymous. To have people sentence you to death indiscriminately." "They can't hear you Turner," said the voice of Wilson Becker through a crackling speaker. Ben's head whipped around to the two-way mirror and he eyeballed himself venomously, "yeah, we turned off the volume right about the time you were talking about a thousand Paul Carters. Nice speech though. Very moving."

Insanity in all its glory.

Pete looks nervously at me as we watch Ben thrashing around furiously in his seat. His neck craned toward where I know the mirror is, and it wouldn't take a proficient lip reader to see the kind of language he's spewing to whoever. Whatever he's said was obviously intended as rabble rousing, given that he started by declaring me as the man to change the country yet again. But Becker obviously wasn't going to let him say his piece if he thought it might sink in any. I don't say anything for a short while and watch Ben's insanity in all its glory. I've really grown to like the guy. Eventually I've seen enough and drag to cursor over the link for Katie. She's seated, obviously, and her big green eyes blink out to me sadly. I'm not ashamed to say that it breaks my heart a little bit. She's always been the bolshy, confident and quirky girl while I've known her. This is another Katie. She looks vulnerable.

Ryan Bracha

Young. Beautiful. I let my gaze linger on her just a moment too long, as Pete clears his throat slightly and speaks.

"Is that your girlfriend?" he asks, but I shake my head to reject the notion.

"No, she's just," I start, but I can't finish the sentence. I don't know what she is, but she's burrowing further and further under my skin, and I can't look at her anymore, so I expand Danny's screen and Pete gasps. My cousin is crying. Not sad, self-pitying tears though, it's something else. My best guess would be pain.

"Everybody!" he wails through his tears, before his tone turns to laughter, "this guard here, is so bad at Fruity Basher. He's been on level three for an hour. Level three!"

Pete stifles a chuckle. Seeing something funny that I don't.

"Private joke?" I ask. Pete smiles affectionately but says nothing, keeping his eyes fixed on my cousin, "is that your boyfriend?"

Pete looks to me, smiles at my own returning of his earlier question, and shakes his head.

"I wish," he says, looking back to Danny, "I'm not his type. We're just friends."

"Really?"

"Yes, really," he says, rolling his eyes, "I've asked him out tons. Made a fool of myself on several occasions."

"If you're his friend then why did you let him go for judgment alone?" I ask, and the smile drops from his face, making way for a much sadder demeanour. I half expected the usual flouncing wall of defence to be raised at this point, so I'm more than surprised when he speaks frankly.

"I wanted to go with him, but he wouldn't let me. They wouldn't let me. The NCC. They didn't need me. That's what they said. They called me useless. I felt useless. This wasn't some clumsy accident," he says, pointing to the purple bruising around his eye and cheek "I wanted to do something, but what could I do Paul?"

I suppose he has a point. I've spent the last day and a half blaming him, but never really got the full measure of what they put Danny and him through. I sigh, and look back to my cousin. The object of his desires.

"Well, you've got your chance to do something now, Pete," I say, expanding Shane's screen, and noticing the ashtray for the first time, "can I have a cigarette?"

He pulls some non-brand British smokes from his pocket and tosses me the pack. I don't smoke very often, but just now I really feel like one. I light it up and my stomach noisily reminds me how empty it is. My body has been dragged along for the ride without a single complaint so far, but now I'm in a reasonably secure hiding place it's making several complaints at once, and I suppose I should oblige it.

"I don't suppose you've got any food in have you?" I ask, Pete nods, "I'm starving."

He rises from the chair beside me and wanders into the kitchenette. Pulling hard on the cigarette and letting the woozy dizziness that comes with a first hit of nicotine in over twenty four hours, I

Ryan Bracha

rise myself and walk to the entrance to the kitchenette, he's got his head in the fridge, pulling out cheese and meat.

"If you really want to help to do something Pete, to help Danny, your friend, then make yourself something too and I'll tell you what you can do over dinner, okay?"

A MODERN BRITAIN #9

GRAHAM ROLLINS WATCHED HIS WIFE AS SHE TENDERLY MADE THE BED FOR THE FIFTH TIME. SHE NEVER GOT BORED OF IT. SHE WOULD PULL THE SHEETS FROM BETWEEN THE SINGLE MATTRESS AND DIVAN BASE, AND THEN TOSS THEM ONTO THE FLOOR IN A PILE, ALONG WITH THE DUVET AND THE PILLOWS. SHE WOULD GAZE DOWN UPON THE BARE, CHEQUERED THIN MATTRESS WITH A SAD SMILE, AND THEN START THE WHOLE PROCEDURE AGAIN. SHE WOULD SMELL THE FABRIC BEFORE PLACING EACH LAYER BACK UPON THE BED. SMOOTHING ANY CREASES OUT WITH THE PALMS OF HER HANDS, AND THEN STANDING BACK TO LOOK AT HER HANDIWORK. GRAHAM STEPPED UP BEHIND HER, AND WRAPPED HIS ARMS AROUND HER. TENSING HIS MUSCLES JUST A TOUCH TO SQUEEZE HER. SHE LIFTED HER HAND TO PLACE IT ON HIS ARM.

Ryan Bracha

SQUEEZED IT. SIGHED. THIS HAD BEEN A
ROUTINE FOR THREE YEARS. SINCE
AARON.
HE HAD TOLD THEM HE WAS GOING TO
PLAY FOOTBALL WITH HIS FRIENDS.
THAT WAS SUCH AN AARON THING.
FOOTBALL. REAL FOOTBALL. NOT THE
ELECTRONIC MONSTROSITY THAT HAD
EMERGED THROUGH THE NETWORK. HE
WAS ALWAYS AN ACTIVE BOY. HE
REMINDED GRAHAM OF HIMSELF WHEN
HE WAS A LAD. CLIMBING TREES,
JUMPING ACROSS STREAMS, KICKING A
FOOTBALL AROUND. HE HAD NO TIME
FOR THE ELECTRONIC AGE THAT WAS
REARING ITS UGLY HEAD. THAT DAY,
WHEN HE WAS SUPPOSED TO BE
PLAYING FOOTBALL. HE DIDN'T. HE WAS
OUT WITH HIS FRIENDS, THAT MUCH
WAS TRUE, BUT THEY HAD DECIDED TO
MAKE A DAY OF CLIMBING THE WALL
OF NO-MAN'S LAND. SEEING WHAT THEY
MIGHT WITNESS ON THE OTHER SIDE.
ONE OF HIS FRIENDS, JAKE, HAD SAID
THAT THERE WAS NOTHING BUT GREEN.
NO PEOPLE CLAMBERING TO DEVOUR

NEW BRITONS LIKE ZOMBIES FROM THE OLD FILMS, LIKE ROBERT LODGE HAD PROMISED. JUST GREEN HILLS AND SHEEP. BUT AARON WAS A ZEALOUS CHILD. HE WANTED TO GO FURTHER. WANTED TO SEE WHAT THE FUSS WAS ALL ABOUT. HIS FRIENDS REFUSED, SO HE WENT ALONE. HE NEVER RETURNED. THE UNKNOWN WAS WHAT GOT TO GRAHAM AND HIS WIFE THE MOST. WHAT HAD HAPPENED TO HIM? GRAHAM HAD TRIED TO GET OVER THERE HIMSELF ON MORE THAN ONE OCCASION. TO FIND HIS BOY, BUT THE RECENT SPATE OF ATTEMPTS BY FORMER SCOTTISH PEOPLE TO INFILTRATE NEW BRITAIN MEANT AN INCREASE OF SECURITY ALONG THE WALL. GRAHAM'S WIFE REFUSED TO ALLOW HIM BACK, LEST HE BE CAPTURED AND JUDGED FOR NON-BRITISH BEHAVIOUR. NOBODY WANTED TO LIVE IN SCOTLAND, EXCEPT SCUM AND RAPISTS, THAT WAS THE OFFICIAL LINE, AND IF YOU WERE SCUM OR A RAPIST, THEN YOU WEREN'T A TRUE

Ryan Bracha

BRITON, AND YOU WOULD BE JUDGED.
SO AS IT WAS, THEY KNEW NOTHING,
NOR WOULD THEY EVER KNOW
ANYTHING ABOUT THE DISAPPEARANCE
OF THEIR SON.
GRAHAM'S WIFE GENTLY RELEASED
HERSELF FROM HIS GRIP, AND BEGAN
HER ROUTINE ONCE AGAIN.

Man of the people.

The speedometer of Pete's car hits a hundred as I floor the accelerator when we hit the junction on the M1 motorway. It's a largely unused road anymore, save for the delivery drivers of provisions ordered on the Sustenance Network. This is one of the roads which are somewhat exempt from speeding laws. Lodge was very selective about his guidelines. It had long been public opinion that motorways should be allowed no maximum speed limits, and ever the man of the people, he obliged to get them onside. Pete's in the passenger seat, his eyes nervously flickering between his handheld computer and the rapidly rising speedo. I didn't think he'd ever go for it, but I kept on planting that seed of finally being able to do something to help me. To help Danny. Eventually he relented, and now he's here. The latest in a long line of sidekicks. He's flicking between the four judgment screens, following the action, and the timers. They're all set to end at the exact same time. Four o'clock tomorrow afternoon. We have little over twenty hours to do this.

What *this* is.

I used to know a man by the name of McGuire. Both back in my old life, and at the time of the regime change. He was a chemistry teacher from somewhere near Glasgow, but lived in

Ryan Bracha

Edinburgh. I met him several times at various education seminars. We always got on. Downed several pints and shots as we enjoyed our time away from our wives. We'd put the world to rights until the early hours, and then go our separate ways. We always kept in touch, and I visited his place many times until Robert Lodge fractured any thin strips of connection between us and the Scots with his short, and pointless war, and subsequent wall building. Being a proud Scot, McGuire remained on the other side of the wall. The reason I'm putting my hopes on such a long shot, is that he would always tell me about the various ways that he could create weaponry and explosives using simple chemistry. Never in any detail, but it's this that I need. Lodge has taken lethal weapons from our grasp, aside from extremely rare illegal firearms, but if I'm going to do what I need to, then I will have to have more than just a Taser at my disposal. The penny has dropped. I need to do something to help them. My friends. I need to get us to the wall, through the wall, and up to Edinburgh without capture. Then I need to find McGuire, convince him to help, and then get back to do what must be done to free them all. In twenty hours. If I'm ever going to prove to myself that I really am worthy of this reputation as the man to free New Britain from Robert Lodge's regime, then this is going to be the time to do it. If I fail this, then I fail them all.

Newcastle.

The junction for Scotch Corner appears and passes at a hundred miles per hour at about half past eight. We've seen barely a soul on the road since we set off, not that I'm particularly surprised, but I am certainly glad of the fact. This far north and you're lucky to see a town for miles. Crews tend to stick predominantly to the more heavily populated main towns and cities so I don't anticipate any major issues until we pass Newcastle, which is a notoriously staunch Lodge supporting city. They love being New British more than most, illustrated quite plainly by the iron statue depicting Robert Lodge's charge against the Scots which stands tall in the city centre. Rumour has it that he used Newcastle as his unofficial base between days of 'talking' with the self-appointed leader of the Scots, Davie Craig. For this fact, Newcastle is an immensely proud city.

Pete still scans The Network for news. A notable development is that there have been a few pockets of violence from people who seem to have taken on the opinion that maybe I'm worth taking a chance on. There's a gang wandering the streets of Manchester, attacking members of small crews in my name, getting away with it too. An anonymous prankster in Liverpool has spray painted the side of a boat in the dock with *Paul Carter for Prime Minister.* In Birmingham a handful of *Pretend Britons* have started a campaign for pretty much the same thing. It's good. It's a start. But it's not enough. Without my new friends. Without Ben, my lieutenant. Shane, my intelligence expert. Danny, my family. Katie. Just, Katie. It's good that the public are taking the ball and running with it, but I need my people. Those I trust.

Played by ear.

Thankfully Newcastle passes without incident. More cars on the road, of course, but as I said, a hundred miles an hour on the motorway is no rarity. It allows speed freak drivers to quell the urge to break the law. By my calculations we're less than an hour from the border. How we're going to get past it is a question I'm yet to deliver an answer to. Some of the parts of this whole things that worked the best were those that were played by ear. This, of course, goes against everything I ever stood for. I was always such a consummate professional, I planned every eventuality down to the last minute detail, but I'm changing. Something in me is changing, and I have to say, it's not entirely unpleasant a feeling. I press my foot to the accelerator and push the machine to hit one-ten but it rattles a touch and I let it go. I can't afford to burn the thing out, not yet.

Robert Lodge won't have it.

"Any news, Garner?"

"None, sir."

"What? He's disappeared into thin air?"

"Apparently so. Wilson Becker and James Finnegan had hoped the judgment of his, ehm, army, might flush him out but he's gone to ground."

"He needs to be found, Garner. The man has made a fool of me and I won't have it. I won't have it I tell you!"

"Indeed, sir."

"Do they have any other known contacts to work with?"

"Not that they have mentioned sir."

"And you didn't think to ask?"

"I-"

"I'll take your expression as a no, Garner. Tell me, what the blazes do I pay you for?"

"To work on your behalf, sir."

"And?"

"To think like you."

"And?"

"To ask the questions that you might ask, sir."

"To ask the questions that I might ask, Garner, correct. You're slipping. If you aren't careful I may just have a good think on whether you're worthy of the role."

"With respect, sir-"

"Yes?"

"Nothing, sir."

"No, I thought not. Get out of my sight, Garner.

Ryan Bracha

I've had just about enough of your
incompetence."
"Sir."

The art of tongue restraint.

"Boss, there's a call from London for you," Oxley
said, stepping tentatively into the viewing room
holding a phone, "it's Garner again."
Wilson Becker sighed and shook his head in
annoyance as he held his hand out for the device.
"Becker," he said curtly, "what can I do for you
now?"
"Quite the tone you have there, Mr Becker. I'll
remind you to show some respect, you're well
aware of who I represent and what trouble I can
make for you."
"Yes, I am. What do you want?"
"Mr Lodge would like to know if you've spoken
with Carter's Network associates, to see if
anybody has heard from him."
"We have a track on his device, Garner. If he gets
in touch with any of his Network associates, we'll
be the first to know, and then you'll be the
second, okay?"
"And what of people he has been in contact with
recently? Anything?"
Becker restrained his tongue, and sighed once
more.
"Look, we're turning over every single stone in
the jackin' city, every single one of 'em has us
drawing a blank. If he's disappeared then you

know what? I don't care. I got four of his own crew, he can't do much alone. He'll slip up in the future and we'll collar him."

"I beg to differ, Mr Becker, need I remind you of why you're pursuing him in the first place? The man is an animal."

"You know what? Why don't you get your own people on it, yeah? Send up a crew of your own if you're so damn itchy to catch the gherkin."

"Care to retract that, Mr Becker? I'll give you only one chance."

Becker felt like throwing the phone through the mirror, like getting up and driving to London and choking Harry jackin' Garner to death with his own stupid tie. He took a breath.

"Okay, I'm sorry, look, we're doing everything we can to track the guy, you have my word that we'll keep you posted at every jackin' turn."

"Okay, good. Be sure that you do. Goodnight Mr Becker. Good luck."

"Yeah, thanks."

We live on a planet.

"No word from your hero, Turner. How you like that?" Becker said as he entered the judgment room, rousing a minimal response from the lunatic, who simply shrugged.

"You don't think that's weird? You don't think he'd have done something by now to assure you he still cares?"

Ryan Bracha

"Sounds to me like you care a whole bunch more than I do about it *Pecker,*" said Ben with a snigger, "what's up? You low on straws to clutch at?"

"No, not really, as far as I'm concerned Carter can do what he wants, he'll slip up before long, my only concern is wiping you off this planet."

"What? You acknowledge that we live on a planet and not just some tiny piece of sherbet island? Did I hear that right? Don't let Lodge hear you say that. He'll have you on a boat back to Australia, no, wait, New Zealand, no, wait, South Africa. No, wait. He'll have you judged, and I don't imagine you'll need twenty four hours to hit your target."

"You're such a dingo, you really are. You know the only reason you're here is because your pal Katie grassed you up?"

"No she didn't," Ben yawned, "you know how I know? Because it's the second time you've said that. You want a reaction? How's this for a reaction?" Ben rocketed a ball of phlegm onto the jacket of Becker's suit, and then grinned, "clean yourself up. Don't get it in your mouth though, you'll get hepatitis, like your boy Teddy."

A change of tactic.

"Okay Katie, here's the thing. Carter's been in touch. He knows you sold him out," Becker said, attracting a weary, and sad nod from his audience, "he says he doesn't care about you.

Says you can say what you want because there's nothing you can do to make him hate you anymore than he does already."

"You're lying," she said despondently, no more tears coming simply because she'd cried herself out, "he knows. He knows I'd never do that."

"Does he though? You've known each other how long? A couple days? Does he *really* know you wouldn't do that?"

"He knows," she whispered. Refused to bring her eyes to Becker's.

"I wouldn't be so sure, princess, he hates you and he's gonna watch you die. Unless, of course, you know where he might be? Why don't you watch *him* die instead?"

Katie finally raised her head and her stare burned into Wilson Becker with hatred. Said nothing for a short while. Blinked.

"Why don't *you,* go and fungus yourself? I'll never grass him up, *never,* I'd rather die than give him up!" Katie yelled before turning to the camera, hoping that the volume was on, "Paul Carter, I would *never* betray you. You're my hero. If I die then I die, but I would never do anything to harm you. Don't listen to Wilson Becker, he's a liar!"

Two miles from the border.

Pete switches it to Danny's judgment screen, and watches the man of his dreams whilst I reflect on the last couple of minutes' viewing. Katie is a mess. Not just visually, but Becker is messing

Ryan Bracha

with her head in a big way, and the more I think of her the more I miss her ways. Her old ways. The happy go lucky, witty girl that latched herself onto me after I somewhat fortuitously saved her life. Those green eyes that sparkle with mischief. I miss that, but the vulnerable side is warming me to her in a big way. She's what I need to ground me. I'm far too uptight. She has barely a serious bone in her body. She could be, I stress that it's only *could*, but she could be the yin to my yang. Ciara was beautiful, but we had the kind of nothing in common that meant aside from the sex we had nothing to talk about. She wasn't interested in me and I wasn't interested in her. Katie, I don't know, she just had that spark that says I'd never be bored, even if I didn't get half of the things she said. I need to save her now more than anything. The revolution, that's something that has to happen to give us all a shot at a better life, but if I get them out of this, and it is a huge if, but if I get them out of this then I will ensure that nothing or nobody gets the opportunity to put that girl in the way of harm again. *Focus.*

"Okay, Pete, we're about two miles from the border. Lodge left two holes in the wall. One at the A1, and one on the A7. Just in case they needed to get back into the country. As far as I know it's reasonable security, but they don't tend to do much for stopping people getting *in* to No-Man's Land, just those that want to get out. Alright?"

Pete nods a nervous nod. This is only the fourth or fifth hardest part of the plan. We still have to negotiate No-Man's Land and find McGuire, *then* we have to get back into New Britain, and rescue our people. All without getting ourselves caught or killed. This promises to be an eventful nineteen or so hours.

"So we're going to continue as we have been. I'm going to need you to keep your head down as we approach the border, just in case there's guns, but like I say, getting *in* shouldn't be an issue, okay?"

"Okay," he says, and there's an air of surrealism around the car, because out of all the people on this planet, the last one I expected to be sitting in a car waiting to burst into the territory of former Scotland with, was Pete. We never truly liked each other. It was more a tolerance. But. We've done okay so far. I don't want to jinx it.

"Right, when I say, get your head down. We're likely to lose The Network shortly after the border, but keep your eyes on it."

He nods again and I press my foot down, not too hard to begin with because I don't want to attract too much attention at the wall. In the distance I can see the faint lights of the security building, and it's at that point that I floor it. Throwing Pete and I back against our seats. Once I'm happy that it's a straight I kill the headlights and press harder and harder onto the pedal. The car shudders like it did before as we pass a hundred, a hundred and ten, and then up to the limit of about one-seventeen. Pete's free hand grips the dashboard, and a couple of men appear from the security building. One shrugs, and the other runs into the middle of the road. I can see he has some sort of weapon trained on us, but we're hurtling too fast.

"Head down, now!" I yell, springing Pete into action as he ducks, out of the route of any anticipated bullets. They don't come. We're going way too fast, and in the dark the guard has nothing to aim at so he dives out of the way as we rocket through the border.

"Keep your heard down, Pete," I say as I flick the lights back on and a number of bullets fly aimlessly around the vehicle, before the guards give it up and in the rear view mirror I see them frantically gesticulating, but nothing more, and we're into No-Man's Land. On our way to what used to be known to the world as Edinburgh. I drop the accelerator a touch, back to ninety. All being well we should be in Edinburgh within the hour, easy.

Skating on thin ice.

Joe had been tasked with checking all of their leads. Seeing if any of them had been behaving particularly strange in the last few hours. The most infuriating part was that they had no particular leads. Carter had done so much under the radar. Joe had already put tracks on the celebrities that the kid Shane had mentioned. Johnny Stiff and Baz Le Shaz, but the truth of it was that one of them was a cripple, and the other had so much more to be doing than responding to daft messages from criminals. Baz Le Shaz was one of the most famous, and successful men in the country. Implicating him in the whole situation without proof would cause so much more grief than help, and Joe was skating on thin ice as it was. He switched off the monitor. Closed his eyes, and just let his mind empty. He'd been hammering this for the last few hours and every road of potential turned into a dead end. He couldn't afford for Becker to fire him. He had children. He had to feed them somehow, and he really did enjoy being a part of the NCC. People feared him for it. Usually. Who was Paul Carter associated with? There was Ben Turner. Caught. Katie Fleming. Caught. Shane Watson. Caught. Danny Carter. Caught. There was nobody missing. Nobody associated with any of those people who-

Joe opened his eyes. Exhaled hard. Switched the monitor back into life. His fingers hammered hard onto the keyboard. Five letters. Then eight. Peter Ferguson. There were several, but he knew what he was doing and narrowed it down to the one he wanted. Joe bypassed a variety of security measures, and requested the track. Nothing. Peter Ferguson had been offline for the last five minutes. He refined his search to six minutes ago. He left both his seat, and the room, quicker than you could say Berwick upon Tweed.

Ryan Bracha

There is nobody.

"They say a car just flew past them, boss, no registration number or anything, they say it was too dark to see," Joe said, his tone dancing dangerously along the line between disappointment at a lack of solid information, and excitement at having provided a lead for once. Wilson Becker eyed him, as if feeling the same danger of whichever emotion Joe might eventually settle on. It turned out, to his benefit, to be the disappointment, but he pushed on.
"It's got to be them, it's too much of a coincidence. Should we get a couple guys out to Ferguson's flat?"
"Who we gonna send Joe? Who we got? We got four watching these rucksacks here. Teddy and Grady are still out of action, Banger's... There is nobody!"
"I thought Finnegan-"
"Finnegan can go fungus himself! This was *my* bust, and he just happened to be in the right place at the right time. We're not going running to him for help."
Joe said nothing, he didn't know what he *could* say now. Becker was losing his grip on the situation once again. Lodge's office was riding his back for answers, and he didn't have any, except that his only lead had just disappeared into No-Man's Land, possibly with the most wanted man in the country.

I'm bored.

"Why's he in No-Man's Land Danny?" Becker asked with a previously unseen urgency. Danny shrugged, prompting the NCC leader to punch him hard in the cheek, throwing his head back against the lip on the backrest on his chair, "who does Pete know up there? Ferguson, it's an old Scottish name, right? Did he have family there?" Danny shrugged.
"I ain't messing here, you tell me what I need to know or I'll have to hurt you."
"You don't have the right," Danny said eventually, his cheek bleeding from the impact of Becker's ring against his skin, "you're the law, remember? Twenty four hours then you can do as you please. Until then, just leave me alone. I'm bored of everything."
Becker seethed. Stared at Carter's cousin. Left the room. Danny chuckled toward the guard in the corner.
"If he's not careful he'll join us on trial."

The beanbags I knew he had.

"He's in Scotland? Wow," Ben said, wide eyed, upon hearing Becker's question, "I'm impressed. Starting to show the beanbags I knew he had."
"So you know why he's there?"
Ben laughed loudly, and hard.
"No, Pecker, I don't, but I'm damn glad he is."
"You are eh? Why would that be?"

Ryan Bracha

Again Ben laughed, shaking his head in what might be construed as pity.

"I dunno. Maybe I'm just happy that he got laid there once and wanted to go see if the lady in question wanted another go. Maybe I'm overjoyed that he just really likes the taste of quality whiskey. Maybe my thing is the fact that he gets a rush of blood to the pants area for the works of Robbie Burns. You getting the message yet? I don't, jackin', care. He's got his own life to lead, and I got mine. The good people of New Britain will let me get going and I'll continue the life I got to lead, maybe I'll head up to Scotland myself."

"It's No-Man's Land," growled Becker, through gritted teeth, losing patience with the nonchalant attitude of Ben Turner. Carter had scored a direct hit when he enlisted the help of this fool.

"No, Mr Pecker, the more educated of us like to refer to it by its maiden name. The one it had before you dingoes got your hands on England. Seriously, you're boring me, leave me alone until my judgment time is up. Man! Can't a guy just get judged by the good English public in peace?"

A lot of road.

I made this journey a lot in my old life, and for some reason I'm surprised that it's much the same now. I suppose I just bought into Lodge's propaganda about Scotland the same as everybody else. I was half expecting some barren wasteland, feral children running around naked, cars either on fire or burned out skeletons of vehicles past. Something more like an accelerated version of my own country south of the border. The drive toward Edinburgh up the A1 is an eerie one. It's pretty much a road amongst fields all the way up to the former capital city. That was always the thing about Scotland in my experience, there's a lot of road, and a lot of green, built up areas are few and far between. Like a tiny, greener Australia. There's no noise but for the sound of the engine rumbling Pete's car to our destination, which suits me. I have no idea what to expect when we get there. The worst case scenario is that McGuire is no longer living, and everything that Lodge said about Scotland is true, that we'll be killed and eaten. Deep fried, of course. Best case is, well, you can appreciate what that is.

Pete has been fiddling with his handheld computer for the last half an hour, trying to attract some manner of signal but of course it's no use. Lodge had any masts around the border dismantled. I leave him to it though, because we don't have a great deal in common, and small talk would be just that. Very very small.

We pass the junction for Pencaitland and Longniddry and it gives me my cue.

"Okay, Pete, we're almost there. We're going to see it get a bit more built up now. If we see anybody, cars or anything like that then keep your eyes forward. Seriously, we have no idea of what these people are capable of, and they may

Ryan Bracha

be very desperate creatures. We need to do our best to blend in."

"Alright," he says with a nod, suddenly becoming stiff, shoulders back, staring straight forward.

"Now you look like a mannequin, just relax, right?"

His shoulders slump, and he exhales.

"Better. Like I say, we don't know what to expect, so we stop for nobody, and we just get to McGuire's as quickly as possible."

Not what I expected.

As anticipated, the landscape becomes more and more grey and built up, and less green as we approach the outer limits of Edinburgh. I'm more than surprised to see the glow of light pollution in the distance. This should not be. Lodge told us what he'd done. He switched off their electricity. He shut them down and left them to fend for themselves. I slow the car down as we leave the A1 at Newcraighall and head into the city. The street lights are illuminated. Every one of them. House lights are on, and there are a few cars on the road, people walking the streets, and a small group of kids are hanging around a bus stop. Pete's eyes remain fixed forward, but I can tell he's wondering the same as I am.

"It just looks normal," he says, briefly allowing his head to turn to witness the area around us.

"I know, I really don't understand," I agree. The city looks as if nothing ever happened. As if the

Lodge effect didn't even nearly touch the place. I really don't get it. I'm not about to drop my guard however, so I roll the car along cautiously, and eventually we pull up outside the house that McGuire used to own. It's a modest semi-detached three bedroom house as far as I remember, always very nicely set up on the inside too. Mrs McGuire had a keen eye for interior decoration, but this is by the by. His wallpaper is the least of my worries. There's a light on in the living room, although the curtains are drawn, so somebody is home, I can only hope that it's McGuire.

"This is it, Pete. Although he's Scottish, he's a good guy, and he was a good friend, so behave accordingly."

Pete smiles a thin smile and nods. I climb out the car, and my legs thank me for it. I've been driving for just shy of three hours, and I now really need a good stretch. Pete's of the same kind of thinking as he slowly spins an invisible hula hoop with his hips. I hear the loud crack of his bones aligning, and the pleasure he felt is apparent in his face. Not a pleasant sight. I approach the door of the house, and I knock tentatively three times. For a brief while nothing happens, and I'm about to knock again but a light clicks on in the hallway, and a distorted figure of somebody behind the patterned glass approaches. A child. The door opens a touch, held firm by the chain which is still on the latch. "Aye?" the kid says, a young lad that I don't recognise, and I'm feeling heavy of heart.

Ryan Bracha

"Hiya, is your daddy home?" I ask in a soft voice reserved for disarming the suspicions of children around strange men. To show him that I'm no threat. He recoils at my English accent however, and slams the door closed. Behind the glass of the door I can hear him calling for his dad, but in a tone I'd rather he didn't, a tone which denotes a threat. Pete has already taken a few steps away from the door, ready for flight. I stand firm. Behind the glass a larger figure pulls the child out of the hall, and then approaches the door. He's holding a weapon. Some sort of bat. I tense up, ready for a fight, and the man behind the door eagerly flicks the chain from the latch and swings the door open. His face is hard. His head bald. His sneer vicious. Without saying a word he leans out of the door and pushes me firmly in the chest, sending me backwards, tripping me over a terracotta plant pot which sits in the front garden. He sends a series of profanities my way in a way that only a Scotsman could deliver, and then he leans over me. I can't help but feel I've made a massive error coming here.

"Please, I'm looking for McGuire," I say, holding the panic from my voice as he holds the bat over me like some Nordic barbarian wielding a war hammer, ready to strike the thing down onto my skull. He pauses.

"An' who might you be?" he asks, not letting a single ounce of threat drop from his voice.

"Carter, Paul Carter, I'm a friend of his."

"Eh? Carter? Whit the bloody hell are you daen' here?"

His face comes close into mine, studying my features. I'm a total mess compared to the last time we saw one another. I take the time to do the same to him. It's McGuire. He's older, harder, and altogether stronger, but it's definitely him.

"I need some help, and I don't have many friends in England anymore."

I smile as his features melt into a softer tone, and he laughs hard, pulling me up from the ground.

"By Christ mate, you're a mess, right enough. Scared ma wean to death, man."

"Yeah, sorry about that."

"Ach, dinnae worry aboot it, he's a tough wee bastart, oor Paddy, c'mon. Who's yer pal?"

"That's Pete, he's my wingman."

"Looks like a bufty," he laughs.

"He is, but he's alright, he's helped me a lot."

"Fair enough, c'mon then, let's get youse inside, the wife'll be over the moon tae see ye."

An enterprising bunch.

Over dinner I've explained as much as I could to McGuire about the bind we're in. Jacob Glover, Banger, Katie, Shane, Ben, Danny. The way New Britain is run. None of it comes as a surprise to him though.

"Aye, I know you're a wanted man, pal. There's not much we don't know aboot whit's happenin' doon there, I hear ye played that bastart Lodge a blinder. Comes oot tellin' yer folk there that he's

Ryan Bracha

caught ye, an' then has tae cut short his ain feed, brilliant. Ah laughed ma arse off."

Pete chokes on his potatoes at the casual use of profanity. So long it's been since he heard it. McGuire laughs.

"Watch yersel' there son, that's good tattie yer aboot tae waste."

Pete takes a drink of water as his face flushes red, and breathes a little before taking another bite of what really is a good dinner.

"How do you know though? Do you have Network access up here?"

"Network, naw, sorry to say we don't. We've got several men on the other side of the wall who do though. Always have done. We get the news from south ay the border aw the time, on the radio like. They package it as a comedy hour. Listen tae aw the daft stuff thay stupit English bawbags have been uptae. Some of the stuff youse get uptae is priceless, it really is. Anyway, that bastart Lodge thought he'd cut us aff, an' he had, to a point, but we've oor ain electricity supply. It's impossible for him tae cut us off totally. He told you lot that we were aw left to die, but we're an enterprisin' bunch us Scots. Invented almost everythin' there is tae invent, you know that?"

I do know this, because he told me on more than one occasion. It's too many to list just now, time is a factor here. I nod and smile that same knowing smile that I used to give him when I heard it the first hundred times.

"So aye, he puts that wall up an' we're celebratin', 'cause it's aw we wanted in the first place. We get left tae dae oor ain thing. You know there's a ferry tae Belfast? We're still in touch with the rest ay the world."

"A ferry? Really?"

This is an interesting development. This is the sort of news that on any other day I'd be over the moon to hear, because I'd on the thing and out of New Britain for the rest of eternity. Because it's today however, it's merely a pipedream that I can one day think about climbing onto and saying goodbye to the shores. I have so much more to do before I can give myself the luxury of that kind of thinking.

"Aye, it leaves Cairnryan once a week. Every Friday. Yer a wanted man, Paul, mebbe you should think aboot getting' on it."

"I can't. I have my friends to think of. I can't just leave them to rot. Maybe one time I might have, but they've been there for me. Plus what about the rest of New Britain? They need to know about Lodge's lies."

McGuire groans in disappointment as he places his cutlery onto the table and looks to me earnestly.

"Ach, so they can aw migrate north? It'll be the Edinburgh festival season aw ower again. No, I'd thank you tae keep oor utopia to yoursel', okay?"

As much as I want to reject his request, I'm in his house, eating dinner that his good lady wife rustled up, and he seems genuinely happy with what his country has become. They've reclaimed the independence they deserve. After a brief moment I smile, and nod.

Ryan Bracha

"Okay, I'll keep it to myself, but if and when I get them out of there, the first place we're headed is here."

"An' it'd be my pleasure to host you and yer pals. Right, you want tae tell me whit youse are needin'?

A MODERN BRITAIN #10

HARRY WAS A PATIENT MAN. A LOYAL MAN. HE HAD SERVED HIS COUNTRY IN SEVERAL MEANINGLESS WARS BEFORE THE CHANGE IN REGIME. HE HAD RISEN THROUGH THE RANKS AND HAD CHOSEN HIS PROFESSIONAL FRIENDS WISELY. HE HAD FOUGHT ALONGSIDE ROBERT LODGE, AND THEN HE HAD FOUGHT *FOR* ROBERT LODGE. HE ADMIRED THE MAN'S TENACITY. HIS CHARM. HIS ABILITY TO MAKE PEOPLE BELIEVE IN WHAT HE HAD TO TELL THEM. IN HIS VISION OF THE FUTURE OF NEW BRITAIN. HE BOUGHT INTO IT MORE THAN MOST AND HE SERVED HIS LEADER WITHOUT QUESTION. BEFORE NOW.
HARRY'S LOYALTY HAD RECENTLY BEEN BROUGHT INTO QUESTION. HIS ABILITY TO PERFORM THE ROLE HE WAS GIVEN WAS IN DOUBT. HARRY WAS NOT A MAN WHO DEALT WELL WITH DOUBT. IT KNOCKED HIS CONFIDENCE. HE QUESTIONED HIS OWN TALENTS. WOULD

Ryan Bracha

HE BE A WORTHY SERVANT OF NEW BRITAIN? WHAT IF ROBERT LODGE CHOSE TO REMOVE HIM FROM HIS POSITION? HARRY WAS A MAN WHO KNEW SECRETS. BIG SECRETS. ROBERT LODGE HAD SEEMINGLY FORGOTTEN ALL OF THE THINGS THEY HAD DONE TOGETHER AS BROTHERS IN ARMS. HE HAD RISEN BEYOND HARRY IN THE GRAND SCHEME. HE REMEMBERED ONLY WHAT HE CHOSE TO REMEMBER. WHAT SUITED HIM TO REMEMBER. HE MADE THE LAWS. HE PAID PEOPLE TO ENFORCE HIS LAWS, AND IF HE DECIDED THAT YOU WERE IN THE WRONG, THEN SO BE IT. IF ROBERT LODGE NO LONGER HAD A USE FOR HARRY THEN HE WOULD BE JUDGED. HE WOULD BE SILENCED. THE RISE OF PAUL CARTER IN RECENT DAYS SPELLED A THREAT TO THE REGIME AND ROBERT LODGE WOULD PLACE HARRY IN THE FIRING LINE BEFORE HE EVER THOUGHT TO DIRTY HIS HANDS. SO HARRY DECIDED TO WORK ON AN INSURANCE POLICY. HE STARTED A DIARY. A VERY PERSONAL

AND POTENTIALLY DANGEROUS DIARY. HE PUT EVERYTHING HE KNEW INTO WRITTEN WORDS. NOT NETWORK BASED DAYLINE WRITTEN WORDS. HE HAD PUT PEN TO PAPER. IN HIS FREE TIME AT HOME, IN THE EVENING THAT PAUL CARTER'S ASSOCIATES WERE BEING JUDGED. THE CONVERSATIONS. THE MEETINGS. THE ACTIONS. HE LEFT NOTHING OUT.

THIS WAS NOT AN ACT WHICH HARRY TOOK LIGHTLY. HE KNEW OF THE RISK HE WAS TAKING. ALL IT WOULD TAKE WAS FOR THE WRONG HANDS TO GRIP THIS VERY PERSONAL AND POTENTIALLY DANGEROUS BOOK, AND IT WOULD CAUSE ABSOLUTE MAYHEM. IN THE RISING LIGHT OF DAWN, HARRY GARNER PUT THE FINISHING TOUCHES TO HIS DIARY. HIS INSURANCE POLICY. HE THEN PLACED IT IN A BOX BENEATH HIS BED, AND HE SHOWERED, BEFORE TAKING HIMSELF BACK TO THE OFFICE, TO FACE WHAT WOULD BECOME THE MOST IMPORTANT DAY OF HIS LIFE.

Ryan Bracha

Technically qualified.

The clock hits midnight and we're in McGuire's cellar. A mild smell of damp lingers in the subterranean air. McGuire has spent the last hour or so over his workstation, mixing a variety of chemicals and household products. He's instructed Pete and I to stay back, since he's the only one technically qualified to do this kind of thing. He's mentioned potassium nitrate, sodium bicarbonate, and sugar for the smoke bombs. I don't really know enough about this kind of thing to really get it, but I said that as long as they did the job then I trusted in his skills. He seemed happy enough with that.

"Now ahm puttin' these wee babies intae tennis balls, awright? Ah widnae hold ontae them too long before ye chuck thum."

"Okay," I say, "you're the boss."

"Ahm gonna do ye some very crude bleach bombs as well, be careful with thum though eh? Ye don't want that goin' off aw over ye. Be careful where ye chuck thum tae, ye don't want to be coatin' yer pals in it."

We aren't terrorists.

By three a.m. we're done, or more specifically McGuire is done. He has us kitted out with more than enough to do the job. By my counting we have tens of smoke bombs, bleach bombs, and several petrol based explosives. We don't want to do anything which might damage the cause, I just want to damage a few people that deserve it. We aren't terrorists. The country had enough of that before Lodge took over. Hell, it was the *reason* Lodge took over. All we need to do is get in, and out with Katie and rest of them in tow. We can work on the nation afterwards.

"How're ye plannin' on getting' back intae England, Paul?" asks McGuire as we're putting our stuff into the back of the car.

"Same way we got in, I guess, floor it and hope for the best," I say, but he's already shaking his head.

"Naw, they'll cut ye doon before ye've got anywhere near the border. Yer gonnae need a distraction."

"Any ideas?"

McGuire's face breaks into a huge grin and his eyes sparkle in the light of the streetlamps.

"Oh aye, ah've got plenty."

Utopia.

"He seems like a nice bloke," says Pete as we're racing down the A1 back to the border, closely followed by McGuire in his car.

"Yeah, he's one of the best, I'm glad he's doing well."

"Can you believe what's happened up here? It's like they've gone back to the eighties."

I know what he means. Everything here is entirely the opposite to how it is down in

Ryan Bracha

England. There's no internet, no real mobile telephony, definitely no Network. Just people getting by and enjoying what they do. McGuire's son Paddy was just playing an old board game with his mother to pass the time before he went willingly to bed to read a book. It reminded me almost of my own childhood, before the information technology boom. This is exactly what McGuire called it. A utopia. This is where we need to be. Away from all of the ridiculous guidelines that Lodge has imposed. Maybe eventually we can climb aboard a ferry to Ireland, Northern Ireland, whatever it's called now, and we can start life afresh. The six of us. If they want to. I know Katie will. I heard what she said. She'd die before she sold me out. I'm going to do my damnedest to return the loyalty. We've seen what a unified and reclusive Britain looks like, and it's a mess. A shambles. We should get out while we can.

I'm aware that I've been thinking silently for a few minutes so I respond quietly and contemplatively.

"Yeah, I know what you mean."

A smart man.

"Would I be right in thinkin' your boy there's Pete Ferguson?" McGuire asks as we stand by the cars. Pete's sitting patiently in the passenger seat, fiddling with his computer.

"Yes, why?"

"They know he's in *No-Man's Land*," he says with a chuckle and emphasis on the government's name for his country, "it's just been aw over the radio. Said he's there wi' you. Don't ask me how they know."

"They probably tracked his device and put two and two together."

McGuire raises his eyebrows and looks into the car. Pete's still fiddling.

"You might want tae tell yer boy tae switch the thing off then; ye'll fall back intae English broadcasting signals a mile or two up the road."

"I will, thanks."

"You ready then pal? You know whit yer daen' eh?"

"I think so yeah."

"Ach, don't think too much, just do. Awright, so ah'll get as close up as ah can, set a few naughty wee fires an' smoke the bastarts oot, then you wheel yersel' back over that bloody border. Aye?"

"Aye aye, boss."

"Away wi' ye, ye radge bastart," McGuire smiles, "good to see ye again Paul, let's hope ah see ye again soon."

I extend my hand and he grasps the thing firmly, pulling me into a close embrace, his breath warms the side of my face as he growls into my ear.

"Don't let the bastarts grind ye doon, Paul, you're a smart man, show thum exactly who they're messin' wi'."

"I intend to, I'll see you soon, McGuire."

Ryan Bracha

"Aye, ye will."

Frantic silhouettes.

"Pete, they know you're with me, you need to turn that thing off, and I mean all the way off. Seriously," I instruct as I climb back into the car and watch the rear lights of McGuire's vehicle disappear across the field. Pete looks at me with a mixture of confusion and disappointment, but I return his serve with one of stern determination. We can't have this jeopardised.

"But, Danny," he says.

"But Danny nothing. He's in the same place as he always was. You know the rules. They can't do anything to him until twenty four hours is up. At worst he's got another bruise for his backchat. I mean it, Pete. We can't have their tracker light up like a Christmas tree when you fall back onto the radar. This is perfect. If they think we're in Scotland they'll not expect us when we show up in the morning. Okay? Turn it off."

He begrudgingly obliges and puts it into the side panel of the door. Even now I can see him looking at it longingly.

"You'll have all the time you want to check The Network when we've done this, I promise."

He nods mournfully, bottom lip quivering. He's such a child. I consider dumping him at the side of the road, very briefly, but steel myself and turn the ignition, rolling the car back onto the highway, and heading closer to the border. The lights go off as we gradually approach the border. Being that it's four in the morning there should only be a skeleton staff on, so if McGuire does what he does best then we can be over the border without much of a fight. Suddenly the night is aglow with the light of flames. It's barely a hundred feet from the security building, and even from here I can see McGuire scampering across the grass in the direction of the structure. Another fire goes up. He disappears into the dark as three men emerge. They're holding weapons and scattering across the field toward the flames. I slowly edge the car forward, my eyes only on the guards. A car horn blares out into the empty night. McGuire. The full beams of his headlights flash once, twice, three times, and the frantic silhouettes of the guards dance around in the bright light. Again McGuire honks the horn, long and hard. This should dampen the sound of our car as I suddenly floor it and rocket the car back into England, New Britain. This time there are no bullets chasing the air around us as the guards scatter like headless chickens as another firebomb smashes into the floor between them. I silently thank McGuire for being such a good man as we speed back toward Yorkshire. Toward Katie. Toward a better future for all of us.

Back in Yorkshire.

"Hey! You wanna turn the lights off? I'm knackered," Ben called to the night guard that

Ryan Bracha

looked into the room through the window on his round of the prisoners, "stupid bandstand, can't even let me get some decent shut-eye."

The timer told him that there were eleven hours remaining. The counter told him that he hadn't even halfway amassed the required votes to judge him guilty. Ben sneered in satisfaction. They were never going to judge him. He'd gained a cult following amongst the fence sitting masses. The people loved a joker. Somebody that they could live vicariously through. Somebody who would say it as it was. He wished a few more people would adopt the same approach. Show the government and the stupid crews that they weren't in total control. Since they'd switched off his microphone though, Ben was completely in the dark as to what, if anything, Carter might come up with. He'd hoped to gee up the country, get them on side, to make the people see what a ridiculous thing their once great nation had become. Their once great empire. It had completely imploded. The one time ruler of half the planet, now a reclusive island with not more than thirty million inhabitants, and a bizarre despot intent on controlling the lot of it.

Glimmer of comfort.

He awoke to the clunk of the night guard closing the door hard at around six, having managed to secure, or endure, three or so hours of broken and fevered sleep. The ache in his foot continued to throb its way up his leg and had begun to reverberate around his hip with every shuffle he made to attempt even a glimmer of comfort in the chair. Danny was exhausted. His efforts to antagonise the staff here had ultimately rewarded him with not much more than a few thumps to the face, and hard stamps to his broken and mangled foot, at least as far as he could see. A few well timed jibes at Wilson Becker, or the guard with the utter lack of Fruity Basher skills had, however, been met with several previously ill-advised LOL and TIJFS from the watching public. Ordinarily these sorts of actions might have been met with a stern warning from the NCC moderator around anti-British behaviour, but just now it was allowed to pass without further comment. Something wasn't right. Perhaps it was that the NCC was already spread thin on the ground, especially with four of them held for judgment at pretty much the same time. Perhaps they simply didn't have the time or resources to focus on anything so utterly trivial as a few typed chuckles of support. Perhaps most promisingly, it meant that they had really just lost control of both the situation, and their fearsome reputation. They were being laughed at, and they were being laugh at to their faces. Danny grinned a tired, and weary smile. Blinked slowly. Looked to the camera.

"I know there's not many watching at this hour, but if you are, how's my cousin getting on?"

Ryan Bracha

He looked to the forum. A few names disappeared. Probably a coincidence and it was just some people that had fallen asleep hours ago and eventually their Network link had timed out. The other names said nothing. Danny smiled knowingly to himself. The laughter and the support were gone, at least for now.

"It doesn't matter anyway, he's a clever bloke, this isn't over yet, not by a long shot. You just watch."

Accustomed to the situation.

Her tummy growled a kind of strangled cat kind of gurgle. She was starving hungry. There was no way they would feed her though, even if it wasn't six in the morning. The night guard passed her room, looked in on her with a cruel smile on his face, before he waved and blew a kiss. The guy gave her the creeps, with his big blonde eyebrows and nerdy glasses. She'd told him as much herself a few hours ago. Asked him if the carpet matched the curtains, with a naughty giggle. She had grown accustomed to the situation. Paul Carter would get her out of this, she just *knew* it. The NCC men were all obviously still in the building somewhere. Wilson Becker had said as much himself, they weren't going to allow Paul Carter the same kind of luxury again. The single night guard was just for show. Give them some sort of false sense of security. She half imagined them all sitting in a pitch black cupboard waiting for him to stroll in there, all invisible to one another except for the cartoonish pure white eyes blinking from the dark, Joe Fatso getting a slap to his mush for stepping on Wilson Becker's toes, and then whispering in a pathetic American accent, "gee, sorry boss," before getting another slap for making the noise and being told to shush. Maybe when Paul Carter did show up, they'd all file out like clowns from a really small car, stumbling into each other in a hilarious slapstick manner. Like the old black and white Laurel and Hardy films that her dad had showed her when she was a kid. Even if he thought it was an empty building Paul Carter wouldn't come in all guns blazing, he was smart, and he would come up with something brilliant. Katie just knew it, and when he busted her out, the first thing she was going to do when he freed her, would be to throw her arms around his neck, and give him the biggest kiss she'd ever given anybody. That was *her* plan, now all he had to do was come up with one of his own.

Change in a big way.

He wasn't asleep, but he made a huge show of showing exactly how asleep he *was.* Head tilted back, open mouthed snoring, doing the catching flies effort that he remembered his dad doing on occasion when he'd fallen asleep in front of the TV after a nightshift, back in the old days. Shane would come downstairs at about this time in the morning to watch the cartoons before school. He'd turn on the telly, arousing a snorting, mouth-slapping noise from his dad, who would rub his eyes, stand up wordlessly and retreat from the room. The heavy thumps of his feet against the stairs as he ascended, and then the creaking springs of the mattress as he climbed into bed with his wife.

Head tilted back kicking out imaginary zeds, Shane half wished that he was in Ireland with his parents, or wherever they had maybe moved onto. Oblivious to the systematic failure of the ideal that Robert Lodge had sold to everybody. But then he would never have been, hopefully, able to help to change what the country had become. It was less about having something to do anymore, it was about change. He could quite easily be an anonymous teenager riding his bike along country lanes in the land across the Irish Sea, kicking a football around, or playing war games with friends across the other side of the world, but then what change could he make? None. That's what. Whatever happened in the next ten hours or so, Shane would be remembered now, for more than just being the runaway son of two defectors who perhaps thought of him on a daily basis but could do nothing to trace. Shane saw the messages of support earlier. People were less scared. They *wanted* what Paul and the rest of them wanted. They pretty much admitted it now. What they didn't know, is that it was what they'd *always* wanted. He saw how Paul spoke when he was addressing either the nation, or Wilson Becker. He was so assured. So confident. He made them see what their lives had become. He made them realise. No, whatever happened from here on in, the country was about to change in a big way, and Shane loved the fact that he was a part of it. To hide his grin he snaffled and made that mouth slapping noise he remembered from his dad, and he heavily and slowly blinked as he feigned returning to the waking world, to see that his guilty counter was seventy five per cent full. Shane frowned, and felt his stomach roll. His head felt light and he breathed a huge and sharp intake. It couldn't be right. He'd done everything that Ben told him to be. He'd acted how he needed to get the public onside. But then Ben had more charisma in one fist than Shane could muster in his whole body. He was obviously irritating somebody out there. He might be remembered for some things when he passed over to the other side, and it looked like one of those things was that he was the first one of Paul Carter's army to be judged guilty.

They had nothing.

"Anything?"
"Nope, nothing."
Becker slammed his hand down hard onto the desk in his office, jerking Joe from his slumber and arousing a jumpy reaction from the rest of the crew. Oxley had been wandering the halls for

Ryan Bracha

hours, putting on the big night guard show, with a hope that one of the rucksacks in the judgment rooms would start bleating for Carter to come and save them, from wherever he was, but they never did. The girl had seemingly pulled herself out of the depths of her self-pity and was now back to some sort of infuriatingly chirpy best. Carter's cousin was just acting plain bizarre. The kid Shane was obviously pushing himself to act up, but it seemed stunted and uncomfortable. Becker had actually visibly shuddered with embarrassment for the kid at one point. It was the equivalent of a middle aged father speaking using fashionable terms with offspring thirty years his junior, and it showed, as the public had made a beeline for the guilty icon whenever he started his act. Ben Turner, well, he was simply being Ben. He was some exception which made a mockery of the whole justice system. A charismatic psycho who fed off the attention of others. For his acts of violence against Teddy and Grady he should have been pushed straight into the guilty chamber and executed, but Becker could do nothing except watch as New Britain allowed him to walk free once again, ready for another bout of lunacy the next time he was dragged before the online court.

It had been several hours and they had nothing. Word had come back from the border that aside from a crazy man trying to set alight the border security building before scarpering back into the safety of the chaotic wastelands of No-Man's Land, there had been no efforts to cross back into

New Britain. Of course there was the possibility that he'd had help, maybe climbed back over the wall and traversed the country back to here, but that was unlikely. If Carter knew the effect that his antics had had on the nation then he would have surfaced by now, eager to take the plaudits for the increasing waves of anarchy that were washing against civilised society in his name. Finnegan had effectively withdrawn their help from this side of the situation to go after some good old fashioned collars, smelling the cash payoff that came with capturing anti-British criminals. Lodge's office was surprisingly and uncharacteristically quiet overnight, but that would of course change as business hours crept into view.

Even though Carter had all but disappeared from the face of the Earth, Wilson Becker had a gut feeling that this would all be on its way to being over before nightfall. Either he'd have the country's most wanted man up for judgment, or he'd be up for it himself after he'd strangled every last breath out of Paul Carter's body, and then ripped his head from his shoulders for the country to see exactly how mortal their new hero was.

Somewhere around the former town of Barnsley.

"But Paul," says Pete, leaning into the window, "what if they don't come?"

Ryan Bracha

"Someone will, whether it's Finnegan or NCC, they can't help themselves. Right now they're looking for you, because they think that if they have you then they have me. I just need enough to turn their heads, whether they come for you or not."

"Okay, I think. So-"

"Yes?"

"Sorry, I just want to make sure I'm doing it right. I don't want to let you, or Danny down," he whines, his hands itching to switch the device on, "how long should I give it?"

"Ten minutes, then run. You know where to go. If I'm not back in two hours, just run."

"What? Run where?"

"I don't know Pete, just run, don't stop to look back, or check The Network for what happened, they'll track you."

"I'm scared," he shivers in the freezing dawn air, "what if I get it wrong?"

"You won't. All you have to do is turn it on, wait, and then go."

"Okay."

"You sure?"

"Yeah. Paul?"

I sigh, we *do not* have the time to go through this again, but I indulge him.

"Yes?"

"Bring him back alive, please. Bring them all back."

"I'll do my best. Ten minutes okay?"

"Okay."

I leave him at the side of a back road which connects an old town that used to be called Barnsley, now another suburb of Greater Sheffield, and the city itself. Sheffield. What a brilliant thing it would be to have it anywhere near the old fashioned vibrancy that Edinburgh was awash with, instead of the stinking grey ghost town that it's become. I can but wish.

The stinking grey ghost town itself peers into view as I push the car over one of its seven hills. The single thing that my hometown has in common with McGuire's utopia north of the border anymore. Seven hills. It used to be as filled to the brim with culture too. Once upon a time. I suppose on a deeper level the fact that Edinburgh is also reportedly built on a volcano could be construed as some sort of common factor, simply because I've got a big urge to start some fires in Sheffield this morning.

The clock in the car reaches ten minutes from when I left Pete. All being well he should be logged into The Network. A minute from now and somebody will be alerted to it. Another minute and he should be headed for the church. Another five minutes and I should be smoking Wilson Becker right out of his cosy little headquarters.

A minute from now.

"Boss, it's Ferguson."
"What?"

Ryan Bracha

"He's back online."

"Where?"

"I dunno, gimme a minute."

Becker simply didn't have the time, or the inclination to give Joe a minute. He strode over to the guy and ripped the device from his sweaty hands. Watched the tracker calibrate, before locating Pete Ferguson twenty miles away.

"He's in Barnsley," Becker growled, tapping the device against his temple. He'd fallen for this trick once too many times. He simply would *not* get burned again. Joe had risen from his seat, an eagerness in his step.

"So we gonna go get him?" he asked, dancing on the spot, still intent on earning the brownie points he lost when he let the bandstand go in the first place. He was now showing the beanbags he should have shown yesterday, instead of peeing his pants and weeping to the nation. Becker shook his head, no.

"Call Finnegan, tell him what's happened, we ain't leaving this building. Carter's gonna show up. I can feel it, and when he does, I'm gonna be the rucksack that takes him down."

Same blue of dawn.

I quietly close the boot of the car, leaving it the corner of the car park of the old Sheffield United football ground. A place which once was held so close to the red half of the people of this city, now another disused reminder of what life used to be. Sheffield United is now a man named Tommy Weeks who plays electronic football on behalf of the city. His bedroom will never be held in the regard that this stadium used to be.

I stick to the edge of the car park as I make my way to the rear of the NCC building. The fence is ripped down from Wilson Becker's vehicular theatrics yesterday, and therefore easy to traverse as I slide into the bushes which branch out in all directions along the fence's length. That same blue of dawn from yesterday at the police station has begun to wake the world, soon to make way for the morning sun. I know for a fact that Becker has gone nowhere, I taunted him way too much yesterday for him to fall for it. I don't need him out of the building, I don't even want him out. The fact of the matter is that if he gets in my way then he can prepare to face all manner of holy hell.

From the bushes I can make out the silhouettes of the vans in the read courtyard, and it gives me an idea for a diversion.

Blatant inaction.

"Boss, you need to see this," a hard breathing Oxley announced as he rushed into the room, almost throwing the door from its hinges.

"See what?"

"Vandals," he huffed, taking a moment to swallow, "they've set fire to one of the vans."

"Huh?"

Ryan Bracha

"Yeah. I saw it from the window, come look!"
Becker followed Oxley from his office to the
hallway of the second floor of the NCC
headquarters. True to Oxley's claims one of the
vans was alight. Contrary to Oxley's belief it
certainly had not been set alight by vandals.
"Carter," Becker said urgently, moving himself
away from the open view of him which Carter
would be afforded, and back into the office. The
rest of his crew were still seated, with their
thumbs up their backsides. Wilson Becker gazed
upon his subordinates with pure disgust at their
blatant inaction. Was he the only one who truly
gave a damn about catching Paul Carter? The
men looked at each other, the floor, anywhere
that wasn't directly at Becker. The first one to
hand was Joe, who received a balled up fist to the
cheek, knocking him to the ground.
"Are you for real? Seriously? We're under attack
and you're all in here doing what? What do I
jackin' pay you for? Huh?!"
Joe looked up to him from his prone position on
the carpet, tears welling in his big pathetic eyes.
"You didn't need to hit me, boss," he whimpered,
but received a boot to the midriff for his
troubles. Then another.
"What? I didn't need to knock some damned
sense into your jackin' skull? Carter's out there
setting fire to our vans and you're doing what?
Sittin' here hiding with your thumb up your-"
Wilson Becker was aware that he had hands
upon him. They tugged gently.

Paul Carter is a Dead Man

"Boss, come on, Joe's scared, we all are. This Carter's a freak."

Becker turned to the owner of the hands. Oxley. His blond eyebrows moved seemingly of their own accord behind the thick rims of his spectacles as he did his utmost to maintain eye contact with his boss.

"You're scared huh?"

"You've seen how he's got the people acting out there, they think he's some sort of messiah. You've seen how he just gets in and out, never gets caught. It ain't natural."

Becker assessed Oxley's words, let the true meaning filter into his brain. They thought Carter was some sort of superhuman rucksack with disappearing skills. They were idiots. Carter was as superhuman as Becker was female.

"You know what ain't natural? A bunch of pansy crewmembers running scared from one man. What? You're more scared of him than you are me? I got that right?"

This question wasn't at all rhetorical, but Becker got his answer in their silence. He let another boot hit Joe firmly in the gut and rounded his desk. He reached into the top drawer and pulled out a .38 snub nose revolver, checked the ammunition and exited the room, leaving Joe to be tended by the rest of his pansy crew.

Becker stomped purposefully through the hall, just wishing that Banger were around. The loyal, unflinching Banger. Had Becker sent Joe, or Oxley, or even Grady to look for Carter alone then he was confident that this would all have

Ryan Bracha

been a hell of a lot easier, having Barry Armstrong by his side. Becker checked the ammunition one more time, before pushing the doors to the stairwell open, and descending to the first floor.

In person.

He was there in the window. Becker. In person. Watching the flames on the van from a couple of McGuire's petrol bombs. It's not doing much aside from aesthetic damage to the paintwork. I sort of hoped for an explosion. Even just a little one. Nothing.

As he stood in the window with his sidekick, disappearing shortly after, I made my way to the front of the building, and am now standing here before the doorway. The exact same spot that I had the guy Joe, bag over his head, kicking at the backs of his knees. Only this time I'm in the middle of a cloud of smoke, a gas mask strapped tightly to my face. I'm feeling vulnerable being this close to the CCTV, but I'm sticking with my gut that if I can't see *it,* then it can't see *me.* Possibly naïve but what can I do? I pull a bleach bomb from my bag and I open the door. The building feels just as empty as it did yesterday, only this time I *know* it's full of Becker's rats, and they're scattered all over the place.

Seriously do not mess with me.

Becker slipped into the corridor. Sidled along the wall and swiftly slid into the room.

"Mr Pecker!" came the call. Turner. Becker turned to the lunatic, whose eyes widened at the sight of a real life, old fashioned firearm.

"My my!" he exclaimed, intrigue in his face, watching the gun as if he were a snake, charmed from a basket in some stinking country out in the far reaches of the planet that Becker refused to acknowledge, "is that a .38 snub nose?"

"Shut up, maggot," Becker instructed, an urgent but hushed tone about him.

"Why? Who's out there? Is it Carter? It' s Carter isn't it? He came to save us all? He shouldn't have, really. I was just about to escape."

Becker levelled the gun at Turner, his face set to seriously-do-not-mess-with-me.

"I said, shut the jack up, maggot."

Turner stopped smiling, his hands out flat as his arms tugged hard against the shackles.

"Hey, look, if I could get my hands in the air I would, but it's just, well, you know, you put me here."

Becker ignored the psycho. Craned his neck to see along the acute angle that he was afforded by the small window to the room. Nothing. He needed to move, quickly.

Ryan Bracha

Bag of tricks.

The smoke bomb sizzles and hisses at the top of the stairs, and I wait. Still there are no voices. This can't be right. They've seen the fire, they must have seen the smoke on the CCTV, and at some point they've got to be wary that something isn't as it should be. Aside from the rapidly diminishing hiss of the smoke bomb it's silent. I do as I've seen in olden day films and I'm sticking low to the ground, close to the wall, as I ascend the stairs. When I reach the doorway that I know leads to the judgment rooms I lay flat against the ground. Beneath the rising smoke. With a single index finger I push the door open, just a touch, and I listen. Nothing. No, that's not right. There's something. It's distant, but it's there. Ben. He's shouting. What he's shouting is not in any way distinguishable, but it's definitely him. I allow my finger to take the strain of the door closing gently again, and I light another smoke bomb. If I'm lucky, they're all I'll need, but let's be honest. I'm hardly likely to be that lucky. Neither is the poor fool that has to bear the brunt of what else I have in my bag of tricks.

A real gun.

"Be quiet nerd, or I'll open up the back of your head, you want that?" Becker hissed at Shane as he entered the room, before the kid had a chance to say anything. Shane watched the gun more than he watched anything else. Becker held it up toward the window in the door and Shane watched it. Held it down by his side as he struggled to see down the corridor, and Shane watched it.

"Is that real?" Shane asked in wide eyed wonderment. A real gun. He'd never seen one before.

"Yeah, and so are the bullets, so just pipe down or each one will show you just how real they are, you understand?"

"Mmhmm." Although the situation was understood clearly, Shane still watched only the gun. His brain struggled to comprehend what was happening. Wilson Becker, in *his* judgment room, with a *gun,* and watching for somebody else along the corridor. Carter? Surely not. But still. Guns were illegal.

"Are you allowed that gun?" he asked, turning to his judgment camera, doing his utmost to convey a message to the outside world that something wasn't right. Becker hissed another warning to be quiet, before he gradually opened the door, slipped through it, and into the corridor once again. Alone in his judgment room Shane turned excitedly to the camera.

"Something's happening, I don't know what, but Wilson Becker just came in here with an illegal gun. A real gun!" he sang, his backside making small leaps from the cushioning of the chair, "I think Paul's come back for us!"

Ryan Bracha

Pretty little head.

The end of the corridor was filled with smoke. It was a harsh smelling chemical sort of smoke, not one which might come from a fire. Becker coughed as he moved into Katie's room. Again he spoke before she had a chance to.
"Shut your mouth or I'll shut it for you," he commanded as he placed the gun on the floor, and began to remove her shackles. Katie looked down curiously, both at the gun, and the NCC chief freeing her.
"What's going on?"
"I said shut your mouth, bitch."
Aware that something wasn't right, and the NCC man was in something of a bind, Katie giggled, and feigned shock, winking to her camera.
"Oh my, Mr Becker, can you use that word? Bobby Lodge'll have you strung up!"
"Bobby Lodge can kiss my beanbags, I've been made a fool of far too much by you lot. You, Carter, Lodge, *Ben jackin' Turner!* You're all gonna see exactly what happens when you make a fool of Wilson Becker! Get up."
Becker dragged Katie to her feet, and out of the view of her camera. He wrapped his boa constrictor of a left arm around her neck and squeezed.
"Okay, so you behave yourself, or one of two things can happen," he whispered into her ear, "one, I squeeze so hard it pops your pretty little head from your pretty little neck. Two, I blow the

pretty little face from your pretty little head with my ugly little gun. Got it?"

Katie endeavoured to nod as best she could, given the restriction placed on her by the arm, and gargled a pained affirmation.

"Good, because you're actually a foxy little bitch, I'd hate to spoil your looks."

Mr Robert Lodge hates being called Bobby.

"Sir, there's a development of the utmost importance."

"Don't tell me Garner, it happened yesterday, you forgot to tell me, and now it's urgent since it's twelve hours old news?"

"Sir?"

"Just tell me."

"Wilson Becker appears to have suffered a breakdown, he has been caught on the NCC judgment cameras with a lethal firearm, and has since removed one of the criminals from their judgment chamber at gunpoint. He referred to you as, ehm, *Bobby* Lodge."

"I hate being called Bobby! My mother gave me the name Robert. If she wanted people to refer to me as Bobby then surely she would have named me Bobby!"

"Indeed sir."

"I am furious, Garner. Absolutely furious."

"As am I, sir."

"This is all your fault, Garner. You know that?"

"Sir?"

Ryan Bracha

"*You* were the one who suggested that we allow Becker to continue on his decided path."

"Me? But sir it was-"

"It was what Garner? Are you about to imply that it was *my* fault? I dare you to, go on, let the implication fall from your idiotic mouth!"

"-"

"I thought so, you're a coward Garner. A coward and an imbecile. I don't know what the hell I was thinking when I gave you the role. Pass me my telephone and then get out of my sight, I'll deal with you later. You see if I don't."

"Sir."

A gun shot rattles out.

I'm standing in the corridor. Gas mask on. Surrounded by tiny smoky particles of potassium nitrate, and sodium bicarbonate. In front of me I can see movement. Silhouettes. It's two people. One much larger than the other. A gasp for air. Katie.

"Katie?" I call, pulling myself closer to the wall in the smoke. A gun shot rattles out. It's loud as hell too. The bullet reaches the window behind me and it shatters.

"Paul Cart-" she begins but is cut off, and it evolves into a strangled gargling.

"Carter!" shouts out the familiar voice with the New Zealand twang, "you've got two options."

One is that I give myself up for Katie. The other is that he kills us both. This is the bet that I have with myself.

"Which are?" I ask, already reaching into my bag for another smoke bomb. The bleach bomb is going nowhere with Katie in the firing line.

"One, you give yourself up and I let your princess go."

Check.

"Two, you just hold out and try to rescue her and I kill the pair of you. How's that?"

There we go. He's not known for his ingenuity.

"I've got a third option, do you want to hear it?" I call out. Stalling him for whatever reason.

"I'm listening."

"I set fire to the building and we all go down. You included."

"Not sure I like the sound of that one, Carter."

"I didn't think you would."

I light another smoke bomb and roll it a few feet in front of me. I just need to keep the screen up whilst I delay the inevitable.

"What the hell are you doing? You can't stay in there forever," Becker says.

"I can try."

"You'll have to come out to cry your tears over Katie's headless corpse in a minute. Now you're getting to the count of three to come out, before I blast your little girlfriend's brains out."

Now he reminds me of my father, when I was a child. Always with his futile countdowns to a punishment that never came. I can't take the chance that this countdown is so futile though,

Ryan Bracha

not with Katie's life on the line. With my back to the wall I edge closer toward them.

"One. Stay still you skanky little rucksack!"

The silhouettes appear again through the smoke. They're in the open. Becker has his arm wrapped tight around Katie's throat. Gun waving forward at the cloud of smoke I'm in. There are no options here. The guy's clearly lost the plot, and we're likely all going to die anyway. In the safety of the smoke I quickly pull a petrol bomb from my bag, and hold the lighter to the rag-cum-fuse.

"Don't be scared Katie. I'm here."

"Two!"

I light the rag, and it flames up quickly. Still Becker waves the gun toward the smoke. I close my eyes and inhale sharply, before I open them and take several steps back and then slam the petrol bomb into the ground as I dive for cover. The flames explode into the corridor and I hear a scream. Katie. A gunshot. Then another. She screams again. I have no idea what I've just done.

Intense heat.

The girl had gone. He let his guard down for just a moment too long, and she slipped out of his grasp. Becker fired a blind shot in her direction. Spun around and fired one back toward where Carter should be. The flames crawled little by little in his direction. Becker roared in frustration, an animalistic savage sound.

"Carter, you're a dead man!"

There was no response. Had the bullet hit him? Was he even there anymore. Becker struggled to see through the smoke and flames. The intense heat drying out his eyes with every point that he attempted to focus through the fire. A noise clunked behind him. A door. Becker spun to level the gun at that end of the corridor. Oxley and Joe. Both men held their hands up, and open palmed in a gesture of surrender.

"Boss," said Joe, his face caked in his own blood, his eyes blinking rapidly, "you can't do this. It's not right."

Becker began to laugh. First it was his shoulders heaving rhythmically, then he laughed loudly.

"I can't do this huh? Who are you to tell me I can't do this Joe? You fat useless lump! You can't do anything."

"Seriously boss, you've lost it. This isn't right," Oxley stepped in, edging closer to his superior, still his hands were held upright, and flat.

"I'll tell you what's not right," Becker said, "people not taking law enforcement seriously. This is what they wanted. It's what *we* wanted. And *Carter,* is allowed to make a mockery of everything, and they love him for it. Tell me how *that* is right. I ain't having it anymore Ox, it's time to punish him properly."

Becker waved the gun in the direction of his subordinates, backing them away.

"I can't let you do it boss."

"Yeah you can, Ox."

A gunshot rang out. A bullet left the barrel of Becker's gun. The same bullet entered the

Ryan Bracha

forehead of one Andrew Oxley. Former member of The Network Cutting Crew. Killed by his own employer. Becker swallowed. Watched the body of his friend and employee fall to the floor. Looked to Joseph Robertson, only witness to the crime. Shot him in the head too. There was one bullet left in his gun.

Bloody corpse.

He's killed two of his own men, and standing there looking at his gun. Katie's gone. I don't know where to but I think she's safe. I hope she's safe. She's got to be safe. Becker stumbles a little. The gun hasn't left his hand but I'm quite sure I know what his next course of action's going to be. I should let him, but for some reason I feel my body rushing through the smoke. The flames. I don't make a sound as I coast along the corridor. Becker brings the gun up to his temple. Mutters something. Is knocked from his feet by me as I plough directly into his kidney with my boot. The gun skitters along the floor, and Becker is momentarily disorientated. I take my chance and I kick him hard, straight in the face. His nose smashes into as many pieces as it's possible for a nose to break into and explodes across his face. He's not waking up from that for a while yet. I stand over his prone body, pulling the gas mask from my face and surveying the mess around me. Two dead crew members. One unconscious crew chief. A hell of a lot of smoke and fire. And no Katie.

"Katie?" I call out, "Katie?"

I face the flames. There's no way she went through there. I fear the worst. Becker shot her. I'm going to find her bloody corpse back behind me and around the corner. This sadness creeps into me. My stomach dances inside me. I was supposed to protect her. I let her down. I still have three others to-

As I turn away from the flames a force hits me hard and scares the life out of me. It's wrapped around me. Arms. Legs. All of it wrapped around me. Kissing me. Her legs are around my waist, her arms around my neck. Her lips on mine. I drop my bag of tricks and hold her there. My hands gripping hard against her backside to hold her up. I'm kissing her. Eventually she pulls her head away from mine. Blinks the tears away from her huge beautiful green eyes. Breathes her awful breath right into my face as she speaks. Only this time I realise how much I've missed it.

"I *knew* you'd come back for me Paul Carter."

Enough killing.

"Come on, we don't have long, Becker's only out cold and the building's still on fire."

This is me speaking as I'm flicking the key in the locks that hold Ben. He's laughing maniacally.

"Aww, killer, you are such a bad ass. Yippee-Kay-Ay muddy funsters! How's it feel eh?"

Ryan Bracha

"How's what feel?"

"Actually fulfilling your potential. Took you long enough."

"I know. I'm sorry."

"Ah don't worry about it. You got there in the end. Where's the others?"

"Katie's getting Shane, come on."

Ben's up out of his feet and dancing around, allowing the blood to flow to the parts of his body that it had forgotten even existed. He skips to the door and looks out into the corridor. Looks back at me, impressed.

"Check you out, you made a jackin' barbecue in here!"

He suddenly stops as he sees Wilson Becker on the floor, and he whistles in appreciation.

"You sure he's not dead? You made a mess of his face."

"No, he's breathing, I checked."

"That's a shame. You mind?"

He's beckoning to the body, as if asking my permission to do something. I give him the nod. Ben takes three steps back into the doorway. Breathes hard. Swings his arms a little, and then begins his run up, before volleying the skull of Wilson Becker. The body moves at least a metre toward the wall, such is the ferocity with which Ben kicked him. He's going to take another run up but I stop him. The man's had enough. There's been enough killing.

Beautiful parasite.

"No-Man's Land?" Katie squeaks at me as the undamaged NCC vehicle we're in exits the car park. Her hand is on my lap whilst I drive. Between gear changes I squeeze onto it. I really have no idea how or when it happened, but she has really got under my skin. Like a beautiful parasite. Into my brain. Into my heart. I make a silent oath to never leave her alone again, "but that's filled with cannibals and psychos!"

"You'd be surprised. Besides, we've got our very own psycho. We'll be fine."

Ben cackles dramatically, slamming a heavy hand onto my shoulder.

"Nah man, we got *two* of our own psychos, Mr Killer."

"But why No-Man's Land?" Danny asks.

"You need to wait until you see it to believe it. Pete and I were as shocked as anybody could be."

"Pete? What do you mean Pete? Where is he?"

"Barnsley. He's a good guy Danny, you could do a lot worse."

Reservoir of emotion.

We pull up to the church, and I sound the horn. Understandably Pete is a little apprehensive to approach the NCC van, so I climb out and I go to get him.

Ryan Bracha

"Pete?" I call, as loud as I can do in a hushed tone. He appears from the bushes. A nervous look on his face.

"Paul? Did it work?"

"Yes. Yes it did, mate."

"Have you got Danny?"

"I have. Yes."

A rush of emotions threatens to drown him as he breaks down crying. Falls to his knees.

"Pete?" Danny's voice is speaking, he's out of the car and limping toward his flatmate, already battling against his own reservoir of emotion.

"He helped me out a lot Danny, really he did. Risked his life three times. For you."

My cousin limps over to Pete, and stands over him. Takes his hand and pulls him upright. As they embrace the pair of them simultaneously break down into heavy loud sobs. Danny pulls away and tenderly holds Pete's chin, before laying on the biggest most disgusting kiss I've ever seen.

Just the man.

On the drive to Scotland Pete and I tell the others what we've done since they were captured, leaving nothing out. McGuire and his homemade bombs. Lodge's lies over what's actually happening across the border. The hilarious episode when he addressed the nation to announce my capture. The pockets of violence that have sprung up in my name. Katie looks at me proudly and plants a kiss on the side of my face at that particular slice of news. The others are telling us how they felt in the judgment rooms. What they did to try and get the country on board. It seems like everybody's done their bit, in one way or another. We might not be an army, but we're certainly a very good team. We have no idea of what's to come next. What Lodge might decide to do. What *we* want to do next. My plan is to take Katie to Edinburgh where Lodge has no jurisdiction. I'm going to clean her up, learn about her properly. I want to make her laugh. I want to make her happy. That's what I want. Enough about me. Enough making me happy, I've found this quirky and tenacious girl, and I want to see what it's like to make somebody else happy for a change.

"Paul Carter," she whispers seductively into my ear, "I've never done it with a murderer before." I smile at her conspiratorially, and whisper back. "I'm sure I know just the man for that particular job."

One week later.

Shane waves at us as he approaches the terminal. He says he'll be back, one day. He knows where to find us. He just wants to get over to Ireland to find his family. He says it's something to do. I wish him all the best. He's a brilliant kid. I've got all the time in the world for him. Katie wipes away a tear as she mutters goodbye to her

Ryan Bracha

friend, and I pull her close to me. Squeezing her shoulder. Smelling her shiny, clean, dark brown hair. I knew she was beautiful, but I really had no idea how precious a diamond was hiding beneath that dirt.

"I hope he finds them," she sniffs.

"I'm sure he will."

We turn away from the ferry port and head back to Ben who's waiting in the car.

We've become a strange little family here in Scotland already. Katie and I, Pete and Danny, and our very own pet psycho Ben. We've been offered a house, by the Scottish leader Davie Craig, no less. He said that anybody who could antagonise Robert Lodge as much as we did were deserving of honorary Scottish-ship. We accepted of course. We still follow what's happening down there. The cracks are beginning to show. The people saw live on The Network what Wilson Becker did. They also saw his execution a couple of days later. Lodge couldn't cover it up. Those small wandering gangs have become larger organisations in such a short space of time. It's only a matter of time before we can all head back to England, as free civilians rather than the most wanted criminals. I can absolutely assure you of that.

Epilogue

"Green, what can I do for you?"

"Sir, there has been a call from the offices of James Finnegan."

"And?"

"He says he lost another two men today, both to roaming gangs of vigilantes."

"That's not ideal, is it Green?"

"Not at all, sir."

"And what would Mr Finnegan like me to do about it?"

"Not entirely sure, sir. But he did mention that these gangs were not British."

"Pretend British?"

"No, sir. He said that they were from No-Man's Land."

"Oh dear."

"Indeed."

"What might you suggest we do, Green?"

"Well, sir, my opinion is that we seek to cauterise this wound as quickly as possible."

"And how might we do that?"

"A call to arms, sir."

"To what end?"

"To neutralise the threat from No-Man's Land. Quickly and efficiently. It's my opinion that Paul Carter is building an army. We should seek to attack them before they attack us."

"Quite. Okay, you have my permission. Call the nation to arms. We will wipe those smug Scottish bandstands off the face of this island once and for all."

Ryan Bracha

Afterword and jackin' acknowledgments

This novel is intended as the first book in a trilogy. Look out for the next instalment, **Harry Garner is a Dead Man** in late 2014.

First off, thank you to my wife, Becks. You know what you do. That's all there is to it.

Cheers to my good mate Gav Wiggan for your quality illustrations and patience when I said that one looked a bit like Hitler. You're a legend.

Fellow authors, and friends, Keith Nixon and Mark Wilson. Two of the best rucksacks you'll ever meet. You fellas have supported me since we met, and it's your words that push me to carry on, to develop, and to continue to keep scraping around the darkest corners of my mind to come up with the sherbet that I do. Seriously, cheers.

To Gayle Karabelen and Craig Furchtenicht for the beta reading.

Cheers to Martin Ward, for coming up with Johnny Stiff. He'll be back, mark my words.

Once again, thanks to you, Mr or Mrs Reader, for sticking it out and buying/stealing my work. I know it's a hard slog sometimes, but the payoff's there, you beanbags just have to work for it.

There's really only one Ryan Bracha on Earth, so you bandstands come find me on Facebook or @ryanbracha on Twitter. Tell me how much you hated my writing. I'll tell you to go fungus yourselves.

Paul Carter is a Dead Man

For some other equally awesome books please visit:

www.paddysdaddypublishing.com

Also you should look forward to the forthcoming release of the first book in my pal Mark Wilson's dEaDINBURGH series, news of which is at paddysdaddy.wordpress.com

For an exclusive and free-to-read series of short stories which further explain the crazy mad world that Mr Robert Lodge has created, to be released once a month for the whole of 2014, please visit The Paddy's Daddy Blog at the same address.

This collection will then be deleted and released as a companion piece prequel, of sorts, in late 2014.

Thanks for your time and efforts in everything people.

Ryan Bracha

Ryan Bracha

13552130R00174

Printed in Poland
by Amazon Fulfillment
Poland Sp. z o.o., Wrocław